Debor...y

FREDRICA ALLEYN

BLACK
lace

Black Lace novels are sexual fantasies.
In real life, make sure you practise safe sex.

First published in 1994 by
Black Lace
332 Ladbroke Grove
London
W10 5AH

Copyright © Fredrica Alleyn 1994

Typeset by CentraCet Limited, Cambridge
Printed and bound by Cox & Wyman Ltd, Reading,
Berks

ISBN 0 352 32945 9

Chapter One

*D*eborah had never felt less like a party in her life, and if it hadn't been for the fact that she needed to re-establish some useful contacts within the publishing industry now that the Americans had taken over Pegasus, the company where she was currently working as a fiction editor, she wouldn't have gone.

As she pulled on the black Lycra skirt and crossed the room to choose a suitable top from her wardrobe, she noticed that her answerphone was flashing. After a moment's hesitation she decided to ignore it. It was bound to be Mick, telling her about some marvellous part he was up for and begging her to take him back again. The simple truth of the matter was, she couldn't afford to take him back either emotionally or financially, and so she left the message for when she returned. She was late enough for the party as it was.

Finally grabbing at a black silk camisole top and a scarlet and black bolero jacket she checked her make-up and hair in the mirror and dashed from the room, hoping she could find a taxi quickly.

She was lucky for once, and by eight-thirty she was at Chrissy's luxury flat in Mayfair, fighting her way through the throng of chattering authors, editors, agents and occasional minor 'party celebrities' who turned up at every possible party on the off-chance of getting their photo in the papers. They were wasting their time here, she thought, because only the publishing trade magazines were likely to be interested in this particular excuse for free food and drink; the introduction of Chrissy's new editorial director.

Chrissy saw her tall, blonde-haired friend cross the room and managed to fight her way to her side. 'I thought you weren't going to make it! What kept you?'

Deborah shrugged. 'The usual things; work, a message from Mick that I . . .'

'I thought you and Mick were finished?'

'We are, but after four years it isn't that easy to remove someone from your life. Besides, I miss him.'

'He was a lazy sponger and you're better off without him,' Chrissy said firmly. 'I'll introduce you to Gavin, he's the new director we've just taken on and he's absolutely gorgeous. He's thirty-one, dark-haired and brooding and best of all, single!'

'One dark-haired brooding man in four years is more than enough thank you, Chrissy. Look, is there any chance we could have a talk about work. The thing is . . .'

'Work?' Chrissy's eyes opened wide and she gazed at Deborah in surprise. 'If you want to talk serious work, ring my secretary and fix a date for lunch, Debbie! Look, I've got to see Gavin. Even if you don't want to meet him there are plenty of people who do, that is what the party's for! Drinks are in the other room. You probably know everyone here.'

As Chrissy turned away, Deborah sighed to herself and drifted towards the far room. Of course she knew everyone there, the trouble was this was the first time she'd been to a party without Mick for a very long time and it hurt. It hurt almost as much as what was happening to her at work.

A bartender had been hired for the evening and he handed Deborah a glass of champagne. She took a sip and then grimaced as she realised it wasn't very good, in fact it was vile. Cheap champagne, loud chatter and not an interesting person in sight she thought to herself, wondering why she hadn't stayed at home. She should have remembered that no one talked serious business at parties like this.

At that precise moment a man walked in through the doorway whom she didn't know and who was certainly interesting. He was huge, at least six foot, three inches tall and built like an American footballer who still had his pads on underneath his cream suit, with its unusually long jacket. At a rough guess Deborah put him in his early forties, and quite apart from his height and build he was noticeable for his thick mop of grey hair and a pair of incredibly piercing blue eyes which were surveying the room intently.

When his eyes found Deborah's his gaze stayed fixed on her and she ran her hand through her long fair hair in an instinctive gesture of femininity. He stared even more intently and then smiled broadly at her, showing a set of impossibly perfect white teeth. He muttered something to the slim, dark-haired man at his side and then walked purposefully towards Deborah. Much to her amusement he didn't have to push his way through the crowd, people seemed to automatically melt away to allow him room.

When he was about three feet away from her, he held out a massive hand. 'Hi, I'm John Pavin III, from America as you'll doubtless have worked out from the accent. My friends all call me Pavin.'

An American! Deborah felt like screaming in frustration. For a moment she'd felt a wonderful surge of sexual attraction, something that hadn't happened to her for so long she'd decided it had vanished along with Mick, and now he had to turn out to be an American, one of the enemy.

John Pavin saw the answering gleam of appreciation die out of the light brown eyes of this exquisite English-rose type beauty and wondered what he could have done wrong.

Deborah managed to hold out her hand in return, but she knew that her voice was cool as she introduced herself. 'I'm Deborah Woods, known to my friends as Debbie, or Debs,' she responded.

'You in publishing?'

'Of course. This *is* a publishing party. Don't tell me you and your countrymen are going to take over Chrissy's publishing house as well. She's spent ten years building this up, can't you leave anything alone?'

'Hey! I'm not buying up anything that belongs to your friend, I'm only here . . .'

'To see if there's anything left worth having?' Deborah finished for him, her cheeks flushing with irrational pent-up fury, really directed at what was happening to her at work.

The American's smile became more cautious and he released her hand, which he'd been holding in a grip so tight it was beginning to hurt. 'Look honey, I don't know what you've got against Americans but I can assure you . . .'

'That you're only here so that you can have a small stake in our wonderful culture? That's bullshit and you know it. Once you take over, culture's a dirty word, and everything gets run by accountants. God, you'd think your own country would be big enough for you, but no, you have to come here and turn us into a load of fast-book companies; the McDonald's of the literary world.'

John Pavin hardly heard the words the gorgeous blonde girl was uttering because he was totally bewitched by her looks and her accent. Tall, slim and,

4

until she'd suddenly turned on him, seemingly cool and remote she'd aroused instant desire in him. The fact that she didn't appear to like him or his fellow countrymen one bit didn't bother him, he was rather enjoying the flush of temper on her cheeks. It helped him picture how she'd look at the height of passion. She also had the most wonderful mouth, the slightly pouting lower lip making an intriguing contrast with the slim upper one. He was a connoisseur of the opposite sex, and knew a passionate woman when he saw one. He'd stake all he owned on Deborah Woods being very passionate indeed, and if he moved at the right pace she might even provide him with some companionship on his remote island in the Orkneys next month. His mouth went dry at the prospect of taking her there to meet his carefully selected group of friends.

'Aren't you going to say anything?' demanded Deborah, having finally run out of accusations to hurl against him concerning the invasion of Americans into the world of British publishing.

The American gave a lopsided grin. 'Deborah, there's not a lot I can say. You see, I'm in oil.'

For the first time in her life Deborah wished that the floor would open up and swallow her. She knew that she'd been behaving badly, haranguing him without provocation, but to discover that he wasn't in publishing at all was unbearable. The hectic colour ebbed from her cheeks and her eyes widened while her lips parted and she stared up at John Pavin in dismay. 'You're not in publishing?'

He shook his head.

'God, I'm so sorry. I mean, it was inexcusable of me. I've had the most ghastly day, well ghastly few weeks to be honest. I came out in a vile mood and . . .'

'And I just happened to step into the firing line, is that right?'

5

Deborah was relieved to find that he didn't seem annoyed, in fact if anything he sounded amused. 'Yes, I'm afraid you did. Look, I think I'll get off home. I wasn't in the mood for a party anyway, and now . . .' She looked up at him again, aware that it was unusual for a man to tower over her in the way he did, and gave an apologetic smile. 'Believe me, I'm not usually this rude. You caught me on a really bad day. I hope everyone else you meet here is a lot nicer than me!'

She turned to go but his right hand moved with surprising speed and caught her by the elbow. 'Did you drive yourself here?'

'No, I came by taxi.'

'I'll run you home.'

'No, honestly that's all right. I couldn't possibly let you. Not after the way I carried on! There are always loads of taxis along this road.'

'Look, it's a pretty boring party and I'm not that keen to stay myself. You'll do me a favour if you let me drive you home. Don't you think you owe me that?'

Deborah hesitated. 'Yes, I suppose I do. Okay, I'll just tell Chrissy I'm going.' She hurried through the rooms looking for her friend, finally finding her with a soulful-looking man who she assumed was the so-called gorgeous Gavin. The large American would have eaten him for breakfast she thought with a smile.

'Chrissy, I'm off,' she whispered. 'I'm really tired and that man over there, the tall American who's like something out of *Dallas* has offered to run me home so I thought I'd go. I'll call you at the office.'

Chrissy's eyes flew to where John Pavin III was waiting by the door. 'Debs, you do know who that is, don't you?'

'Sure, someone big in oil. Well, big in anything come to that!'

'Debbie, he is *the* John Pavin III, one of the thirty wealthiest men in America. He also has the reputation of being an incredible womaniser and fantastic in bed, although none of his ex-wives or girlfriends ever talk about him so we don't really know any juicy details.'

'He's running me home, Chrissy, not taking me through the Kama Sutra page by page. I must go, see you soon.'

'If he does offer to go through the Kama Sutra I should let him!' laughed Chrissy as her friend walked away. And when she turned back to chat animatedly with her new editorial director he didn't seem quite as attractive to her as he had done before she'd taken a good look at the Texan millionaire.

Deborah had expected a large, tasteless car, but John Pavin was driving a black Saab and he drove surprisingly carefully through the London streets as she directed him to her flat. She couldn't help noticing the size of his hands on the steering wheel, the wide spread of the fingers and the way his nails were cut neatly back. She wondered what hands like that would feel like on her breasts and thighs. Mick's hands had been slender and light, artistic hands she'd called them. There was nothing artistic about this man's hands, but they looked very capable.

'Still mad at me?' he asked abruptly.

Deborah jumped, wondering what on earth she was doing letting her thoughts wander like that. Since she and Mick had parted three months earlier she'd only had two brief, unsatisfactory one-night stands and had resolved to put sex on the back burner for a while. She decided her erotic daydreaming must be the result of the sudden lack of sex in her life.

'Of course I'm not mad at you,' she replied quickly. 'It wouldn't be logical considering you're in oil! Mind you, I can't help wondering what you were doing at a publishing party that was held to introduce Chrissy's new editorial director to everyone who counts?'

'I went with a friend,' he said casually. 'The friend is

7

in publishing, so it's probably a good job you let rip at me and not him!'

'What company's he connected with?' queried Deborah.

'I've no idea. To be honest, I'm not a reader. Is there anywhere round here I can park?'

'If we're lucky there should be a space round the back of the flats, yes look, over there. Would you like to come in for coffee?' she added, thinking it was the least she could do after her earlier rudeness.

The American slid the car smoothly into the space and followed Deborah on foot round to the front entrance of the flats and up the stairs to her top floor apartment.

'I'm afraid it's a bit untidy,' she said awkwardly, remembering the way she'd dashed out earlier. 'I wasn't expecting anyone to come back with me.'

He looked carefully at her. 'I don't have to stay for coffee. If you'd rather I went . . .?'

Deborah shook her head. She definitely didn't want him to leave. There was something about him that was extremely attractive but she wasn't sure if it was the almost overwhelming impression of rugged masculinity or the fact that she now knew he was rich and powerful that was attracting her. She'd always found successful men irresistible, until she met Mick, who was the complete opposite.

'There should be somewhere you can sit down,' she promised him with a laugh, and opened her front door. The laugh died in her throat and she stared around her flat in horror. Clothes, CDs, pictures and ornaments were strewn all over the floor and where her TV and video had stood there was now just an empty space.

'Hey, you weren't exaggerating!' the American said softly. 'This is probably the biggest mess you can get.'

'I've been burgled, you idiot!' snapped Deborah, her legs turning weak. 'Even I'm not stupid enough to mislay my television set. And look at my CD rack, half of my favourite operas are missing. I'd better check the bedroom.'

'Wait!' The American caught hold of her arm. 'Let me go. Someone might still be here.'

Deborah hadn't thought of that, and she moved quickly towards the phone. 'I'm calling the police. No doubt they'll tell me it's happening to someone every four minutes but I still think they should be told. Besides, if any of my jewellery's gone I'd like it back. Some of it's been handed down from . . .' She tailed off as she saw a note written in Mick's familiar hand pinned to the cork board over the telephone.

Couldn't get you on the answerphone so came and took my things anyway. I couldn't find my red silk shirt anywhere. Please send it on when it finally surfaces. By the way, I got the job. Hope you're missing me but knowing you, you'll miss the TV and video more.

Mick

Deborah stared at the note then snatched it down and crumpled it up into a ball. 'How could he?' she shouted furiously. 'He had no right to take half the things he has. He never paid for anything while he lived here. I kept him for four years and now he has the nerve to turn round and . . .'

'Who?' asked the American. 'Just who the hell's done this?'

Deborah had forgotten he was there for a moment. When she looked at him, he saw that her eyes were filling with tears. 'I'm sorry, John. It's my ex-lover. We split up three months ago and he's been on at me to take him back. Now he's obviously lost patience and decided to move out everything he considers his, but nothing was his apart from his personal possessions, nothing at all!'

9

'Tell me where he lives and I'll go round and fetch your stuff back,' he said swiftly.

Deborah didn't know whether to laugh or cry at the thought of this huge, muscular man turning up on Mick's doorstep and marching out with her TV while her ex-lover looked on.

'No. It doesn't matter,' she said slowly. 'It's better that he's gone for good, I just wish he'd done it in a nicer way.'

'I guess it wasn't a friendly split?'

'No, John, it wasn't.' Deborah's hands were clasped tightly together in front of her and she was rigid with shock and tension.

The American moved closer to her. 'Call me Pavin, honey. I hated my father and when he died I didn't want people calling me by his name. Let's face it, John Junior isn't exactly appropriate for someone of my build.'

Deborah began to laugh, but all at once the laughter turned to tears and she suddenly found that she was sobbing uncontrollably. Gently, Pavin led her to the sofa, swept the assortment of clothes off it and then sat her carefully down facing him, their bodies close together. He kept one large hand on the back of her neck, letting his fingers massage the rigid tendons lightly, while occasionally allowing his fingers to stray to the roots of her blonde hair.

Even through her tears Deborah was aware of his touch. And when his other hand began to rub small circles between her shoulder blades she found herself turning towards him and the next thing she knew she was buried against his huge chest and sobbing away all the tensions and strains of the past three months.

Pavin let her cry herself out. He kept his arms around her and held her firmly against him. Then when the tears eased, his hands massaged carefully all over her back and upper arms as she moved closer so that he could feel her breasts pressing against him.

10

Deborah had forgotten what it was like to have a man comfort her. Mick had always been the one in need of comfort. Every failed audition, every rejection of any kind, had resulted in childlike sulks that would go on for days if she didn't pamper him and shower him with affection. To have a man taking care of her was bliss, and when the tears finally ended and Pavin put a finger beneath her chin, raising her face towards him, she closed her eyes and waited with eager excitement for his kiss.

It wasn't the kind of kiss she'd expected. He looked the sort of man who'd ravish you with his mouth, kissing hard and forcefully, but he tickled the corners of her mouth with the tip of his tongue, teasing her so that she strained upwards for closer contact and he then let his tongue slide inside her mouth for a brief second before returning to the corners again. Deborah found that she was twisting her head in an attempt to feel his tongue inside her mouth more often.

After a while, Pavin slid Deborah into a reclining position and then bent her head back more, supporting it at the back with one large hand that covered both the base of her skull and the nape of her neck. He then carefully parted her lips with his tongue before licking all round the inside of her mouth in deliciously sensuous movements that aroused her whole body so that she was achingly aware of every one of her erogenous zones.

He continued to kiss in this way for several minutes and then, as Deborah pressed her body up towards him, he finally thrust his tongue deeply into her mouth and at once she longed to feel his penis thrusting inside her as well and she tightened her arms round his neck, trying desperately to communicate her longing for more intimate contact.

Once he was certain that this was what Deborah wanted, Pavin picked her up off the sofa and carried her through into the bedroom, still teasing her mouth

11

with little licks and flicks of his tongue. Then he laid her on the bed and moved away for a moment.

'Don't go!' said Deborah frantically, terrified that he was about to desert her. She opened her eyes, which had been closed to savour the sensations caused by his kissing, and saw that he was quickly stripping off his clothes. As she'd thought, although he was a very big man there was no fat on him, it was all well-toned muscle and she shivered with excitement at the thought of what was to come.

Sitting up she began to peel off her bolero, but Pavin shook his head. 'Let me,' he said harshly, his own arousal evident in his huge erect penis and the slight huskiness of his voice.

Obediently Deborah waited until he sat on the bed next to her and began to unfasten the jacket buttons one by one and then he slid it off her shoulder tantalisingly slowly. After that his fingers slid beneath the bottom of her black silk camisole top, gliding over her skin and brushing the undersides of her bare breasts as he eased it over her head.

He lowered his head for a moment and kissed each of her already erect nipples, and then he pulled the Lycra skirt down over her legs, unfastened her black stockings and peeled them down her legs and over her feet before finally slipping a thumb under the sides of her cut-away briefs and inching them from between her already damp thighs.

No one had ever taken so long to undress her and by the time she was naked her body was screaming for the touch of his hands and mouth, but to her surprise he promptly left the room, only to return a few seconds later with a bottle of baby lotion that he'd found in the bathroom.

'You're tense, honey. You need a massage,' he said softly. He then slipped her onto her face with one easy movement and she heard him rub some of the lotion

12

between the palms of his hands before lightly pressing across the admittedly tight muscles of her neck and shoulders.

Deborah turned her face to the left and felt his hands gliding across her, slowly increasing their pressure as he reached beneath the soft flesh to the taut muscles and joints beneath.

After that he travelled on down the sides of her spine and across the base of her back, working with extra vigilance on the area between the small bones above her buttocks. Deborah groaned and pressed her pubic bone down against the mattress to try and get some stimulation on her rapidly engorging vulva.

With a soft laugh, Pavin at last turned her onto her back again, and now his hands crossed the front of her shoulders and swept down the valley between her breasts, but he never once touched the swollen breast tissue itself or the tight, hard little nipples that were frantic for contact. Instead he spread the lotion around her stomach in circular movements and, as his hands pushed the skin of her tight abdomen upwards, she could feel a small tug on the hood of her clitoris as it moved and pinpoints of promised pleasure began to spark there.

Pavin watched Deborah closely. Her whole body was becoming restless, her breasts engorged with the veins showing dark blue through her fair skin and the nipples so tight he knew they must be hurting, but still he waited. Now his hands parted her willing thighs and he moved down the bed, keeping her legs apart with his vast forearms while he massaged the delicate skin of her inner thighs but he didn't touch her swollen outer labia despite the tell-tale beads of moisture he could see on her fine pubic hair.

His rhythmic stimulation of her body was driving Deborah into a frenzy. She wanted to scream at him to touch her between her thighs, to suck on her throbbing

13

nipples and release the mounting tension, and yet at the same time she was enjoying the glorious feeling of heightened sexuality. She wanted release and yet she didn't want the lovemaking to end.

Pavin lay on his side, his head level with Deborah's breasts and as his hands moved lazily down the outside of her long legs he suddenly stabbed at her left nipple with his tongue and as her eyes flew open he took the whole nipple into his mouth and then drew back his head so that her nipple was fully extended to a point where it was almost painful. Then he slowly rolled his tongue around the tip before releasing it.

Deborah's breathing was becoming more and more rapid and her hips moved in reflexive jerks as he continued to arouse her without touching the core of her pleasure. As he took all the nipple and surrounding areola into his mouth he let his free hand move down her stomach so that the heel of his hand was resting on her pubic bone and his fingers were finally where she wanted them to be; between her thighs.

Now his touch was incredibly light and sensitive. His fingertips eased her outer sex lips apart and then danced gently over the slippery flesh beneath until they located her throbbing clitoris. Deborah arched up to meet him.

'No, keep still. It's better this way,' he whispered, raising his head from her breast for a moment. Deborah obeyed him. No one had ever made love to her this well before and she certainly wasn't going to argue now.

For a moment he rested the tip of one finger very softly against the tip of her clitoris, and then he tapped at it lightly and Deborah gasped as pleasure shot through her, zig-zagging its way right up through her abdomen to where he was once again sucking on her engorged breasts.

Now the tapping continued, increasing in pressure and speed until her entire pubic area seemed to be on fire and the heavy aching pleasure grew and grew but without reaching a climax. Deborah moaned, twisting and turning as she tried to bring about her release, but Pavin knew what he was doing. As beads of perspiration formed on her top lip and her abdomen tightened yet more he stopped drumming on the clitoris and instead slid two fingers up from beneath it so that it stood out between the V-shape of the join. Then he pressed down with the two fingers while at the same time increasing the pressure on the trapped stem of Deborah's screaming bud.

She'd never known sensations like it, and as he pressed down against the inner folds and squeezed the clitoris like a pip, he at last triggered her climax and her whole body went rigid as she was suffused with orgasmic waves of ecstasy that rolled over her in an endless stream until she thought she might pass out from the pleasure.

When the last spasms of excitement had finally died away, Deborah opened her eyes to find Pavin looking down at her, a smile of pleasure on his lips. She smiled back at him, and then felt his hands grasp her at the waist and turn her to face him so that they were both on their sides. She lifted her top leg over his hip as he pulled her against him, and for a moment felt the tip of his swollen penis playing at the entrance to her vagina before, with a sudden thrust, he was inside her and the slight ache that had remained within her even after her shattering climax was finally stilled by the comforting thickness of him deep within her.

Pavin used his hands on her hips to move her backwards and forwards on him, slowly at first but then more rapidly, the rhythm increasing as their mutual excitement mounted. Deborah closed her eyes, but immediately Pavin stopped moving.

'Look at me,' he said firmly. 'I want to watch your face as you come.'

15

Even the words added to her excitement, and this time she kept her eyes open and saw his pupils dilate as he approached his own climax but he seemed to know that hers was still a little way away because he withdrew slightly, and moved his penis around just inside her vaginal opening in small circles that aroused the nerve endings situated at the entrance. Once again the darts of pleasure grew and her breasts strained towards his chest, the nipples brushing against the thick hairs that covered him there.

Now that she was near, he gripped her nipples even harder and began to move her vigorously so that she could feel him thrusting to fill the whole length of her and then withdrawing slightly as her body was pushed backwards, and all the time she stared into his piercing blue eyes and saw her own excitement reflected back at her.

The sensations expanded to cover her whole body, she was suffused with heat and knew that her climax was only seconds away. 'I'm coming!' she told him, because Mick had always wanted to know so that he could stop worrying about control and let himself go too.

At once Pavin stopped moving and held her body motionless. Deborah nearly screamed at him in frustration. 'I was nearly there!' she whispered. 'Didn't you understand what I said?'

He smiled. 'Sure I heard. That's why I stopped. It's always better to wait a little. Makes it all the better in the end.'

Experience had shown Deborah that the opposite was true. If for some reason Mick had stopped too near the vital moment she'd never managed to get it back and had usually ended up faking her climax. Pavin saw the doubt in her eyes.

'Trust me, Debs. Just wait a moment and you'll see.'

She had no choice because his hands held her tightly

by the hips and she wasn't strong enough to move unless he released her. For several minutes they lay face to face, their breathing gradually slowing, and then just as the last of the sexual tingles were dying away, Pavin began to move her again. He used the same tempo, building up from slow thrusts to quick, only this time as her excitement mounted he became fiercer and her body slammed into his every time he pulled her up against him.

Now the sensations were like red tongues of fire scorching her as her clitoris ground against his lower body every time their flesh met, and suddenly she felt as though her whole stomach was swelling visibly with the pressure of the approaching orgasm, and her breath came in short gasps as she prayed silently that he wouldn't stop again.

He didn't. Instead he watched her eyes widening in anticipation and, just seconds before she climaxed, he reached behind her and inserted the tip of his little finger into her tight anus so that it seemed to Deborah every nerve ending possible was being stimulated and she arched her belly into his as her second climax of the evening tore through her.

Pavin heard her cry out with excitement and this, coupled with the feeling of her breasts and belly thrusting against him, finally triggered his own orgasm and he went rigid, his teeth clenched as a small groan escaped from between his lips.

Deborah felt him shuddering and wrapped her arms round his broad back, feeling the thin film of perspiration that was covering his skin and relishing the closeness and the physical satiation.

For a long time they lay entwined, their eyes finally closed now that they were finished, and Deborah felt his heartbeat slowing against her breast. Finally he withdrew and sat up, glancing at the watch that he'd left on the bedside table.

17

'I'll have to be going, Debbie,' he said reluctantly.

She felt surprisingly bereft. It wasn't as though she knew him well, and she certainly hadn't intended to go to bed with him tonight, but now that she had she didn't want to lose him. He'd just given her the best sex she'd ever had and quite apart from that she found him incredibly attractive.

'Of course,' she said coolly, hoping he couldn't tell quite what an impact he'd made on her.

Pavin dressed swiftly and she pulled on a robe to see him to the door. He glanced around at the mess made by Mick. 'I'll send someone round to help you clear this lot up tomorrow.'

'There's no need. I know where it all belongs. I was just mad at the way he'd done it behind my back. Somehow it doesn't seem so bad now!'

Pavin grinned at her. 'Good! I'll ring you, Debbie. What's your number?'

She gave it to him, he jotted it down in a notebook, kissed her very softly on the lips and then left without a backward glance. Deborah hugged her robe tightly about her. She knew that she ought to take a shower, but didn't want to lose the distinctive smell of him that was all over her at the moment. Instead she made herself a pot of tea and sat in the kitchen drinking cup after cup and wondering if and when he'd call her again.

When she finally went to bed she told herself that even if he didn't call he'd certainly helped her get over Mick. Just the same, she hoped that he did. It hadn't felt like a one-night stand to her, and she didn't want to think that was all it had been to him.

She finally fell asleep re-playing their lovemaking in her mind.

Chapter Two

*A*fter three days had passed without Deborah hearing a word from Pavin, she reluctantly decided that she'd been nothing more than an enjoyable one-night stand. Since, on the two previous occasions she'd slept with men since her affair with Mick ended, she'd been the one to leave calls unanswered, she supposed there was a kind of justice in this, but that didn't stop it hurting. The sex had been fantastic and she'd felt really attracted to him. Apparently the feeling hadn't been mutual.

Exactly a week to the day after she'd met the American at Chrissy's party, she was called to her managing director's office and told officially that she would not be promoted to fill the vacancy of senior fiction editor at Pegasus, despite her eight years as deputy.

'It's nothing personal,' the managing director assured her, his eyes fixed firmly on his desk top rather than meeting hers. 'It's simply that the current policy here is for new faces. We have to bring in fresh blood, liven ourselves up, create a new image.'

'I'll have to go then,' said Deborah firmly, having had

plenty of time to prepare herself for this since rumours had been circulating for several weeks.

'If that's what you want, then of course you must, but no one at Pegasus would dream of asking you to go. We value all you've done for us,' responded the managing director tonelessly.

Deborah wished that she could tell him exactly what she thought of him and the spineless way he was carrying out the new American owner's demands, but that would mean she'd find it difficult to work anywhere else and so she swallowed her pride, told him she'd like to leave as soon as possible and left his office.

Even Deborah was surprised though when her secretary began helping her pack up her personal possessions that very afternoon, and by the time she left the office at five-thirty she knew that she wouldn't ever be going back. She'd receive a generous cheque in lieu of notice no doubt, but as far as work was concerned her years at Pegasus were over.

Once back at her flat she swore aloud for a good five minutes, threw all her belongings into a corner of the living room and then ran herself a deep bath. She emptied half a bottle of bubble bath into it, then stripped off her clothes, collected a bottle of white wine from the fridge and took it together with a glass into the bathroom. She'd drown her sorrows in comfort.

Just as she was about to step into the bath, the doorbell went. She waited, hoping the caller would go away, but within seconds the buzzer was sounding again. This time it was a long impatient ring forcing her to pull on her towelling robe and go and see who it was. She slipped the chain on first and peeped out, then clutched her robe more tightly round her in amazement.

'Pavin!'

His eyes flickered over her and his mouth widened in the familiar grin that made her stomach turn over.

'Seems I called at just the right time. Can I come in, or has some lucky guy beaten me to it?'

With shaking fingers she slipped the chain off and opened the door. 'No, I'm quite alone. I was just going to take a bath. What on earth brought you here this evening? I thought you were probably back in the States by now.'

He draped a heavy arm round her shoulders. 'Without contacting you? That would have been pretty unlikely after the time we had together! No, I've been caught up in some unexpected business, that's all. Hey, nice smell!'

'It's my bubble bath. I lost my job today, at least I handed in my notice, and I was about to drown my sorrows.'

'Fine, I'll watch you.'

Suddenly Deborah felt unexpectedly shy. Considering how intimate they'd been on their first evening she knew it was stupid but she still felt herself beginning to blush.

Pavin saw the tell-tale colour staining her fair skin and was delighted. He loved to see a woman blush, especially when it was due to sexual excitement, mixed with modesty. She was delicious, he thought to himself, and she'd be the perfect guest to make up the numbers on his private Orkney island. All he had to do now was persuade her to come.

'You don't mind, do you?' he continued with a smile. 'If you like I promise not to touch!'

'Of course I don't mind, it's only that you've taken me by surprise.'

In the bathroom, which seemed far too small to contain someone of Pavin's size, she let her robe fall to the floor and stepped into the tub. He sat himself down on the top of the wicker clothes basket and Deborah hoped it would take the strain. She slid beneath the

21

bubbles until only her face and toes were peeking out at opposite ends.

'How come you lost your job?' Pavin asked conversationally.

'The Americans have brought someone in over me, and after eight years I'd expected to get promoted. I had to go, and the directors knew that. They didn't make me redundant because of the cost, they just made it impossible for me to stay.'

'That's business, honey. Aren't you going to wash at all?'

She slid into a sitting position and began to use the sponge on her shoulders and breasts, knowing full well that Pavin was watching her like a hawk and feeling her nipples spring to attention the moment the sponge touched them.

When she'd spent as long as she possibly could on her upper body she lifted one long leg from the water and began to sponge that. Pavin leant forward. 'Can't I help?'

Her body longed for him to touch her again, but part of her resented the fact that he hadn't made contact for so long. 'I can manage,' she said at last.

'You *are* mad at me, Debbie! Why?'

She shrugged, struggling to reach her toes and aware that Pavin was laughing at her efforts. 'I suppose I thought you might have at least called to let me know you were busy.'

'I've only just got my second divorce finalised. I quite like not having to answer to anybody right now.'

'Fine.'

Pavin mentally filed away the fact that she was more attracted to him than she was letting on and wasn't going to give in easily. That suited him. He preferred difficult conquests. 'Come on, let me at least soap your back.'

Deborah threw the sponge at him. He caught it

neatly, and moving very lightly for such a big man made his way round the cramped bathroom until he was kneeling on the floor behind her. He then soaped her back with large circular movements before sluicing off all the bubbles with the bathwater.

She was about to take the sponge back when she felt his hands on her waist. He was easing her up into a standing position and then the sponge was sliding between her thighs, caressing the responsive skin on the insides of her knees and up towards her pubic hair. He ignored her genitals but instead slid the sponge round beneath her and soaped each of her buttocks in turn, squeezing the sponge so that trickles of warm soapy fluid ran down the crease between them, some of it running beneath her to tickle at her outer labia.

Deborah wriggled, and Pavin laughed before pressing down on her shoulders so that she was once again sitting in the tub, somewhat surprised that he hadn't touched her more intimate parts.

'Don't you have a shower?' he asked, holding out the large but somewhat frayed bath towel she'd laid out for herself.

'Not in this flat.'

'I guess a tub's got more potential, but only a big one. I doubt if I could get in that little thing on my own, let alone with you! Come on, let's get you dry.'

Deborah couldn't think why she wasn't more resentful of the way he was taking over. Normally she liked her independence, and for a time it had quite suited her that Mick had been the dependent one. This American couldn't have been more opposite in manner and approach but somehow that only increased the attraction for her. Her carefully controlled life at work and home was falling apart around her, and for once she was grateful to let someone else take over.

Pavin swung Deborah out and onto her feet, then rubbed her briskly all over with the towel. This time his touch was far less delicate than the first time he'd touched her, but as the blood coursed through her veins she found this highly exciting.

'Dry?' he asked shortly.

Deborah nodded.

At that, Pavin removed the towel, threw it on the bathroom floor and carried her in his arms to her bedroom. There he lowered her to the bed for a moment, but as she started to lie back he shook his head. 'No, stand up and face me.'

Obediently she did as he asked.

'Now undress me,' he said softly.

A pulse began to beat rapidly in her throat and she found that her fingers were shaking as she fumbled with the tiny buttons of his shirt front. When his jacket and shirt were off at last, she knelt down, took off his shoes then began to undo the wide leather belt that held his trousers up. After that she slowly opened the zip and eased the trouser legs down until they reached the floor and he could step out of them. He then lifted each foot in turn and she took off his socks. Finally she hooked her hands in the sides of his boxer shorts and began to ease them off him, but they got caught on his erection and she had to stop and reach inside the buttoned fly to release him before she was finally able to remove the last barrier between them.

Once he was naked he drew her to him, wrapping his arms round her back and moving her slowly from side to side so that her nipples rubbed against his chest, caught in the curly hair there and grew tighter and tighter with her rising excitement and the friction.

Pavin lowered his arms slightly so that they were round the back of her waist. 'Wrap your arms round the back of my neck and your legs round my waist,' he murmured. Deborah hesitated. She was tall for a girl and it wasn't something any of her previous lovers had ever suggested. Then she realised that for a man of

Pavin's height and strength it would be easy, and quickly she followed his instruction. As her legs closed round his waist his hands tightened on her back and moved a fraction lower so that he could angle her hips more towards him. Then, with one swift, almost brutal thrust he was inside her and instinctively she used her arms to help pull herself up and down on him while he stood firmly braced, his muscles rigid with tension and his eyes strangely impassive as he stared into her face.

'Move faster,' he whispered. 'Don't worry about me, make it good for yourself.'

She loved it when he talked to her. Mick had rarely spoken during sex and to be told to be totally selfish was irresistible. She moved as rapidly as she could, hanging back as far as her extended arms would let her so that her long fair hair tickled between her shoulder-blades adding a new touch of sensuality.

Pavin shifted his weight slightly, making some small adjustment, and suddenly Deborah's clitoris was being indirectly stimulated so that with every move she made she could feel that tiny nub of nerve endings swelling with excitement. Now her face had a sheen of perspiration on it and her eyes were half-closed as pre-orgasmic tension began to grip her.

Pavin was filling her with his rock-hard erection, her body had found its rhythm and was steadily climbing to its peak of fulfilment and Deborah was totally lost in the pleasure of it when suddenly Pavin lowered her so that her upper torso was resting on the bed and now her arms let go of the back of his neck and spread themselves across the width of the mattress as he bent over her, put his hands beneath her hips and without withdrawing was able to move himself inside her.

He was thrusting almost savagely now. His hands, free at last, gripped her swollen sensitive breasts and his fingers dug into their tender sides as he squeezed

25

and squeezed until finally Deborah felt that she would have to cry out because he was hurting her.

She looked up at him and he was watching her closely, almost as though he was waiting for her to speak. 'You're hurting me,' she whispered.

'Wait,' he whispered back. 'Trust me, just go with it.'

She bit on her bottom lip, but before she could protest again, the streaks of excitement that were leaping up through her body every time he lunged into her were joined by flashes of pain-edged pleasure from her breasts and when the two sensations became one she heard herself start to cry out with excitement. Then her whole body was suffused with one incredible wave of tension that exploded into a ball of fire which engulfed her entire body in heat and she felt her toes curl up with a new and glorious kind of orgasm that she'd never experienced before.

Her body was still throbbing with the dying pulsations of her climax when Pavin finally reached his own and once again his top lip drew back over his teeth and the smallest of groans escaped him as his body went rigid for a few seconds before he lowered himself carefully onto the bed next to her, his hands still wrapped round her tender breasts, but loosely now. In the post-orgasmic minutes that followed, his large fingers moved with exquisite gentleness over the sore breast tissue in such a tender way it was difficult to imagine these were the same fingers that had gripped her so harshly. Deborah turned her face into his shoulder and laid one arm across his chest. It had certainly been a new experience for her, and she had to admit that she'd enjoyed it.

After a while Pavin tweaked one of her nipples. 'Come on, let's go out and eat. Good sex always gives me an appetite. Where would you like to go?'

'I don't mind. I quite like Italian or Chinese.'

He shook his head. 'How about seafood? I know a

26

great place not far from here, and it's never too crowded either.'

Deborah didn't really mind where they went and so she agreed. She dressed quickly in a pair of black velvet leggings and a long multi-coloured silk top. Pavin, who was wearing a suit in exactly the same design as the one he'd worn when she'd met him but this time light brown in colour, nodded approvingly. 'You look good. Leggings show off your legs well. Do you know what you remind me of?'

'No!' laughed Deborah.

'One of those highly-strung racehorses, all slender legs and nerves.'

'I'll have you know I'm extremely capable,' protested Deborah.

'Hey, that was a compliment. I didn't mean neurotic kind of nervy, I meant sensuous, you know – sensitive nerve endings, erogenous zones, that kind of thing.'

Once again, Deborah blushed. 'That's not the kind of thing Englishmen ever say, Pavin.'

'More fool them. Come on, the car's outside.'

Within twenty minutes they were sitting at a secluded table, a platter of seafood in front of them and a bottle of champagne standing in its ice bucket at Pavin's right elbow.

'Tell me about yourself,' said Deborah. 'What exactly do you do in oil?'

'Not a lot these days. I made my money by luck a few years back, now I'm a kind of freelance troubleshooter for the oil rigs in your North Sea. I have a company based on the North Mainland of the Orkneys and there's an expert for almost any kind of problem available on demand. Most of my team are freelance so they take other work as well, but they know that when I call, it takes priority.'

'So you're in Scotland a lot?'

'Quite a bit. The real reason I'm here now is that

27

about this time of year I spend a couple of weeks on this little island I own off the North Mainland. A group of friends always join me, they're all employees but friends as well. They bring their wives, lovers or whatever and we have a good, relaxing time. We all enjoy the same kind of thing, if you know what I mean.'

Deborah stared at him. 'You *own* an island in the Orkneys?'

He shrugged. 'It's no big deal. Only sheep lived there before I brought it, and it's the best place in the world for total privacy. In the winter you can be cut off for weeks at a time, but now – in mid-summer – that doesn't happen. It's just that no one can come unless I invite them.'

'Are there many houses on the island?'

'Nope! The truth is, I rather indulged myself when I bought the place. It still had the ruins of this old castle on it, nestling under the slope of a hill facing out to sea, and I thought why not restore it? You know, do it up like it used to be. I got an historian in to help with ideas, and an architect the historian recommended, then between the three of us we kind of rebuilt the castle, only with modern plumbing. Showers too, would you believe!'

Pavin's face was alight with enthusiasm and Deborah felt touched by such childlike pleasure. 'So you've got your very own castle?'

'That's it, honey.'

'And all your friends stay in it when they come for their holiday?'

'Sure; it makes for a real cosy couple of weeks. On sunny days there's no place on earth like it. Talk about getting away from it all!'

'But what is there to do?' asked Deborah.

Pavin refilled her champagne glass. 'I've had a swimming pool put in, the sea's too damned cold for my

28

liking, and there's a sauna, a gym, all that kind of thing, plus the scenery.'

'I suppose you can walk for miles.'

He gave a half-smile. 'Sure, if that's what you want to do.'

'You must have to choose your guests carefully. All shut up together like that, it wouldn't do to have people who don't get on.'

Pavin lifted his glass to her. 'You're right there, but I'm a pretty good judge of people and most of us have been staying there for a few years now. Last year I took my wife, but this year . . .'

'Did she like the island?'

Pavin nodded. 'Sure, and the idea of being the lady of the manor. The trouble was, she didn't ever really get on that well with the others. She wouldn't mix in, if you get my meaning.'

Deborah nodded. 'Probably because she was used to being the boss's wife.'

'I don't think it was that exactly.' Pavin leant across the table and, picking up a king prawn from Deborah's plate, pulled off its head and then popped it into her mouth. The gesture was extraordinarily intimate and at the same time sexual. She felt a surge of desire for him. He saw the dilation of her eyes and moved his left leg beneath the table, so that their calves brushed against each other.

'How would you like a couple of weeks on my island, Debbie?' he asked softly.

Her mouth had already gone dry at the touch of his leg against hers. Now she realised he'd slipped off a shoe and one foot was resting on her knee, teasing the flesh beneath her leggings and then sliding on up until it came to the join between her thighs. At the same time he fed her another prawn, running a finger beneath her bottom lip where a tiny drop of mayonnaise had spilt.

A dull aching throb was starting up between her legs

29

and it was as much as she could do to swallow the prawn in order to answer him. 'I don't know if I could,' she muttered as his big toe rubbed very softly along the seam of her leggings which exactly divided her sex lips.

'Why not? You're out of a job and fancy free.'

'Your friends might not like me,' she protested, her voice rising as the toe increased its pressure between her sex lips and she felt currents of electricity shoot up through her pubic mound.

'Sure they would. Any friend of mine is a friend of theirs. And you don't have to worry. We're all intelligent, sensible people. There's no risk involved.'

Deborah couldn't think what he meant. She supposed some women would be nervous at the possibility of being marooned on a remote island for a few weeks, but Pavin had already said this didn't happen in summer and anyway if the men were troubleshooters in the oil business they must know how to cope with all kinds of emergencies.

'It's just that I don't know you that well, and I really ought to start looking for another job,' she muttered.

Pavin's foot curled round her entire sex mound and with tiny movements he gently palpated the flesh beneath the velvet leggings. Deborah felt herself becoming damp there and her cheeks were hot with desire. She glanced around to see if anyone could see what was happening, but there was no one near them.

'You look a little warm,' the American remarked casually, and only the dancing light in his eyes betrayed his amusement.

Deborah swallowed hard. Suddenly she wasn't interested in her food any more, all she wanted was the feel of this man's hands on her body, and the bliss of another of the intense climaxes he was able to give her.

He obviously read her mind. 'Drink up the champagne and we'll go,' he told her. 'You *are* going to come on holiday with me, aren't you?'

Deborah stared at him. It almost seemed as though the query was an ultimatum. If she said yes, then he'd go back to her flat now and finish what he'd started during the meal. If she said no, he wouldn't. But then she told herself she was being stupid. If it was an ultimatum he'd have spelt it out, not left her to guess.

Pavin withdrew his foot from between her thighs and knew exactly what she was thinking. It *was* an ultimatum, or at least a test. He needed to know if she was the kind of girl willing to take a risk, the kind who'd adapt to the type of holiday they all liked in the castle on his own private island.

'Why not!' exclaimed Deborah with a laugh. 'As you say, there's nothing to keep me here at the moment, and after the holiday I might be able to see things more clearly.'

'Sure you will. Besides, we'll have a lot of fun together and if you ask me you haven't been having enough fun lately. Mind you, we seem to be making up for that lost time right now!'

He put his arm round her waist as they left the restaurant, and Deborah had no idea that as far as John Pavin III was concerned, this holiday would quite possibly turn her into exactly the kind of woman he wanted for his third wife. The first two had both ended up disappointing him, but he had a feeling that Deborah wouldn't. Not that she understood about the holiday yet, but that didn't worry him. She'd soon learn, and enjoy herself in the process.

Once back at her flat, Deborah turned to him with a laugh. 'Would you like coffee? We left the restaurant in rather indecent haste!'

'Sure. Do you have a proper coffee maker?'

'Sorry, only instant.'

As Deborah reached up into one of her cupboards for the jar, Pavin glanced around the room. The kitchen table was large and solid, and as she turned back to him

31

he caught hold of her by the waist and pushed her across the table on her back, his hands sliding up the sides of her legs to pull down her leggings.

Deborah made a token protest, but really it was what she wanted, what she needed and had needed ever since his toe had danced along her sex lips throughout their meal.

Once the leggings and panties were off, Pavin pulled her towards the foot of the table and then lowered his head so that for the first time his mouth was covering her sex. Deborah's hands gripped the sides of the table and she felt her labia swelling as he sucked gently on the juices that were flowing from her opening. Then his tongue darted inside her vagina and out again, curling along the silky channel between the inner lips and spreading her with her own moisture.

He alternately licked and sucked until her hips were thrusting up at him in frantic despair as her frustrated clitoris throbbed and screamed for attention. When he still ignored it she moved a hand to it herself but he pushed her arm firmly away and exhaled very gently on the glistening bud to cool its heated pulsations.

It seemed that he was going to keep ignoring it for ever, and then just when Deborah felt sure she'd go out of her mind with need, Pavin lightly ran the tip of his tongue along the shaft of the clitoris and when she jerked and gasped he moved one hand, held back the small hood of flesh that covered the clitoris and kept the hood back so that it couldn't retract.

Exposed and vulnerable, the centre of her pleasure waited and Deborah's whole body went tense with expectation as Pavin delayed the moment of contact, then suddenly he stabbed at the clitoris again and again so that Deborah screamed aloud with the overwhelming intensity of feelings, feelings that were too much for her to bear but the clitoris couldn't escape because he still kept the hood held back. Now, although Deborah wanted him to stop he didn't, but instead kept flicking at the tight bunch of sensitive nerve endings so that Deborah's orgasm was suddenly swamped by another one, one that ached and tore through her causing her whole body to thrash on the hard wooden table. She felt her stomach muscles rippling with the harsh contractions that were sending incredible darting messages to every part of her body from the tips of her fingers to the ends of her toes. Then she was crying out, begging him to stop because if he didn't she felt sure that she would break into a thousand pieces.

Finally he released the fleshy hood, the clitoris retracted and then he turned her onto her face, unzipped his trousers and a few moments later was entering her from behind. Every thrust rubbed her entire pelvic area against the table so that when he came so did she and this time when she'd finished she closed her eyes in total exhaustion.

Pavin picked her up, carried her though into the living room and laid her down in one of the easy chairs before making the coffee himself and carrying the cups through to her as she dozed in the high-backed chair.

'That was incredible!' she murmured.

He sat on the sofa opposite and watched her from beneath lowered lids as she smiled dreamily to herself and absently fingered her breasts where they were sore from the friction against the table top.

'I'm going to be out of town for the next few days,' he said at last. 'Can you be ready to go by Friday week?'

At that moment Deborah would have been ready to go with him that evening, and so she smiled and nodded without really thinking about what she was promising.

'One of my men will collect you and you can fly to Glasgow together. After that it's a plane to the Orkneys and then my helicopter will fly you to the island itself.'

'Won't you be with me?' she asked in surprise.

33

'It doesn't look as though that will be possible. I'll be on the island to meet you though, that I can promise. Don't look so worried, sweetheart, no one's ever got lost finding their way there!'

'Do you call me "honey" and "sweetheart" because you can't remember my name or as an endearment?' asked Deborah lightly.

Pavin grinned. 'A bit of both I guess. Now, I've got to go, Debbie. Pack a couple of cardigans, the nights are long but cool even in June. If you've any problems ring this number. My secretary can always contact me within an hour of your call. Okay?'

She felt slightly bemused. 'So that's it, until the holiday?'

He put a hand gently on the back of her neck. 'You rest up, get yourself some new clothes and before you know it we'll be together again. I can't wait either, but sometimes even I have to work!'

She kissed him passionately and then they parted. Only after the door had closed behind him did she begin to wonder if she was doing the right thing.

Chapter Three

On the Thursday before she was due to leave for the Orkney islands, Deborah rang Chrissy at home. At first Chrissy sounded guarded, but once she realised that Deborah wasn't going to ask her for a job she became more friendly.

'I don't quite see your problem, Debs,' she commented after hearing about the forthcoming holiday. 'What's worrying you?'

'Well, I hardly know the man, do I! It's one thing to have a tempestuous affair in the safety of London, and quite another to go off to some remote island and stay with a group of unknown people for two weeks. What if they're all weirdos?'

Chrissy hesitated. 'Does Pavin seem the kind of man to have weird friends?'

'I suppose not, it's just that once or twice I catch him looking at me in a rather peculiar way, as though he's trying to work out how I tick or something, and he was a bit evasive about what they actually do on this island.'

'For heaven's sake, Debbie! What can they do apart from go for walks, enjoy the luxury of a millionaire's castle and make passionate love whenever they feel like it? Most girls would jump at the chance.'

'But a remote island's a bit worrying.'

Chrissy laughed. 'You're not being carried off to the Far East, you're only going to the far north of Britain! Honestly, if I were you I'd be off like a shot. From what I can gather your American friend is considered quite a catch.'

'I haven't caught him, I'm just having an affair with him.'

'Then enjoy it. You spent four years looking after Mick, supporting him financially and massaging his monstrous ego whenever it flagged. You deserve a break like this. As a matter of fact . . .'

'Yes?' asked Deborah curiously.

Chrissy lowered her voice. 'I probably shouldn't tell you this because she swore me to secrecy, but since she's now living abroad with some boring European count I don't think it matters.'

'Who is? And what doesn't matter?' pressed Deborah.

'You remember Diane Pashley, that small girl with the fabulous figure who worked in publicity for me a couple of years ago?'

'Yes.'

'Well, she went to stay on this island with her boyfriend just before she met her count.'

'With Pavin?' asked Deborah in amazement.

'No, not *with* him, but it was certainly his island and he and his wife of the time were there. Diane went with someone called Brian. I never met him but Diane was dead keen. I remember that when she came back she said it was the most incredible holiday of her life but she and Brian had found they weren't really suited. As far as I can remember she never saw him again.'

'Did she say anything about Pavin?' asked Deborah eagerly.

'She certainly did. In fact, she went on about him so

much that I wondered if the pair of them had had some kind of fling during the holiday and that was why she and Brian broke up, but I could be wrong. What I do know for certain is that the castle's the last word in luxury, the scenery's out of this world and you'd be stark staring mad not to go.'

'Yes, I suppose I would.'

Chrissy could hear that there were still lingering doubts in her friend's voice. 'Tell you what, Debbie. If you don't ring me within two days of when you're supposed to return, I'll alert the entire police force and Interpol for good measure, how's that?'

At last Deborah laughed. 'That sounds very reassuring. I honestly don't know why I'm worried, there's just something I can't put my finger on that's bothering me.'

'If what I hear's true, Pavin will put his finger on it for you pretty damn fast!' laughed Chrissy.

'That's none of your business!' giggled Deborah as she hung up.

Chrissy had put her mind at rest, and now she was ready to go. Her cases were packed, and a friend was going to come round to water her plants while she was away. Also, she had to admit that the thought of seeing Pavin again after what seemed an eternity was very exciting.

The trouble with you is, you've got out of the habit of having a good time and now feel guilty about it, she told herself sternly as she got into her bed for the last time before her holiday. Go with the flow as they say! With that comforting thought she fell asleep.

At eleven the next morning a well-built man in his late twenties, wearing a dark suit, white shirt and blue tie with a small yellow 'P' on it, arrived at her front door to escort her as far as Glasgow.

He was polite, well-spoken and agreeable but when she tried to ask him anything about the island he retreated into silence, indicating with a slight shrug that he knew nothing about the place. After a time, Deborah read a book because chatty conversation didn't seem to be his strong suit.

Two and a half hours later they were changing planes and at last she was actually on her way to Orkney. The flight ended at the Grimsetter aerodrome by Inganess Bay. Almost as soon as she and her companion, whose name she never did learn, had left the plane she was whisked into a waiting helicopter with 'Pavin Oil Co.' emblazoned on its side, then strapped in and whirled into the sky on the final leg of her journey to 'Pavinsay' as he had named his island.

When she'd found her courage, Deborah glanced out of the helicopter window and saw the scattering of islands dotted around the grey-blue sea, all formed over the centuries by the pounding of the waves. They were of various shapes and sizes, and none of them looked particularly hospitable. Considering that Pavin had assured her the sea was calm in summer, she thought the white caps on the waves surprising and could feel the helicopter being blown around by the wind.

When they at last descended towards Pavinsay she saw at once the large castle looking out over the sea, exactly as he'd described it to her, but its size took her breath away.

The landing pad was outside the castle grounds, and as the pilot helped her out, warning her to duck low, Pavin himself came striding across the greeny-brown scrubland to meet her.

He was wearing black jeans and a black and white plaid shirt, and as Deborah was taken into his arms and enfolded in a warm bear hug she realised that although he'd seemed perfectly at home in his suits and evening dress this was probably the way he was meant to be. Despite his money and position the sheer size and presence of him demanded a rugged, outdoor setting like this island provided. Fleetingly she wondered exactly how deep his veneer of sophistication went, and whether at heart he was more primitive than she'd imagined. A shiver of excited anticipation ran through her.

'How was the journey?' he asked after he'd finished kissing her enthusiastically.

'Fine, although I hadn't expected it to be quite so windy,' she added as a gust of wind caught her hair and blew it across her face.

Pavin smoothed it behind her ears and then kept her face between his hands as he stared down at her. 'You're exactly as I remembered you, beautiful!' he said softly. 'The others are going to adore you.'

'I hope you're right. Does the wind ever drop?'

He looked puzzled. 'What? Oh, the wind. Yeah, sure it drops. This is a bit unusual for mid-summer. Not that it will bother us. The castle walls are seven feet thick, you won't even hear it blowing. Come on, everyone else in already here and dying to meet you.'

He turned to the co-pilot, pressed some money into his hand and within seconds the helicopter had taken off again, disappearing towards the mainland.

'Don't you keep it here?' she asked in surprise.

'Hell, no. What's the point? When I need it I call them up on the mainland. If it stayed here I'd have to put the pilots up as well, and they're not exactly the kind we want for the holiday break!'

He laughed, and Deborah wanted to ask him what kind of people he did want, but she was struggling to keep up with his long strides. The wind was taking her breath away and somehow she never got round to it.

All around the castle was a red stone wall and at the entrance to the front drive stood a pair of huge wrought-iron gates with a stone eagle, wings outspread, standing on a plinth on each side. Deborah glanced up at their gaping mouths and sharp beaks and shivered again.

'Cold, honey?' Pavin's arm rubbed briskly over her back and shoulders. 'Let's get you inside.'

Still stunned by the splendour of the castle, Deborah let him lead her across the rectangle around which the main part of the castle was built. Glancing up she saw a man and woman looking down at her from a balustrade and Pavin, following the direction of her gaze, waved at them. The man waved back but the woman turned away and disappeared from view.

'Paul and Tansy Woolcott,' said Pavin by way of explanation. 'He's my figure man, a whizz with numbers, don't know what I'd do without him to keep an eye on my accountants. You'll like him.'

'What about his wife?' asked Deborah as they climbed the white steps to the heavy double oak doors that swung open beneath Pavin's hands.

'Tansy? Well, she can be difficult to take to at first but once you get to know her you'll get on fine. She's a bit more up-front than you British are used to!'

Deborah didn't answer him. She couldn't because she was staring in astonishment at the hall in which they were standing. Everything was made of wood, from the high arching beams to the beautiful minstrel's gallery, and antlers hung from every possible space. Old wooden chests and tables were dotted around the area while a heavy iron chandelier containing six huge candles hung suspended by three thick chains from one of the cross-beams.

'It's a reconstruction of a fourteenth-century great hall,' said Pavin casually. 'You can look over the place later. Right now they're all in the blue drawing room and dying to meet you. We mustn't keep them waiting.'

'I can't think that I matter that much!' laughed Deborah. 'After all, I'm here with you.'

'We're like a big family once we get to this island,' he explained, flashing her one of his wide, reassuring smiles. 'But don't worry, I know you'll fit in real well.'

He led her through a door at the far end of the entrance hall which had been concealed by a thick embroidered curtain made to look like a wall-hanging, and then up a staircase with intricately carved bannisters in dark oak; its surrounding walls covered in swags and picture frames of white plaster that stood out against a grey-blue background that exactly matched the colour of the sea outside.

On a half-landing there were two more doors, and one of those was slightly open. From within Deborah could hear the soft hum of voices, but as Pavin pushed it fully open the voices died away and as Deborah walked into a vast, rectangular-shaped room whose carpets, curtains and wall coverings were all of varying shades of blue, eight pairs of eyes turned towards her.

Despite the ornate splendour of the room and the marvellous pictures and ornaments that decorated the walls and surfaces, it was the people who held Deborah rooted to the spot. For just one split second, before Pavin introduced her and they all smiled and uttered greetings, she saw in their eyes a strange mixture of excitement, curiosity and surprise. The men all looked curious, their gaze intense and assessing while the women were unable to hide a kind of surprised astonishment that totally bewildered her. Instinctively she shrunk against Pavin, and at once his arm was round her and he was propelling her forward into the midst of the group.

'Didn't I tell you she was lovely!' he said enthusiastically. 'Deborah, this is Paul, you saw him up on the balustrade just now, and this is his wife Tansy.'

As Deborah took their outstretched hands and smiled at them she realised that Tansy was probably older than her husband, although with his slim build and fair boyish good looks it was quite possible that he was older than he seemed. His wife was nearly as tall as Deborah, and extremely curvaceous. Her full breasts

41

seemed perilously close to falling out of the low-scooped neckline of her summer dress and although her waist was small her hips were rounded and extremely feminine. She had light brown hair which she wore piled up casually on top of her head, and as she greeted Deborah she managed to touch Pavin intimately on the chest at the same time.

'She's just as lovely as you said, darling. Welcome to Pavinsay, Deborah, or can we call you Debbie?'

'Of course. It's certainly a beautiful castle. I never expected it to be this big.'

'Plenty more surprises in store for you yet, I can assure you!' laughed Paul, and for a moment Deborah thought that Pavin seemed displeased by the remark because she felt his hand tighten on her arm.

'I'm Brian Forster,' said another man in a precise New England tone. 'Welcome indeed, Debbie. We're in need of some fresh young thing to brighten our little group.'

Deborah remembered Chrissy mentioning that it was someone called Brian who'd taken Diane to the island a couple of years earlier and she wondered if this was the same man. He was almost exactly her height, slim and wiry with straight black hair and dark brown eyes that shone with a sharp intelligence.

'This is my wife, Lizzie,' he went on, pushing forward a slim, olive-skinned girl with long brown ringlets whose dark doe-shaped eyes seemed anxious. 'Smile for God's sake,' he added more sharply. 'Deborah is here on holiday.'

Obediently his wife smiled, but to Deborah's amazement tears suddenly filled her eyes and she quickly turned away from the newcomer and busied herself pouring drinks at a nearby table.

'I'm Flora,' announced a petite, brown-haired girl in a pair of cut-off denims and red T-shirt. 'I'm Pavin's secretary on the mainland. I've worked for him for the past three years and hope I'm becoming indispensable!'

42

Pavin laughed. 'Of course you are, honey. Why, but for you who would have made Deborah's travel arrangements?'

'I expect I could have made them for myself,' said Deborah shortly, rather resenting the inference that she was too dim to manage to get herself from London to the Orkneys without help from his secretary.

'Nice to have it done for you though, wasn't it?' asked Flora.

'Yes, of course, I'm very grateful.'

'Debbie used to be an editor for a big publishing house,' explained Pavin. 'I don't suppose she ever had to make her own travel arrangements, did you sweetheart?'

'No, because I never went out of London,' retorted Deborah.

Brian Forster laughed. 'There you are, Flora, not everyone needs you!'

As Flora flushed with irritation a tall curly-haired man put his arm round her. 'I need you, Flora.' He smiled at Deborah. 'I'm Richard Ford. I don't know if Pavin's mentioned me but I'm his P.A., or perhaps general dogsbody would be nearer the truth. We're all very pleased you could get here.'

'Where are Celia and Martin?' asked Pavin, taking a large whisky from Elizabeth's outstretched hand. As he took it he reached out his free hand and gently stroked the side of her face where the tears that Deborah had spotted earlier had now dried. 'You okay?' he whispered tenderly, and Deborah stared at the pair of them, wondering if at some time they'd been involved in an affair that had gone wrong or been brought to an abrupt close by her husband.

Elizabeth nodded, rubbed her cheek against the palm of his hand and then moved quietly away to pour drinks for the rest of the group. Deborah found that she was feeling distinctly awkward. Although the group

43

had expanded to include her in the circle they still seemed to be watching her and making judgements.

However, after a couple of sherries she began to feel more relaxed, and almost immediately Pavin – who had been at the far side of the group in conversation with Flora – came back to her.

'I'll show you where we're sleeping, Debbie. We'll meet up with the rest of you at dinner time, okay?'

Brian Forster smiled thinly while Flora immediately became deeply involved in a conversation with Paul Woolcott and his voluptuous wife.

Deborah followed Pavin out of the room and up the second half of the stairway to the floor above. 'What's the other room, next to the Blue Room?' she asked curiously.

'The dining hall. It used to be the great hall but it's been changed a bit to make it more homely. This is the west end of the original main part of the castle. There's only our bedroom and ante-rooms up here. At the east end there's a recreation room but the other bedrooms are all in the south-west tower. That's got four floors with a bedroom and bathroom on each floor, which explains the number of guests here.'

'So we're on our own on this floor?'

'Quite alone, honey. There, what do you think?'

As the American pushed open the double doors, Deborah stared at the room that was to be her bedroom for the next fortnight in astonishment. She'd expected opulence; tapestries, glorious window drapes and pictures. Instead the high-ceilinged room looked like a throwback to the Elizabethan age. An enormous four-poster bed dominated it, the dark oak plinth and corner posts all intricately carved, while soft grey curtains hung beside the posts and a grey silk-fringed canopy formed a ceiling beneath which they would sleep and make love.

The room was roofed with double-framed oak beams,

while a dark oak writing table and chair, a single cabinet with a drawer above it and a slightly incongruous chaise longue pushed against one wall, were all the furniture there was.

'Pretty good huh?' asked Pavin with a proud smile.

Deborah swallowed hard. 'It's certainly impressive.'

His smile faded. 'You don't like it?'

'It's nice to look at, but I suppose I'd expected something a bit more modern. Where do I keep my clothes and things?'

'The dressing room's full of closets and there's a king-sized bathroom too, so you've got more mod cons than in that flat of yours.'

She realised he'd upset him. 'I wasn't criticising, just astonished! I mean, this is like stepping back in time.'

Pavin smiled again. 'That's right! I wanted to create that feeling. Hell, anyone can go and live it up in four-star splendour in some swanky hotel. I wanted something different.'

'Well, you certainly got it.' She glanced around more slowly. 'Pavin, is that a TV console? Because if it is, they definitely didn't have those in Elizabethan times!'

He pushed a button, set on the small writing table, and dark panels slid across to cover the offending set. 'You're right, but it's useful for entertainment purposes.'

Deborah perched awkwardly on the edge of the high bed, but was relieved to find that the mattress was very comfortable. 'What kind of programmes do you like?'

'All sorts,' he replied vaguely. 'Mostly we rely on videos out here. Ordinary reception's not that good. I've got my own generator because otherwise we wouldn't get any electricity at all and then how could I use my electric toothbrush?'

He sat on the bed next to her and fondled the nape of her neck beneath her fall of blonde hair. 'Did you miss me, Debbie?'

'Yes, desperately.'

'Where's your hairbrush? I'd like to brush your hair.'

She handed him a small brush from her handbag, one that she used when blow-drying her hair, but he shook his head, went over to the writing desk, opened the drawer and pulled out a large, silver-backed brush. 'This is the kind of thing I meant. Those bits of plastic aren't the same at all. Close your eyes and you'll see what I mean.'

Deborah lowered her lids and felt the bristles moving slowly and rhythmically through her hair. He brushed lightly at first and then more firmly, beginning at her scalp and running the brush down the hair where it fell over her shoulders. Deborah sighed, her shoulders relaxed as her whole scalp began to tingle and her mind started to float off.

When he finally stopped she opened her eyes in surprise. 'What's the matter?'

'Can't have you falling asleep on me! Lie back on the bed a minute.' She hitched herself higher up the bed and within seconds Pavin had removed her skirt and briefs leaving her naked from the waist down. Then he lay beside her, propped up on one arm, and kissed her lightly on the corner of her mouth.

'Spread your legs wider,' he whispered in her ear, then his tongue was swirling around her ear lobe and she wriggled sensuously, spreading her legs obediently as she did so.

Pavin's left hand travelled across her stomach making swirling movements as it went, and then his fingers edged further down and brushed softly past the opening of her vagina. She moved slightly, expecting him to use a finger to penetrate her, but he ignored the movement and simply brushed upwards towards her stomach once more, again letting his fingers drift against the vaginal opening but without any great pressure.

It was tantalising and she wriggled again. 'Keep still, Debbie,' he murmured. 'Don't be in such a hurry. We've two weeks ahead of us, remember. Now keep your legs wide apart.'

He began to kiss her deeply on the mouth, his tongue penetrating her lips and sliding along her gums before darting between her teeth while at the same time his fingers continued their relentless brushing against her vaginal opening.

Deborah could feel herself getting more and more moist as his kisses became increasingly passionate and the fingers persisted in their relentless, insidious arousal. Eventually, when she couldn't repress a moan of desire, he let the pads of two of his fingers caress around the area of her clitoris. She could feel the bud swelling but he was careful not to touch it, only the surrounding moist, tingling tissue.

Deep within her abdomen, Deborah felt an ache starting, while between her legs her flesh seemed to tighten and it felt as though hidden strings were drawing her internal tissue towards a point somewhere beneath her pubic bone.

'Please touch me there,' she gasped as Pavin moved his mouth from hers.

'Where?' he asked, eyebrows raised in a query as he looked down at her frantic expression.

'On it!' she whispered, although she felt like screaming the words.

'You mean here?' One of his fingertips strayed to the shaft of the clitoris and caressed the side with such light pressure that only the jerk of her hips told her it had really happened.

'Yes, but more, please Pavin. I don't want to wait any longer.'

'Sure you do, it's fun like this.'

Deborah wasn't certain he was right. The whole of the lower half of her body was so tense it was painful and because her legs were spread wide at his direction she could even feel tiny movements of air against her straining swollen vulva.

Pavin moved his mouth to her breasts and licked right across them, his tongue moving in a broad band across both nipples. Then he moved it back again and soon her breasts were swelling too and all the time he continued to stroke her vulva with the lightest of touches as she felt her juices flowing more than ever before in her life.

It seemed to go on for hours and Deborah could hear herself moaning and crying out while her head turned from side to side and she squirmed beneath his touch. Her breath was coming in short gasps and her hands dug into Pavin's upper arms, the nails raking at the flesh beneath his shirt-sleeves.

'Guess you've still got a lot to learn about patience,' he said with a laugh. And as Deborah closed her eyes in relieved anticipation of sweet release he drew a silk handkerchief from his pocket and with amazing delicacy trailed the pointed corner of it across the very tip of Deborah's straining nub of pleasure while at the same time he sat up and abruptly took her left nipple in his right hand, pinching it fiercely between thumb and forefinger.

The combination of the softly trailing silk and the streak of unexpected pain radiating through her tightly engorged breast resulted in a climax that made Deborah scream out and arch her back upwards, thrusting her belly high into the air so that Pavin could easily bend his head and lick at the tiny droplets of perspiration that were running from her naval down to her pubic hair.

This seemed to stop her climax from ebbing away as it would normally have done. Instead the waves of long-awaited release continued to ripple through her stomach and deep inside her she ached with a need for him to fill her but Pavin had no intention of doing that at this stage in the day.

Once Deborah's climax had at last ended and her body was still he stroked her cheek quietly for a few minutes, then started to climb off the bed. 'We'd better get ready for dinner. You can bath first. I've got one or two things to see to.'

Deborah stared up at him, one hand catching at his wrist. 'Aren't you going to finish making love?'

'You mean you want more?'

'I want you inside me!' she exclaimed, bemused.

'Later, honey. The night is young as they say. By the way, we dress for dinner. I've got a dress here that I bought for you just before I left London. I'd like you to wear that. It's a kind of bluey-pink, you'll find it in the first closet of the dressing room. It's meant to cling, so don't worry about wearing anything under it except for hold-ups if you like. They won't spoil the line.'

Still exhausted by the way he'd made love to her, Deborah tried to gather herself together. 'I've brought lots of clothes of my own,' she protested.

'And you'll have plenty of time to wear them, but tonight, just for me, why not wear the one I bought?'

Deborah sighed. 'All right.'

Pavin's head lifted and he stared at her. 'Hey, come on! It's not like I'm trying to order you about, Debbie. I just want to see what you look like in a dress that I chose for you. It's a present and I thought after this afternoon it would be nice to see you in it. If you really don't like it, then fine, wear something you've brought. It's no big deal.'

Deborah looked back at him. He was probably right, it wasn't any big deal and it was nice to know he'd been thinking of her while he was still in London. The trouble was, the expression on his face didn't match his words and for the first time she realised that when he wasn't smiling his face was quite hard, and the corners of his mouth actually turned down in repose. For the first time she could see the hard-headed businessman beneath the benevolent and slightly misleading air of geniality that he used most of the time.

'If it's as nice as you think, then how can I refuse?' she asked.

Pavin's mouth turned up again as he smiled at her. 'That's my girl! You should find everything you need in the bathroom off the dressing room, but should anything be missing pull the tasselled cord and eventually one of the staff will find their way up here.'

'Or I could just call you,' she pointed out.

'Sure, you can always call me.' He waited until Deborah had left the room and then went to the innocuous-looking table opposite the foot of the bed. There he pushed a button to stop the filming. He knew that he'd positioned Deborah perfectly, with her feet pointing towards the camera, her legs spread wide so that her every reaction would have been recorded for them all to watch at a later date. He did hope she'd take to the entertainment that lay ahead that evening. It was always the first night that was the most difficult. After that they'd never had any problems, except with Angela, and even on the day he'd married her he'd known it was a mistake. His weakness for tall, slim blondes had let him down then, only this time he felt sure he'd found one who would share his sexual tastes as well.

After taking a bath in the largest bathtub she'd ever seen, presumably especially designed to take Pavin and partner, she thought to herself with a smile, Deborah used one of the fluffy towels to dry off and then checked through the closet for the dress Pavin had described.

When she took it off the hanger she knew that he was right, it would look marvellous on her. It was made of the softest silk; the colour a blend of pastel blues and pinks, and although it had a high neck there were large cut-away sections over the shoulders, between the breasts, down the middle of her spine and even on the tops of her thighs just below the hipbones. It was a sensuous dress, both in feel and style and once she'd pulled it on she was astonished at her appearance.

Where it touched her skin it really clung, emphasising her rounded breasts and narrow hips and the cut-outs gave the impression of showing far more than they actually did. She stood in front of the floor-length mirror in the dressing room and turned from side to side admiring herself in it. Behind her, reflected in the mirror, she saw Pavin come into the room.

He whistled softly. 'You look stunning!'

'I feel stunning. It's a fantastic dress, Pavin. Thank you!'

He rested his hands on her hips and her stomach twitched as she leant back slightly to rest against the comforting breadth of him. 'You can show your appreciation later. Why not put your hair up on top of your head? That would go with the elegance of the dress, don't you think?'

Deborah nodded. 'You're right, and I've got some pearl earrings that would look fantastic.'

'No underwear?'

She laughed. 'No, no underwear, only the hold-up stockings you left so conveniently on the cupboard shelf. Will you men all be in evening dress?'

'Of course. While you're finishing off your face, I'll use the tub. The gong should sound at eight-fifteen, then we'll go down.'

As Deborah carefully made up her eyes and sprayed herself with Laura Biagiotti's 'Venezia' perfume she found that she was really looking forward to making her entrance at dinner on Pavin's arm and already her body was looking forward to later that night when they returned to the privacy of their bedroom.

Chest-deep in bath water, Pavin was looking forward to the evening as well, but for rather different reasons.

Chapter Four

*A*t exactly eight-fifteen the gong summoned everyone inside the castle to dinner, and Pavin escorted
Deborah down the staircase, her hand resting lightly on
the sleeve of his dark dinner jacket.

This time they went through the second of the two
doors on the first floor of the castle. If their bedroom
was sparse, this dining hall more than made up for it.
The heavily-polished wooden floor had a rectangle of
Persian carpet on it that left a four-foot border round
the room. An ornate ceiling covered with paintings and
carved figures supported the largest chandelier Deborah
had ever seen in her life, while the long, damask-
covered dining table could easily have seated twenty
people. Large candelabras stood on pedestals at regular
intervals along the walls, which were themselves
covered either in embroidered tapestries or by huge
paintings which, after a second glance, Deborah
realised were graphic Chinese erotica. The colours were
all variations on peacock-blue intershot with gold, and
she was completely overwhelmed by the rich splendour
of the room.

They were the last to arrive and as soon as they

entered the men went to the table and pulled out the chairs for the women. Pavin pulled out a chair at the far end of the table for Deborah, then went to sit at the opposite end himself. She looked down the expanse of table and wished that they were closer. Somehow, like their bedroom, although for a very different reason, this wasn't what she'd expected from the holiday either. It was like dining out in a stately home, rather than having a restful holiday on a remote island.

Pavin caught her glance. 'Don't worry, sweetheart,' he boomed. 'We don't use this room every night. There's a cosy little dining room in the new wing, and we sometimes even have barbecues in the cove.'

'Only then we don't bother dressing for dinner,' said Brian softly. He was sitting on Deborah's right and she turned to him, seeing once more the glint of sharp intelligence in his narrow pale face.

'I'm Martin,' said the man on her left, and she was quite relieved to hear another English accent. 'Sorry we missed your arrival. Celia and I were using the games room.'

'What were you playing?' asked Deborah.

Brian gave a laugh. 'Yes, do tell us Martin, what were you and Celia playing? She certainly looks well after it whatever it was!'

The blond-haired Englishman ignored Brian and glanced down the table to where his wife, a small, rather sullen-looking girl wearing a low-cut dress of sapphire blue, was sitting next to Paul Woolcott. 'Don't take any notice of Brian, he just likes to cause trouble. I'm afraid Celia's not in a very good mood today. Too much wine last night.'

'Wine was it?' put in Brian.

'So tell me,' continued Martin smoothly. 'How did you and Pavin come to meet? He certainly seems to have learnt the secret of discovering leggy blonde beauties wherever he goes.'

53

As Deborah began to explain about the party where they'd first met and the misunderstanding about Pavin's work, Pavin watched her like a hawk from his end of the table. Although she was talking mostly to Martin he could tell that she was very aware of Brian, and that pleased him. Brian was his right-hand man, and Angela's inability to get on with him during their holiday had contributed to their divorce.

After a while, certain that Deborah was quite content, Pavin turned his attention to Brian's wife Elizabeth, or Lizzie as her husband always called her. She was the perfect wife for a man like Brian, but not really to Pavin's taste although he'd had a great deal of pleasure from her during their last group holiday.

The food was excellent, the wines superb and when the maids arrived to clear the plates, Pavin stood up and moved towards the door. 'Coffee in the library I think. We can play a game of cards or something in there. It's much more comfortable than here.'

Tansy Woolcott glanced at Celia Craig and their eyes both held the same unspoken question. What would Deborah do once the games began?

The library turned out to be in the east wing, having been added on to the original ruined building. Although the same style had been maintained, Deborah found the room far more relaxing with its high, book-lined walls, comfortable tapestry-covered sofas and chairs, and watercolour paintings. It was also warm, with wall-to-wall carpeting and in the huge fireplace a log fire burnt.

'Even in summer there's a chill at night,' explained Pavin gesturing towards the fireplace. 'I don't have the central heating on in June, but anyway this is more homely don't you think?'

Deborah laughed. 'I think your definition of homely and mine are rather different!'

Silver coffee pots and thin, bone china cups were

already in the room and Flora Stewart quickly bustled round pouring it for everyone. Her dress was black, shot through with red and silver threads, resting just above her knee in length and with puffed cap sleeves, while a sparkling diamond necklace hung in the deep V of her exposed tanned flesh.

'What's it to be then?' asked Paul Woolcott, prompted by Tansy. 'Strip poker?'

They all looked at Deborah, who was perched on the arm of Pavin's chair as he absent-mindedly stroked the flesh through one of the keyholes over her left hip. She laughed. 'Sorry, I'll have to pass. I can't play poker.'

'Pity,' said Brian shortly. 'Well, we can't leave you out on the first night. How about that new board game that Paul designed last year?'

Pavin nodded approvingly. 'Sounds good to me. Don't worry, Debbie, it's easy. I'll help you as we go along.'

'What's it called?' asked Deborah, who hadn't expected to find herself playing some kind of advanced Trivial Pursuits on her first evening.

'Fines and Favours,' laughed Flora. 'It's an adult board game.'

'I hope I'm up to it,' said Deborah.

'We're the ones who have to worry about that!' laughed Pavin, but Deborah wasn't sure why the others found the remark so funny.

As two of the tables were pushed together and the board game set up, Pavin explained the rules to Deborah who nestled up close to him on the carpet. 'It's really a friendship game,' he told her. 'We all start out on our own, and when we meet someone new on a party, dinner or blind date square we have to draw a card from the pack. The cards are either forfeits or favours. You choose your friend before drawing the card, and they either do you a favour or choose a forfeit for you. Once that's been accomplished to the satisfac-

55

tion of everyone playing then the pair of you are "friends". The idea is that the game finishes when everyone is part of one big group, rather like us here on the island.'

'What do you mean by "do you a favour"?' asked Deborah.

'Why don't we start, and then you'll see,' said Martin briskly.

'Great!' enthused Pavin. 'Let play commence.'

At first the game seemed quite boring to Deborah. She moved her counter when it was her turn, gained a sports car and a penthouse suite, lost her job – rather to Pavin's amusement – but didn't go to any parties or dinners or have a blind date.

Then, on his fourth throw, Brian landed on a party square. A strange tension gripped the group, and when Deborah looked around she realised that everyone was watching her. 'I choose Flora as the girl I meet,' said Brian slowly. Flora didn't look particularly thrilled, but she held out the pack of cards and watched as Paul drew one out. 'A favour! Right, let me think. Flora, I want you to take off Lizzie's blouse as a favour to me.'

Deborah couldn't believe she'd heard him correctly, and then decided it must be his idea of a joke. She looked up at Pavin, but he was watching Flora, his eyes sharp. 'Is Brian serious?' she whispered.

He looked down at her. 'Sure, honey. I told you it was an adult game.'

'But . . .'

'But what?' he asked softly.

'I couldn't do anything like that. I mean, they're all strangers!'

'I told you it was a friendship game. The idea is that after this they're not strangers anymore. Sssh now, let's see how Flora does.'

Flora walked round the outside of the sitting group until she was standing behind Elizabeth, who slowly

56

turned to face the other woman and then held out her hands so that Flora could pull her to her feet.

Brian's eyes were alight with excitement as Flora, her fingers shaking a little, began to unfasten the tiny pearl buttons that ran down the frilled front of his wife's cream satin blouse. She did it very slowly, and as the blouse opened she folded it back so that Elizabeth's breasts, unfettered by any bra, were gradually exposed to the silent watchers.

When all the buttons were undone, Flora ran her hands up the outsides of the sleeves and then slipped the garment off Elizabeth's shoulders leaving her upper body entirely bare. Deborah couldn't hold back her gasp of astonishment, for hanging from Elizabeth's small but rigid nipples were two tiny rings. Flora's hand reached towards one of them.

'No!' said Pavin sharply. 'You were only asked to remove the blouse.'

Flora flushed and lowered her eyes, obviously distressed by Pavin's displeasure.

'I don't think that can count,' drawled Brian. 'Pity, but you screwed up there in your enthusiasm, Flora. Looks as though I'm still on my own.'

There were murmurs of agreement from the group and as Elizabeth sat down topless, Tansy threw a five that meant she landed on a candlelit dinner for two square. She turned to her husband. 'I choose you as my dinner companion.' Her card was a forfeit and this amused her husband.

'Right Tansy, your forfeit is, you've got to get Pavin erect without touching him with your mouth or your hands.'

Deborah started to get to her feet but Pavin's hands pushed against her shoulders. 'Stay where you are. Just relax and enjoy yourself. It's only a game.'

'I don't want to watch her with you,' retorted Deborah, but deep down there was a part of her that did.

57

She wanted to see how another woman would arouse this man without using either hands or mouth, but she didn't want to think of him wanting anyone in the room but her. In the end she remained seated, her face warm with conflicting sexual emotions.

Pavin smiled at Tansy and stood up. 'Where do you want me, sweetheart?'

Tansy considered for a moment. 'Sitting on the big chair there. I take it he's allowed to unzip himself?' she added to her husband. Paul nodded. 'Sure, it's just your hands that can't move!'

After Pavin had unzipped himself and settled in the chair, Tansy slowly began a sensuous striptease. In the flickering light from the fire her full figure gleamed and her surprisingly large, firm breasts remained upright as she bent to peel off her stockings.

'Your plastic surgeon did a good job!' laughed Brian, and Tansy shot him a look of annoyance before returning her attention to Pavin. He seemed to be thoroughly enjoying himself, and when Tansy lay full length on the carpet at his feet, her rounded body totally naked, and extended one shapely leg until her foot was between his thighs he let his head fall back slightly to savour the sensation.

As Tansy worked her foot along the seam of his trousers, Deborah remembered the scene in the restaurant when Pavin had pleasured her with his toe and she knew just the kind of sensations he was experiencing. Then, as his erection slowly emerged from the opening in his trousers, Tansy got onto her knees and bent her head so that her long curly hair could brush against the sensitive tip of his penis and all the time she wriggled her body between his large, muscular thighs so that whenever she looked up he could see her ripe, aroused breasts.

Within a very short space of time, Pavin was undoubtedly fully erect, and when a tiny tell-tale drop of clear fluid appeared at the end, Tansy stopped and turned to face the rest of the group. 'Is that enough?' she asked sweetly. Everyone except Deborah clapped her and it was agreed that she and Paul were now 'friends'.

After that the game quickly gathered pace, but for quite a time Deborah escaped attention until Richard, Pavin's tall personal assistant, landed on a party square and chose her. His card was a favour and she waited nervously to see what he'd ask.

'As it's your first time here I'll make this simple,' he said reassuringly, and she relaxed slightly. 'Just take off your dress, that will do fine.' He glanced at Pavin as he spoke and both men smiled.

Deborah's whole body went stiff with shock. Now she knew why Pavin had insisted that she left off her underwear. He'd guessed that something like this would happen and wanted her to have as little on as possible. She turned to him helplessly. 'I can't!' she muttered.

'Come on, Debbie,' urged Celia, her previously sullen expression lifting. 'It isn't much to ask and then you're in.'

'Mind you, you can still get used in forfeits,' Brian reminded her, but Deborah wasn't bothered about the future, only this moment in time.

'Don't spoil the game, honey,' said Pavin, running a hand through her hair and letting his fingers lightly massage her scalp. 'Be good and we'll have a nice time later on.'

Deborah knew very well it was the moment of no return. If she didn't join in then she wasn't going to fit in. She might remain on the island, although somehow she doubted it, but she certainly wasn't going to be a part of what Pavin called his family group. The old Debbie, the one who'd held down a good job in publishing and looked after Mick for so long, would never have played the game, but she reminded herself that she was a new Debbie now and the whole point of the holiday was to have a change.

After all, no one outside the group would ever know and once she returned to London she'd probably never see any of them again, so what did it matter? Besides, a part of her that she'd never known existed before wanted to show off her figure, which she knew was good and would be admired by most of the men present.

'All right,' she said decisively, and she heard Pavin let out a slow breath of relief. Before she could change her mind she was on her feet, and deftly unfastening the hook and eye at the back of her collar she shrugged off the dress, which fell in a pool of silk at her feet. She then stepped out of it wearing just her cream high-heeled sandals and the white, lace-topped hold-up silk stockings.

She heard one or two swift intakes of breath and then Richard clapped softly. 'Well done, Deborah! Welcome to the group.'

'He means the games group,' said Flora coolly.

'How do you know what he means, Flora?' enquired Brian. 'Are you as close to Richard as you are to Pavin?'

'Pavin's my boss when we're at work, Richard works with me,' Flora retorted. 'I think I know both of them pretty well.'

'We all know you do!' gurgled Tansy.

Pavin, who could hardly take his eyes from Deborah, frowned. 'Can we get on with the game, please. You can sit down now, darling. If you don't you'll distract me so much I won't be able to play!'

At first Deborah felt extremely uncomfortable, sitting virtually naked on the floor between Pavin and Elizabeth, but since no one else was fully clothed now except Pavin she supposed it didn't matter too much and she even made sure to sit straight-backed to show off her breasts to their full advantage.

The very last person to gain entry to the whole group turned out to be Elizabeth. When she finally landed on a blind date square she chose Pavin and then drew a forfeit card.

She stood before the American, dressed only in French knickers and high heels and her body trembled from head to toe as she waited to hear what forfeit he'd decide upon. Deborah glanced up at her lover, wondering why Elizabeth seemed nervous, but the look on his face startled her. It was so calculating, as though he was trying to work out something far more complicated than just a piece of sexual frivolity for the doe-eyed girl waiting almost submissively in front of him.

'I hoped you'd choose me, Elizabeth,' he said at last. 'After our last holiday I think you should forfeit the privilege of hiding the one piece of jewellery you've kept from us this evening.'

Deborah saw Elizabeth swallow. Her slim neck went taut and she threw a glance at her husband. Brian seemed composed enough but his eyes were narrowed and he was watching Pavin closely.

'Come on,' Pavin urged her. 'We're all waiting. Do you want me to remove the panties myself?'

It looked as though he'd have to because Elizabeth was standing frozen in front of him while everyone else in the room watched with bright eyes and flushed faces so that Deborah realised there must be more to this request than she'd thought.

When Pavin stood up as well he towered over the waiting girl and she seemed almost like a child compared to him, although Deborah guessed that she was about twenty-two or three. For a long moment he paused, and then he thrust his thumbs into the sides of her French knickers and jerked them sharply down her

61

legs, lifting one foot out after the other with unusual roughness.

Elizabeth didn't seem to mind, in fact Deborah could see that her nipples were swiftly becoming erect and her breathing quickening as Pavin roughly spread her feet wider apart on the carpet and then turned her back to face the rest of them.

Hanging down between her legs was another gold ring, like the ones through each of her nipples, but this one was clearly attached to her clitoris. Deborah shivered at the thought of what it must have felt like to have it inserted.

'Pretty isn't it?' Pavin remarked to them all, and then he was on his knees in front of the girl and very carefully he hooked the little finger of his left hand through the ring, resting it against the bottom of the circle.

Elizabeth's legs began to shake, her nipple rings moved gently as her breasts swelled and her eyes were enormous in her face. There wasn't a sound in the room as they all waited.

Deborah realised that the clitoral ring was moving, slowly descending as Elizabeth's clitoris expanded with sexual arousal simply because Pavin had his finger resting inside the ring and could pull on it at any time. Her breathing began to rasp in her throat and still he waited, his eyes fixed upon her face, and then he curled his little finger tightly round the slim gold hoop and tugged.

Elizabeth's whole body jolted. Her mouth opened and her abdomen went rigid as the pain that Deborah knew she must be feeling seared through her. But she didn't look like a woman in pain, she looked like a woman in the grip of ecstasy. Pavin released the ring. 'That's all, Elizabeth. I just wanted them to see the ring.'

Elizabeth's eyes snapped open and she stared down

at him in shocked bewilderment, obviously devastated that he was stopping at this point. 'You stay standing there,' added Pavin, 'I'll just sit down with the others and have a good look at your unusual wedding ring.'

They all continued to stare at Elizabeth's fine-boned tense body, especially Brian who looked as though he too was enjoying himself more than at any other time that evening. When she finally realised that Pavin was serious, and that he had no intention of touching her again, Elizabeth's legs went stiff and then her whole body was suffused with shudders as her muscles twitched and jumped in a tiny climax that totally baffled Deborah.

'Why did she come?' she whispered to Pavin.

'She gets off on pain and cruelty, Debbie; both mental and physical. I guess I judged the mental cruelty about right by leaving her alone when I did. She certainly seems to have enjoyed it. More of a favour than a forfeit in the end!'

Deborah turned her face into his shoulder. The game was over and she wasn't sure that she wanted to take part in any more. These people were clearly going to lead her into a new world where she might discover more about herself than she cared to know.

'Not time for bed yet, is it?' asked Martin Craig. 'Celia's never ready to sleep before one in the morning.'

'No, but she's always ready for bed!' laughed Paul Woolcott.

'Martin says I've already worn him out for the day,' said Celia sulkily. 'He obviously needs this holiday to build up his strength. You work him too hard, Pavin.'

Pavin, who was absent-mindedly stroking Deborah's bare breasts, looked across at the small Welsh girl with her short dark hair and thickly lashed coal-black eyes. 'Perhaps I do, but even if he's tired I'm sure someone else can keep you amused. Paul? Brian? How about it?'

Flora, who was watching her boss with this blonde-haired English girl, who seemed likely to prove a threat to her own ambitions to become Mrs John Pavin the third unless she managed to do something about it, looked annoyed. 'Brian and I were going for a swim before we turned in.'

Brian stood up and stretched. He was rather like a leopard, Deborah thought to herself. There was so much coiled energy there, just waiting for a chance to unleash itself and also more than a hint of danger about him.

'Tell you what,' Brian said lightly. 'Why don't Flora and Celia play the water game? I'll spend the night with the winner.'

'Yes, let's do that!' said Tansy excitedly. 'I love that game. We can all take part, can't we?'

'Sure,' said Pavin. 'It will be an experience for Deborah just to watch. You can play another time, honey,' he added in an undertone.

'I'm not sure I'll want to,' she retorted, pulling away from him and slipping into her dress. 'I thought we were going to bed now?'

'After the game, Debbie. You'll be even more in the mood by then.'

She didn't think she needed anything to put her in the mood for Pavin's lovemaking since she'd been looking forward to it all evening, but the others were leaving the room and when Pavin caught hold of her hand she decided to go along with him.

'Is Brian really going to make love to either Flora or Celia tonight?' she asked as they made their way to the guest bedrooms in the south-west tower.

'I guess so.'

'But what about Elizabeth?'

Pavin sighed. 'Debbie, I told you before you came here, we're all one big happy family on this island. Everyone's free to do as they please just for these two weeks. We take sensible precautions, there's no risk of disease, so where's the harm?'

'You mean none of the women here mind sharing their husbands?'

'Why should they? They get plenty of attention from all the men themselves, no one gets short-changed.'

'Well I'm not having anyone but you make love to me,' Deborah replied fiercely.

Pavin laughed. 'You are a funny girl! In a few days you'll be singing a completely different tune.'

'I won't! I came here to be with you, not . . .'

'You *are* with me,' he said irritably. 'Now just be quiet, honey. If you don't approach things like this in a receptive frame of mind then you might as well not bother to come along.'

'I don't want to leave you,' she said softly.

'Fine, then we can watch together. I promise you it's a very stimulating game, for onlookers as well as participants.'

The staircase in the south-west tower was made up of flights of wide stone steps round a central pillar of solid masonry, and the brick walls were cold to the touch.

'Which room?' asked Celia.

'I think ours would be best. It's got two beds in it for a start,' said Paul.

'They've got the Chinese room, you'll like it,' Pavin assured Deborah as they climbed to the third floor. Deborah wasn't bothered about the room, only what was going to happen once they were inside it.

In many ways Paul and Tansy had a more comfortable room than Pavin and Deborah. Certainly it was in a more modern style, with oriental rugs on the polished floor, heavy patterned wallpaper depicting oriental birds and trees, while Chinese cabinets and lacquered tables all held Chinese vases and basins.

At the far end of the room two beds, both slightly larger than a normal single, were set on blocks of wood and covered with white bedspreads that were fringed with the same pattern as the wallpaper. All the paint-work was white and the general impression was of lightness and colour.

'What happens now?' whispered Deborah.

'Just sit with me and you'll see,' murmured Pavin, lowering himself into the largest chair in the room and pulling Deborah onto his lap. Flora and Celia were busy slipping off their clothes, stripping until they were entirely nude. Then they walked, without any apparent self-consciousness, to the two beds and stood waiting at the foot of them.

Deborah thought that Flora had slightly the better figure. Her breasts were small but firm and the nipples an unusually light pink while the surrounding areolae were smaller than on most women and again light in colour. Her waist was tiny and her hips attractively rounded.

Celia was far slimmer. Her breasts were tiny, but the nipples and areolae were larger than Flora's and darker in colour. She too had a small waist, but she was also slim round the hips, giving an almost boyish impression except for her well-rounded buttocks.

Richard Ford, who Deborah remembered was Pavin's PA, came into the room carrying two pieces of black leather that looked like mini-skirts and two shallow glass bowls. Celia and Flora took the leather garments from him and began to ease them up over their legs.

The women pulled them up until the top edge rested about an inch below their breasts, which meant that the hem was just touching the beginning of their pubic hair. The leather was tight, and as they both lay down on the beds the effect of the garments was to make them look more exposed than when they were entirely naked because now it was their breasts, genitals and legs that were on show, emphasised by the absence of any sight of their lower chest and abdomen.

Once they were lying flat on their backs, the black

leather garments clinging tightly to every curve and flattening their abdomens, Brian and Paul each took one of the shallow glass bowls from Richard and placed them on the women's stomachs.

'What are they doing?' whispered Deborah, her hand clutching the top of Pavin's arm.

'The bowls are filled with water,' he explained patiently. 'The idea is that both the women are stimulated in exactly the same way, at the same time but obviously by two different men, and they have to keep as still as possible because as soon as the water level in one of the bowls drops below a line that's marked round the rim the game's over and the winner is the one who spilt the least water.'

Deborah remembered the way her own stomach would arch and ripple during sexual arousal and she wondered how on earth it would be possible to learn the kind of control Pavin was describing. 'Watch closely,' he added. 'You might like to take part one day.'

Deborah didn't think that very likely, but she found that she was leaning forward on Pavin's lap in order to get an unrestricted view as the game began.

First of all, Tansy handed each of the men a jar of lotion and everyone in the room watched eagerly as the men moved to the sides of the two beds and looked down on the waiting women. 'It's the heat jelly,' Brian told Flora, who gave a tiny cry. Even that made the water in the bowl move, and as though she realised the danger, Celia said nothing despite the fact that Paul was standing by her with the same cream.

Pavin nodded at the two men. 'Right, you may begin!'

Slowly they started to rub the cream into the two women's breasts. Flora had only ever had it used on her once before and had found it highly stimulating. It smelt of fresh mangoes and when Brian's fingers began to work it in to her breast tissue it seemed pleasant and

67

not over-arousing, but she knew that its secret lay in the fact that the more his fingers touched it the warmer it grew. If it was blown on, then a tingling deep heat would spread right through the tissue that it was covering.

Brian, his sharp face a study in concentration, moved his fingers around the outside of Flora's breasts and then up to the more delicate areolae until finally he was massaging it into her nipples and she could feel the warmth suffusing them. Almost without thinking she pushed her breasts upwards in a voluptuous stretching movement that immediately had the water in the glass bowl slopping dangerously near the top. She strained to keep her body still, forcing down the tight ripples of excitement that were threatening to invade her body.

Pavin and the rest of the group watched Flora's efforts in excited silence. Her breasts were always highly sensitive, and they could guess at the difficulty she must be experiencing. She bit on her bottom lip to try and distract herself from the pleasure, and attempted to keep her abdominal muscles rigid when Brian lowered his head and blew softly on the already warm breasts.

He blew lightly but steadily and now the heat was coursing through the blue veins of her breasts, and darts of excitement shot downwards through her constrained belly to below the hem of the rubber garment so that her outer labia started to spread backwards of their own accord in the beginning of sexual arousal.

Celia was struggling too. Her breasts weren't as sensitive as Flora's, but Paul had a lighter touch than Brian and he also left her nipples free of the lotion for longer than Brian did so that the nipples felt cold compared with the warm breast tissue. This contrast made Celia's nipples stand proudly erect which meant that when he did finally massage the lotion directly on to them they were highly aroused and her stomach

68

jerked involuntarily when the heat started to make itself felt.

That one small jerk meant that a single drop of water spilt onto the constricting leather garment, and although the failure line was still a long way off she gritted her teeth in concentration, determined that it would be she and not Flora who had Brian in her bed that night.

Leaving the lotion on the women's breasts, the men finally turned their attention to below the hem of the leather. First they each called forward one of the women, Tansy to help Brian and Elizabeth for Paul, and they carefully spread the prone women's legs further apart, making sure that they didn't disturb the liquid in the bowl as they did so. Once the legs were spread more widely, the two assistants held the competing women's outer labia apart which meant that the men had easier access for their attentions.

Deborah could feel a tightness in the pit of her stomach and her own breasts seemed almost as swollen as those she could see on the beds in front of her. She was becoming incredibly stimulated by what she was watching, and knew that she was shamingly damp between her thighs. When Pavin squeezed the top of her leg she almost jumped out of her skin at the physical contact, so aroused was her flesh.

'You like watching then?' he asked quietly. She refused to answer, but knew that her body had already told him the truth. 'I said it would be exciting,' he reminded her and then fell silent as Brian and Paul began to lightly caress the inside of the women's thighs.

Paul's fingers skimmed up Celia's thighs and into the joins at the top of her legs. There they played with the soft folds of skin, pulling them to the side a little so that the hood of the clitoris moved and stimulated the bud beneath. Brian chose to press the heel of his hand firmly against the opening of Flora's vagina, leaving his fingers free to roam along her moist inner channels in a tantalising dance that skimmed the paper-thin membranes and caused her to lubricate even more from her vagina. Carefully he took some of her moisture and then spread it up the inner channels until Flora felt as though she was just a mass of melting, damp flesh with leaping nerve ends that were sending frantic messages of arousal up through her entire vulva and even higher until they travelled beneath the increasingly tight leather garment that was now painfully restrictive.

Both of the women began to breathe through their open mouths, hoping to slow down their body's responses and keep their climax from engulfing them. When Brian unexpectedly turned his hand palm upwards and then slid his middle finger inside Flora so that he could beat a tattoo on her G spot she was unable to stop the tearing wave of pleasure that forced its way beneath the leather and now it was her turn to spill some of the water.

Tansy and Elizabeth, who were standing by the competitors' hips and facing towards the men, were as flushed as Flora and Celia. They both longed to reach down and touch the other women themselves, touch them close to the stem of the clitoris and precipitate the orgasms that would end the competition, but they knew better.

By this time both the women on the beds were beginning to struggle desperately against the sensations caused by all their swelling flesh. The leather garments, initially merely a close fit, seemed wickedly constraining as their stomachs swelled with passion and their breasts were becoming mottled with the flush of arousal.

Now Richard handed each of the men a long brown object made of latex. It was a vibrator that could twist and rotate within the vaginal walls, while at the base, situated just above the handle which the men were grasping, was a ball covered in tiny probes with padded ends that would further excite the flesh around the clitoris.

Both Flora and Celia gasped aloud as the probes were slid into their vaginas, already lubricated with their own excitement, and then when the twisting vibrations began the women bore down as hard as they could in order to prevent the contractions from affecting the balance of the shallow bowls.

Their muscular control was incredible and Deborah watched with wide eyes and a rising excitement that made her long to run from the room with Pavin to their huge Elizabethan bed so that he could give her the satisfaction these women were striving to hold at bay. Her breasts were so tight with desire they hurt, and when Pavin cupped one in a large hand she strained against his fingers and rubbed the nipple against the palm of his hand through the silk material of her dress. Her excitement delighted him.

In the meantime the women on the bed were suddenly given a moment's respite as the probes were withdrawn, but it was only brief because then their skilled tormentors dropped to their knees and began to use their tongues, flicking, licking and skimming the entire vulva of both women so that their parted legs started to tremble and Flora began to groan with the sensations.

'No! No!' she moaned, as Brian's tongue circled her throbbing bud making it stand up even more proudly. 'I can't bear it, I can't!'

Celia could hear Flora, but she was suffering just as much because Paul was using his tongue like a penis and thrusting it quickly in and out of her vagina while at the same time pressing lightly on her pubic bone to force the clitoral hood downwards over the highly sensitive tip of her bud. Now she too began to cry out. 'Stop! Not there, Paul! Please, not there!'

With both women crying out, their breasts still

covered in the warm lotion which was never allowed to cool completely because Tansy and Elizabeth would occasionally massage it carefully into the skin again, and their entire sex mounds constantly stimulated, the air of sexual tension in the room was electric.

Quite a lot of water had now spilt from both bowls, but there was very little difference between the two women as the men moved and together lightly stabbed with the very tips of their tongues at the acutely sensitive opening to the despairing women's urethras.

It was Flora who reacted first. She gave a loud shriek of ecstasy mixed with frustration and her back arched causing her stomach to jerk up into the air and the glass bowl slipped from its tight leather base and fell to the bed beneath, spilling the contents as it went.

Only a few seconds later, Celia too was ravaged by an intense orgasm whose pleasure was almost spoilt for her by the tightness of the leather round her taut belly and the violence of the long-suppressed waves of contractions.

Deborah had never watched another woman brought to a climax before. She had never even watched another man and woman in any kind of sex play, and if anyone had suggested it to her she would have refused indignantly, but now she had to admit to herself that watching the two skilled men and the women fighting against their natural responses had been the most arousing thing she'd ever done.

Celia struggled upright into a sitting position. 'I guess I won!' she said with a grin.

Brian looked levelly at her. 'I guess you did. We'll go to the dungeon I think.'

For a moment, a look of hesitation crossed Celia's features, but then she saw Flora's look of misery and grinned in triumph. 'Bliss! Sleep well, Flora. Better luck next time.'

'Come on,' Pavin whispered in Deborah's ear. 'I can't

wait any longer. Now it really is time for us to go to bed.'

Deborah nodded, her mouth too dry for her to speak, and while the others chatted amongst themselves Pavin hurried her from the room. Only Flora saw them leave and Pavin's haste simply added to her misery at losing out to Celia moments earlier. She tried not to imagine what might happen in his bedroom so far away from the rest of them all during the next few hours.

Chapter Five

When they reached the privacy of their own bedroom, Deborah expected Pavin to tear off his clothes as fast as she was shedding hers, but he didn't. Instead he watched her as she peeled down her hold-up stockings and then, when she was entirely nude, slipped off his dinner jacket and shoes and stretched out on the chaise longue which he'd pushed to the foot of the bed.

'Lie down,' he said softly. 'Lie on your back, propped up against the pillows and tell me what you and Mick used to do.'

Deborah stared at him. 'You want to know what I did with Mick? But why? He and I are finished.'

He smiled reassuringly. 'Sure, I know that, but you were together for four years. Something must have kept you with him and since he was neither rich nor – as far as I've heard – particularly agreeable I'm assuming it was the sex. So, tell me about it.'

'I don't want to talk about Mick; I want you,' retorted Deborah, her body still on fire from the scene they'd just witnessed.

'I want you, but I like to prolong things a little. If you

get too worked up you can always play with yourself while you're talking. That excites me like hell.'

Deborah shook her head. 'I won't.'

Pavin yawned. 'Then I guess it's time for sleep. It's been one hell of a long day.'

'Look, this is stupid. We both want to make love, so why have I got to talk about Mick at a moment like this?' Deborah was utterly bewildered.

'I like hearing about the way other people make love. That's part of the pleasure of these holidays, I get to hear and see everything. You like it too, otherwise you wouldn't have got so worked up watching Celia and Flora. Come on, Debbie. Tell me about Mick. Where did he touch you first?'

Deborah couldn't remember ever having felt such overwhelming desire for any man before this, and this made her decide to go along with him. After all, he was right. She had enjoyed watching the two women being pleasured earlier, and perhaps she'd even enjoy this if she did it the right way.

'Do you mean in bed, or out of it?' she asked with a slight smile.

Pavin's blue eyes gleamed in appreciation. 'We'll deal with in bed tonight, save the more exotic stuff for another time.'

'He always began by running a hand over one of my breasts,' she said quietly, her mind going back to the early days when it had been good between her and Mick.

'You'll have to speak up, I can hardly hear you. How hard did he touch you? Lightly, like a feather, or more firmly?'

'Quite hard, all his touches were hard.'

Pavin took off his bow tie and began to undo the buttons on his dress shirt. 'Show me how hard he touched you.'

Deborah found that she couldn't take her eyes away

from Pavin's, slowly her right hand moved and she let the fingers trail down over her left breast.

'Go on,' said Pavin huskily. 'Show me what he'd do next.'

'Then he'd run his hand back up again, like this,' Deborah told him, watching the excitement growing in the American's eyes. 'When he got to the nipple he'd take it between two fingers and pinch it until it stood erect.'

'Was that good?'

'Not always. Sometimes I wished that he'd be more gentle.'

'Didn't you ask him?'

She shook her head. 'You couldn't ever criticise Mick. He had a very short temper and I think he suffered from low self-esteem.'

Pavin chuckled. 'More likely he was conceited. Do it then, pinch your nipple the way he used to.'

Deborah rolled the tight tip of her burgeoning nipple between two fingers and immediately it stood up proudly from the expanding areola while her entire breast began to grow.

'Open your legs wide,' Pavin urged her. 'I want to see your excitement increasing as you talk. That's right. Now, what used to happen next?'

'He'd slide the palm of his hand down over my stomach and between my legs.' Her voice dropped as she spoke because she knew from the look in Pavin's eyes that she was expected to do this, but she wanted him to do it for her.

Pavin merely continued to watch, his eyes narrowing as she tentatively slid her hand down her body and across the pubic mound until it was between her wide-spread thighs. 'Now show me how he used his fingers on you.'

'Please Pavin, I don't want to. He wasn't that good at

it. Won't you do it for me? I need to be touched the way you touch me.'

Pavin, his dress shirt now open to show his firmly muscled torso, rose from the chaise longue, but only to remove his socks and trousers, then he sat down again. 'You must have liked it. You were with him for four years. Show me.'

Deborah rubbed her fingers in firm circular motions across her entire vulva, and as the heavy friction caused the already aroused flesh to spark with flickers of desire and she started to tighten in anticipation of a climax, she remembered that sometimes it had been good. There had been days when she'd wanted Mick's hands to be almost rough and instant gratification had been her aim. It was only later, when they were used to each other and he refused to try variations, that she'd gone off their sex life.

Pavin saw her mouth open slightly and between her legs he could see tell-tale beads of moisture signifying her increasing arousal. 'Keep going.' His voice was deep, his own breathing quickening at the sight of this long-legged blonde bringing herself to a climax as she remembered her previous lover. 'Doesn't it feel good?'

'Yes!' she gasped.

'You see, I told you it must have been. Tell me when you're nearly there. I want you to show me how he triggered your climax.'

The tightness of sexual tension was spreading all around Deborah's vulva. Her thighs were trembling, her belly rounded and taut and the heat generated by her hand's movements was glorious.

'I'm nearly there!' she gasped. 'This is when he used to . . .'

Pavin moved very fast. One moment Deborah's hand was between her widespread thighs and the next he'd grasped it in one of his own and then both her hands were pinned up behind her head, one of his legs was between hers and she was left on the very brink of her orgasm but unable to move.

'No, Pavin!' she wailed. 'That's not fair! Do it for me then, please! I've been waiting all evening for this. I don't think it's funny.'

'It isn't meant to be funny,' he told her, his face above hers. 'You didn't really think I was going to let you come imagining some other man's hands on you, did you? I just wanted to see you arouse yourself, and that seemed the best way.'

At some point he'd taken off the last of his clothes and his huge, naked body was balanced above her as he stared down into her eyes that were burning with sexual need. Between her legs a dreadful, bitter-sweet ache was suffusing Deborah and she tried to move against Pavin's thigh to ease it, but he shifted his body so that clitoral contact was impossible.

'Just wait a few more minutes, honey,' he whispered in her ear as she twisted and turned trying to free her hands from his grip. 'I'm going to give you one of the best orgasms of your life, I promise. Turn on your stomach.'

As he spoke he released her hands and then flipped her over before she could protest. He kept her legs spread widely apart and inserted one of the numerous pillows beneath her hips. Deborah, whose swollen breasts and abdomen were even grateful for the contact with the satin sheets of the bed, wondered anxiously what was going to happen next.

Pavin knelt between her parted legs and ran one hand slowly down her spine, tracing the outline of each of the cheeks of her smooth bottom before carrying on down the backs of each of her thighs in turn. At the back of her knees he swirled his fingers in tiny circles and saw her calf muscles tighten with the increasing sexual tension.

Deborah's whole body was screaming out for satisfaction. Mentally and physically she had been aroused to the point of no return over the past few hours and yet still satisfaction was being withheld. She felt one of Pavin's fingers slide up her love channels until he could insert the tip into her vaginal opening. Her internal muscles contracted fiercely about it, attempting to use it as a substitute for his penis but he bent his head to nuzzle the nape of her neck and once more urged her to wait just a little longer.

Then, as she lay trembling with thwarted desire, he let three fingers slide palm down inside her so that they were touching the front wall of her vagina, that was facing the bed. The touch was so welcome to her starved senses that she moaned in gratitude.

'Now move your pelvis, Debbie,' he urged her. 'Try rotating it and rolling from side to side. I want to see what suits you best.'

She obeyed him, and at one point, just as she was halfway through a rotation, a delicious sensation swept through her whole body and she groaned aloud. Her reaction encouraged Pavin to increase the pressure on this particular spot, and as he felt her juices increasing around his fingers he eased his other hand beneath her body just above her pubic hair and pressed there as well.

The combination of the fingers pressing on her front vaginal wall from the inside and outside at once drove Deborah into delirium. She cried out 'Yes! Yes!' and the hot flooding feeling began to travel down her legs and up through her belly as well as all through her swollen vulva and yet she still hadn't climaxed. The unbelievably intense sensations of sexual excitement simply continued to climb and she began to move her lower body around without even realising it, wanting the feeling to increase and perversely to end as well.

Pavin's self-control was stretched to its limit by her passionate response and now he let the fingers that were inside her slip out so that he could insert the tip of his penis, while at the same time the hand that had been pressing down above her pubic bone moved lower and as he rotated his blood-suffused organ just inside her vaginal opening he managed to stimulate her clitoris by manipulating its covering hood with his fingers. It was this that finally gave the frenzied, swollen, aching yet pleasure-soaked Deborah her release.

She felt the moment of almost unbearable tightness that preceded her climaxes and then she seemed to burst and every inch of her was racked by muscular contractions that had her heaving and twisting in uncontrollable spasms beneath Pavin as he too reached his long-delayed climax within her tight pulsating warmth.

Even after the peak of her orgasm had passed, Deborah continued to twitch and squirm on the bed, her body totally out of her control as it recovered from the intense experiences of the entire day.

Pavin, who as soon as he had finished had withdrawn and was now lying next to her on the bed, laid a protective arm across her back and murmured soothingly until finally she was able to rest.

'Do you know what I'd like to do now?' he asked her. Deborah shook her head, too exhausted to speak. 'I'd like to bring you to another climax. I'd like to see you thrashing around again, you look so incredible when you finally lose control.'

'I couldn't,' moaned Deborah in mock-horror.

'Sure you could, but not tonight. It's something you'll learn though before the holiday's over.'

'I thought you were never going to let me come,' she whispered as she drifted off to sleep.

He smiled against her hair. 'Wasn't it worth the wait?'

'Yes,' she agreed sleepily. 'In the end it was.'

'That's all that matters then.'

Very soon they both slept, Deborah curled up against

80

Pavin's chest while his arms stayed around her for most of the night.

'Coffee, sir,' said a young girl's voice lightly.

Deborah opened her eyes and realised that she was lying naked in Pavin's arms without even a sheet over her while a maid of about nineteen put a tray of coffee down on the chaise longue, where Pavin had watched her arousing herself a few hours earlier.

Pavin opened one eye, grunted and closed it again. The maid then drew back the curtains, smiled shyly at Deborah and asked her if she wanted a bath run.

'That would be great!' enthused Deborah, trying to pull a sheet discreetly over herself. Then she realised that she had to climb over the bed to reach the coffee and hadn't any nightclothes near at hand so she had to wait for the maid to disappear into the bathroom before she could get herself a welcome cup.

'One for you, Pavin?' she asked brightly.

He groaned again. 'I'm not a morning person, honey. You go ahead. I'll probably give breakfast a miss. You'll find everyone in the main hall. After you've eaten why not go for a walk, explore the island a bit? I'll join you later.' With that he closed his eyes, turned on his side and went back to sleep.

Deborah finished the coffee, deliciously hot and strong with cream and sugar, and then washed in the deep, scented bath the maid had run before pulling on a pair of light denim jeans and a short-sleeved T-shirt in coral pink. That combined with a pair of canvas shoes on her feet seemed about right for touring the island.

Both Tansy and Paul Woolcott were already eating when Deborah arrived for breakfast. So too was Celia, the winner of the previous night's water game, but there was no sign of Flora nor of Brian or Elizabeth Forster. Richard Ford was there though and she was astonished to find herself wondering if the dark curly

81

hair that covered his head also covered his body. She had never before considered men in such an intimate way and wondered what was happening to her on Pavinsay. Whatever it was, it seemed to agree with her.

'You look well rested!' laughed Tansy. 'It's not how Pavin's women usually look in the mornings.'

Celia glanced at Deborah. 'Do you want to come for a walk when you've eaten? I usually take some kind of exercise after breakfast and you really ought to see the place on a lovely morning like this.'

Deborah was surprised. Celia hadn't seemed particularly friendly the previous day, but she smiled her thanks. 'That would be great. Pavin suggested I had a look round. He doesn't want to get out of bed yet!'

'Even when he does he'll be closeted with my husband. Believe me, it's never all play and no work with Pavin, not even on these holidays as Martin's learnt to his cost.'

'Come off it,' said Tansy. 'The most Martin does is go through a couple of balance sheets in the course of a fortnight. That's not as likely to kill him as a couple of nights with you!'

Everyone laughed except for Celia who turned away from Tansy. 'At least I don't have to resort to surgery to keep my husband interested,' she said loudly and then nibbled daintily on a piece of toast.

Deborah, after examining the contents of the various silver-covered dishes that were laid out along the side tables, settled on scrambled eggs, bacon and tomatoes, plus more of the strong coffee that she'd enjoyed in bed. After that she had two slices of wholemeal toast and dark, bitter marmalade.

'Something's given you an appetite,' remarked Celia. 'Ready to go now?'

They walked out of the main castle entrance, along the gravel drive that curved between two immaculate expanses of lush green lawn, and then started along a path leading down towards the sea.

'If you want to go right round the island it's about a mile,' said Celia. 'But there are plenty of shorter walks, and it's probably best if I show you some of the things close to the castle today. You can explore further afield another time. Not that there's very far to go. The whole place isn't more than half a mile across. It's really just a castle with very big grounds!'

'It's magnificent!' exclaimed Deborah as they followed the path down the gradual incline. 'What are those birds?'

Celia shrugged. 'No idea, honey. Cormorants or shags I guess. Martin's the expert on wildlife. He'll spend hours taking pictures of seals in the bay and stuff like that. I just like the fresh air.'

Deborah looked down at the cove below them. The sand was very white and the cliffs around it brick-red in colour. Most of the hills on the island were more like large slopes and the grass wasn't lush but a kind of browny-green scrub.

'I can't see any trees!' she exclaimed.

'Kinda weird that, I know,' agreed Celia. 'My theory is that Pavin sneezed one day and they all blew down! Probably Martin can give you a real boring explanation about geographical conditions, but who the hell cares? If you're into history though you must visit one of the cairns sometime. They're these underground burial places with low passageways, and if you go with the right guy it can be some experience!'

Despite talking, Celia was walking at a fast pace and Deborah had a job to keep up with her. Eventually Celia slowed. 'Sorry, I'm rushing you. Guess you get out of shape working in London. I spend most of my time in Florida where you just work out, go to beauty salons and eat salads. Means I'm up to these holidays though!'

'Are you all from America, apart from Martin?' asked

Deborah as they descended the last few feet to the sandy cove.

'No, Flora is the genuine Scottish article. I mean with a name like Flora Stewart she'd have to be, wouldn't she? I think Elizabeth is half Portuguese, but I'm not sure. Brian's kind of cagey about where they met. As for me, I was born in Wales! I went to America on a walking holiday as soon as I was old enough to leave and ended up in Florida.'

'How did you meet Martin then?'

'I met him right here. I worked for Pavin as a temp a few years back. We sort of clicked, he asked me on one of these holidays and that's where I met Martin. His British reserve drove me insane with lust. Now it just drives me insane!'

They reached the beach and both women took off their shoes. 'I didn't really know exactly what kind of holiday this was going to be,' confessed Deborah.

'Pavin prefers it that way,' laughed Celia. 'He likes to see how people react in strange situations. You're enjoying yourself, aren't you?'

Deborah nodded. 'Yes, although if I'd known in advance I don't suppose I'd have come.'

'That's the whole point. You're meant to discover another side to yourself on Pavinsay.'

'But doesn't anyone mind sharing their partners? Surely Elizabeth must have hated knowing her husband was with you last night?'

Celia turned to face the taller blonde woman. 'Sweetie, you can be quite sure someone was taking very good care of little Lizzie while Brian and I were busy in the dungeon. That's how it works here. No one gets left out.'

'And no one ever minds what's happening?'

Celia gazed out over the now calm sea. 'Maybe they do, but they're wise enough not to say because if you complain you don't get asked again and believe me the pluses outweigh the minuses. All the men here are very different which is fun, and most of us keep quiet just for a chance to spend a few hours with Pavin.'

Deborah tried not to show her shock. 'Pavin joins in with everyone too?'

Celia laughed. 'It's his party, he can do whatever he likes and yes, that means joining in. Why? Did you think he'd only make love to you while you were here?'

'I hadn't thought about it,' lied Deborah.

'Well think about it now, then it won't come as a nasty surprise. Just remember that when he's busy elsewhere you'll be having such a good time you won't mind a bit. One word of advice though. Keep your eye on Flora. She's worked for Pavin for several years now and once he'd divorced Angela she expected to be the next Mrs Pavin. Your arrival's put her nose out of joint, and if she can get you to kick up any kind of scene to displease Pavin she will. So if you want to hang on to him, and something tells me you do, then watch her carefully.'

'I hardly know Pavin,' responded Deborah.

'Doesn't stop instant attraction.'

Deborah knew that was true. He drew her to him like a flame attracts a moth, but she wasn't going to confess that to Celia. 'Who's that?' she asked, pointing to where a woman was lying stretched out naked on a rush mat in a corner of the cove.

'Tansy, she likes to get her plastic boobs a nice golden brown.'

Deborah laughed. 'Has she really had them done?'

'Sure. She's a couple of years older than Paul and doesn't want to sag before he does! Actually, she really went to the surgeon to have her clitoral hood removed and he threw the breast job in as a cheap extra.'

Deborah stopped walking. 'She had what removed?'

'I know it sounds weird but she had her clitoral hood taken away. She says it's like a bloke being circumcised

85

and means it makes it much easier for men to find that vital little spot.'

'But it mean's it's got no protection.'

Celia gave a strange smile. 'Yeah, which is something Brian really maximises to the full. Come on, we'll go across and I'll get her to show you.'

Tansy was lying on her back, her full, perfectly formed breasts pointing upwards to the clear blue sky. Although the sun was out, Deborah couldn't help thinking she must be freezing in the morning air.

'Hi!' said Celia casually.

Tansy took of her sunglasses and propped herself up on one elbow. 'Oh, it's you.'

'Expecting someone else?'

'Richard said he might join me later. You know he enjoys fresh air!'

Celia giggled. 'I sometimes think the beach barbecues are just for his benefit. I was showing Debbie round some of the island.'

Tansy gave Deborah a half-smile. 'Do you like it? Or is it only Pavin that interests you?'

'I think the whole place is fantastic!' responded Deborah.

'That's more than his last wife did. She complained it was always freezing cold here and that there weren't any shops. I suppose you haven't yet reached the stage of needing shops to keep you entertained!'

'Leave her alone,' said Celia. 'It's not a crime to fancy Pavin or we'd all be in prison! Actually, I wanted you to show her what that surgeon did for you.'

Tansy indicated her thrusting breasts. 'He stopped these sagging for a start.'

'Not that,' said Celia with a sigh. 'Show her what he did lower down.'

Tansy looked up at the waiting Deborah. 'Stand at my feet then and I'll show you.'

Deborah walked round until she was between Tansy's legs, then the other woman put her hands down and pulled apart her outer sex lips. 'There, what do you think?'

Deborah didn't know what she thought. There, high up at the top of the sex lips, just beneath the pubic bone, was a tiny little button of light pink flesh with no familiar fold of skin half-concealing it.

'It's fantastic having it like this,' enthused Tansy, seeing the look of uncertainty on the blonde woman's face. 'Let's face it, even the most incompetent man can't miss it now! As for the experts, well let's just say they have a field day. There's also the added bonus of self-stimulation. I only need to wear a pair of tight bikini pants and I start getting aroused!'

'But what happens when you don't want to be aroused? Surely it must be painful then?' asked Deborah.

'I just leave off underwear, though to be honest it isn't often that I don't want to be stimulated! You can touch it if you like.'

Celia was standing at Tansy's head and she looked curiously at Deborah, clearly interested to see what her reaction would be. Deborah's first instinct was to refuse, but there was an undeniable fascination about the situation that tempted her.

'Lick your finger first,' added Tansy. 'There's nothing worse than a dry, clumsy touch.'

Deborah licked her middle finger and crouched down between Tansy's thighs. 'How do you like it touched?'

Tansy smiled. 'Probably the same way as you do. Use your imagination, honey.'

Celia's dark eyes were fixed on Deborah's face as the young Englishwoman slowly ran her finger, damp with her own saliva, along the side of the exposed clitoris. Tansy drew in her breath and Deborah felt a strange surge of power. Very carefully she let her finger circle

87

the nub, watching it swell and suffuse with blood as it responded to her stimulation.

'Don't stop now!' begged Tansy, spreading her legs wider. 'You've got a super touch.'

There was a tightness around Deborah's chest. Breathing seemed difficult and her own legs were trembling as much as Tansy's as she removed her finger for a moment, slid three of them into her mouth and then used all three to tease around the increasingly prominent clitoris.

Suddenly the bud moved slightly as Tansy gave a small moan. 'It's about now that a clitoris starts to retract,' explained Celia. 'The stimulation must be too intense or something, but of course Tansy's can't. Don't worry, she likes it like this. Just increase the pressure a bit.'

'No!' said Tansy sharply. 'Don't increase it, keep it as it was.'

But Deborah was aroused by Celia's words and she ignored the squirming woman's plea and pressed her fingers more firmly against the sides of the still-swelling sex button.

Tansy moved her hands to slow Deborah's movement, but just then a shadow fell over the three women and when Deborah glanced up she saw that Richard was standing over them, dressed in a pair of swimming trunks.

He caught hold of Tansy's hands and pinned them above her head to the beach mat. 'Carry on, Debbie,' he urged her. 'This is what she really likes.'

Tansy's top teeth were biting into her bottom lip as she tried to twist away from Deborah's touch but Richard held her firmly and Deborah continued to stimulate each side of the shaft until Tansy's head was rolling from side to side and tiny mewing sounds came out of her mouth. As her stomach began to clench into a tight ball, Deborah stroked across the top of the permanently exposed clitoris with the very tip of one long nail and at that Tansy screamed aloud and her legs went rigid as a climax tore through her.

Celia clapped lightly. 'Well done, Debbie! That was great. Wasn't it great, Tansy?'

Tansy lifted her head and stared at the newcomer to their group. 'You're not quite what I expected, Deborah. Somehow I think Flora's in for a nasty surprise. You've definitely got hidden depths. Don't you think so, Richard?'

Richard smiled at Deborah. 'I can't wait for my turn with you! Enjoy the rest of your walk, girls. Tansy and I will be busy for the next hour or so.'

Celia put her arm through Deborah's and they walked to the edge of the sea where Deborah dipped her hands in the salt water.

'You enjoyed that, didn't you?' said Celia.

It was a statement rather than a question and Deborah didn't answer it. She was slightly shocked to realise that it was the truth. She had enjoyed it. Not only her ability to give another woman such pleasure but also the fact that Tansy hadn't been able to stop her. That once Richard joined in and kept Tansy from directing the show, the sense of sexual power had been an aphrodisiac in itself.

'Come on, you can face your new knowledge later!' continued Celia with a small laugh. 'Let's finish our walk. By the time we get back to the castle the others should have made up their minds what they want to do today.'

When they finally got back, the big dining hall was deserted. 'I think nearly everyone's in the east wing, madam,' explained the same maid who'd brought Pavin and Deborah their coffee that morning. 'Mr Pavin said for you to join them when you returned.'

'We'd better go then,' said Celia. 'Will you be joining us at all today, Sara?'

The maid lowered her head. 'This afternoon, madam.'

'Lovely! Martin will be pleased.'

'What was all that about?' asked Deborah as they went out through the courtyard to the east wing.

'Most of the staff who work here join us from time to time. It livens up their dreary days and adds a little spice to the proceedings! Sara is a particular favourite. She plays the role of an old-fashioned serving maid so well that Martin has difficulty containing himself. You English get really hung up on class, don't you?'

'But what does she do?'

'Takes part in our home movies.'

'What home movies?' asked Deborah.

Celia seemed surprised Deborah didn't know. 'Pavin's a home movie buff. He likes to make films, appear in films and view them on his own console. You must have seen that, you are sharing his bedroom.'

'I saw a TV set yes, and he said something about watching videos because the TV shows were so poor.'

'That's one way of explaining it. It sounds as though we might be making a film this afternoon. I hope so. They're out of this world.'

'I never photograph well,' said Deborah.

Celia raised her eyebrows. 'I wouldn't say that, Debbie.'

'How would you know? You've never seen a picture of me.'

But Celia didn't respond, simply pushed open the doors that led into what Pavin had described as his personal recreation centre.

'Is this where the swimming pool and gym are?' asked Deborah.

'Among other things, yes. I expect they're in the small lounge though. That's where we always meet to discuss entertainment. Come on, it's up these steps.'

The room where Pavin, Elizabeth, Brian, Flora and

Paul were gathered was certainly smaller than any of the others Deborah had seen so far. The tone of the warm pink carpet was echoed in the plaster and marble reliefs around the fireplace, along the tops of the walls and on the ceiling. Portraits of stern-faced men in Highland costume hung on three walls and a large gold-framed mirror was on the wall opposite the door. The furniture seemed more modern, Regency style Deborah thought, and she wondered why Pavin had decided to mix styles so haphazardly.

'Have a good walk, sweetheart?' he called from where he was leaning against the fireplace, whisky glass in hand as he talked to Brian.

'Lovely thanks. It's a super morning, and your island's so beautiful.'

'Did you see Tansy or Richard?' asked Flora. 'They were meant to be here.'

'Sorry, no. We saw a lot of birds and a few seals, but no humans,' said Celia smoothly.

'Is that right, Debbie?' Pavin asked her, noticing that she was blushing slightly.

'Yes, of course. I mean, they might have been around but I was concentrating on the scenery.'

'It's no big deal,' said Paul. 'They're both free agents, Flora.'

'They know we always meet here on the first full day of the holiday.'

'They'll turn up soon enough,' said Brian. 'Anyway, they won't mind what we decide on. Deborah's the newcomer. We have to make sure she's happy with the itinerary!'

'I like to keep records of each of these holidays,' Pavin explained to Deborah, handing her a glass of bucks fizz. 'You wouldn't mind coming along to the filming after lunch, would you honey?'

'What kind of a record?' asked Deborah.

91

Pavin grinned. 'I like to show how well we all get along.'

'They're sex films,' said Flora crisply. 'Everyone's expected to take part. You can't just come and watch.'

For the first time since she'd met him, Deborah saw Pavin's face go dark with anger and he turned on his secretary. 'Who asked you to speak, Flora?'

Flora was clearly taken aback by his anger. 'I was only telling the truth. You were hardly being honest.'

'I think it's up to me how I describe things to my own special guest, and none of your affair,' he retorted.

'Come on, Pavin, she had to know before we began,' drawled Brian. 'What do you say, Debbie? Are you in or not?'

Deborah glanced at Pavin for guidance but he was staring down into his whisky glass, and leaving it entirely up to her.

Celia moved to Deborah's elbow. 'You'll love it,' she whispered softly. 'Remember that scene in the cove? Well, that's the kind of thing it is. You'll only do the things you want to do. If something turns you off then you give it a miss. Don't flunk out now, that's what Flora wants.'

'If I don't like it, can I leave?' asked Deborah.

Now Pavin did lift his head to look at her. 'Sure, you can leave any time, but it would mean leaving the island as well.'

Deborah looked round the room. Some of them were smiling at her in encouragement, but Flora wasn't. Flora's eyes were cool and Deborah knew that Celia had told her the truth, and that the best thing that she could do as far as Flora was concerned was say no.

Luckily, she didn't really want to say no. She was enjoying herself. Everything here was totally different, and she knew that if she were still in London she'd be shocked by them all, but here on Pavinsay it seemed quite acceptable. They were in their own world, and it was a world she wanted to savour to the full before she returned to her previous, rather conventional life.

'Sounds like fun,' she said positively.

Pavin raised his glass to her. 'Great! You won't regret it, I promise you. We'll only have a light lunch, a buffet in the small library would be best. I'll arrange that for twelve-thirty. In the meantime, do what you like. Deborah, how about joining me for a swim and a sauna?'

She drank the last of her bucks fizz then crossed the room so that he could put an arm round her, and all the time she was very aware of Flora's smouldering resentment.

'See you later then!' called Brian. 'I'm glad you've come, Deborah. You're a definite asset to our little gathering.'

Pavin's arm hugged her closer to his side. 'See, I told you they'd like you.'

'I can't believe I'm behaving like this,' confessed Deborah. 'I mean, it just isn't me.'

'Sure it is, otherwise you wouldn't do it. What you mean is, you didn't know it was you before you came here. The island's a very liberating place. Now, let's see what kind of a swimmer you are.'

Chapter Six

Deborah found that despite her swim – when Pavin had proved himself outstandingly proficient at the crawl while she moved slowly up and down the deliciously warm pool using the breaststroke – and their sauna together when he'd caressed her and covered her with kisses and tiny bites that aroused her appetite for full sex, but failed to satisfy it, she wasn't hungry at lunch time. She guessed that it was nerves; fear of the unknown things she would be expected to do and watch during the filming this afternoon, that was closing her stomach against food.

Pavin noticed and tried to reassure her. 'You'll have a great time, honey. From what Tansy tells me you're not slow to take part in group games!'

'She told you what happened in the cove?' asked Deborah in surprise.

'Tansy's been coming here for some time; she knows better than to lie to me,' he said smoothly.

'I'm sorry about that, it was only that I . . .'

Pavin turned away from her to speak to Flora and Deborah was left alone, wondering how annoyed Pavin really was that she'd denied seeing either Tansy or Richard when out on her walk.

Just before two o'clock everyone went off to their various rooms to get ready for the filming. Deborah wandered around the bedroom and wondered what on earth she should wear.

Pavin, who was pulling on linen slacks and a tight T-shirt that emphasised his powerful muscles, eventually got tired of her indecision. 'Wear that short blue dress with the V-neck. And don't bother with any undergarments except a suspender belt and stockings. Oh yes, and put on your highest heels. They make your legs look even longer.'

Deborah paused. 'Pavin, I'm not sure I can do this.'

'Sure you can, sweetheart. You've enjoyed everything so far. Why should this be any different?'

'I don't fancy performing in front of other people.'

'You like watching other people; it seems only fair to offer them the same enjoyment. Come on, once we're underway you'll be fine.'

Quickly she pulled on the dress, fastened a pair of sheer blue stockings to the blue suspender belt then hurried down the staircase after Pavin, her high heels clicking loudly on the steps. To her surprise when they reached the ground floor he opened a small panel in the wall of the entrance hall and ducked down through the gap. 'This way,' he called over his shoulder, his voice echoing back to her. Deborah obeyed, and then stumbled in the dim light of the passageway. 'Hold on to my shoulders, there are some steps to go down,' Pavin said.

'Where do you do your filming? I had no idea this part of the castle even existed.'

He laughed. 'It used to be the dungeon, where undesired guests were left to die of starvation or spies had their secrets torn from them I guess. Now it's our film studio.'

Deborah shivered. 'It's freezing cold.'

'Couldn't get the central heating this far, but the dungeon itself is fine. We keep a log fire burning there day and night. Here we are, you can straighten up now.'

At the bottom of the steep flight of stairs the ceiling rose again and then Deborah was following Pavin through a thick wooden door with a tiny peep-hole in the top, into the room where the filming was to take place.

'You're late,' said Brian.

'I'm never late; you must be early!' responded Pavin. 'Okay, I thought we'd start with Richard and me welcoming Flora to the holiday.'

Deborah clutched hold of Pavin's arm. 'Don't leave me,' she whispered.

'I'm needed on set, Debbie. Brian will take care of you!'

She watched desolately as he strode away from her into the middle of the flagstone floor. Brian and Elizabeth came to stand by her, and she felt Elizabeth's hand rest on her arm in a soft, sympathetic gesture.

'It's just a game,' she whispered. 'Don't worry about it. It's you Pavin's really keen on.'

'Elizabeth!' said Brian warningly, and at once her hand was removed and she fell silent.

'Where's the cameraman?' asked Deborah.

Brian laughed. 'We don't have a film crew. The cameras are all concealed, and the lighting's been adjusted so that we get really good results. It cost a fortune, but then what's money to a man like Pavin?'

'Quiet!' called Paul Woolcott who seemed to be directing this part of the afternoon, and at once the room was silent.

There were chairs round the walls of the dungeon and Deborah, seeing that Brian and Elizabeth had already sat down, decided to follow suit. As she began to lower herself, Brian caught hold of her by the waist and pulled her towards him. 'Sit on my lap, Debbie. That way I can tell you what's going on if you lose track of the plot!'

For a moment she resisted, but then she realised that there was no point and allowed him to pull her onto his knees. As she sat down her dress rode up and she could feel his heavy denim jeans against the smooth flesh of her upper thighs.

At that moment a door on the opposite side of the room opened and Flora walked slowly in. She was wearing a transparent, long-sleeved white muslin blouse which reached to mid-thigh and nothing else apart from a G-string and a black garter. Her short brown hair had been coaxed into tight curls and her make-up was subtle except for the eyes where her lids had been heavily darkened with a charcoal-grey colour, while black kohl had been used to emphasise their shape. The effect was to make her look languorous and undeniably sexy.

Richard, wearing the same outfit as Pavin, moved towards Flora and putting his hands on each side of her face kissed her deeply, his tongue invading her mouth forcefully. Flora's head went back and while Richard kept kissing her, Pavin began to unbutton the muslin blouse and then he slipped it off her and his teeth nibbled lightly on each of her nipples in turn.

Watching him, Deborah felt a heavy stirring in the pit of her stomach, as though it was her nipples he was teasing and not Flora's. She moved slightly on Brian's lap and he smiled to himself, knowing that her turn would come, although in a very different way.

Now Richard had finished kissing Flora, and he moved behind her, drawing her arms back as he went so that he had her wrists held behind her, pushing her rapidly engorging breasts into even more prominence. Pavin licked them very lightly, working from the undersides up and Flora's eyes closed as she gave a moan of pleasure.

Now Richard was sliding to his knees, his tongue travelling the length of Flora's spine as he went, until he could suck at the tender tissue right at the base of her spine where her flesh dipped inwards.

This was clearly something Flora found hightly stimulating because she began to move her breasts to and fro so that Pavin's tongue could stimulate her nipples more strongly. For a moment Pavin acquiesced, but then he left her straining breats and instead hooked one of his fingers inside the top of her G-string and pulled it upwards so that it split her outer lips and pressed against the vulnerable inner tissue.

Flora uttered a whimper that could have been pleasure or discomfort, and then the two men were lifting her and moving her across to a flat couch where they lay her face down, arms hanging to the floor and her feet just dangling over the opposite end.

Flora seemed quite oblivious of the onlookers, she was squirming frantically against the raised pattern on the sofa trying to keep her breasts aroused while Pavin slowly teased the G-string from between her outer lips and then slid it, damp from her secretions, down her legs and off over her feet until it fell to the floor and she was naked except for her garter.

Now Richard, his erection clearly visible within his linen slacks, placed a ribbed, air-filled cushion beneath Flora's squirming hips which raised the cheeks of her bottom up into the air giving all the spectators a far clearer view of what was to come.

Pavin, after slipping off his T-shirt and slacks so that his swollen penis was free of all constraint, slipped on a thin plastic glove like those used by surgeons, then squirted some cream onto it from a tube he'd taken from his jeans pocket. The air was filled with the scent of cherries and Deborah assumed he was going to spread it over Flora's back and buttocks then lick it off her, but instead he smeared it carefully around his index finger, then parted Flora's buttocks with his free hand whilst slipping the lubricated digit into her tightly closed anus. Flora's head lifted from the sofa and there was an expression of anguish on her features.

'She's not too keen on this,' Brian whispered in Deborah's ear. 'That's why he's having to take it so slowly. Once he's got her going she'll be fine. It's odd how some women resist such pleasure.'

Deborah didn't think it odd at all. It certainly wasn't a form of lovemaking that had ever attracted her. However, as Pavin's covered finger carefully moved within Flora's rectum, the cool cream lubricating the highly sensitive walls, and his free hand massaged her back reassuringly, the sensations started to take over for Flora and her mouth slackened with increasing pleasure.

When he was sure she was relaxed again, Pavin withdrew his latex-covered finger, stripped off the glove and then picked up a multi-speed vibrator with a plughead that Deborah thought had to be at least two and a half inches wide, while the shaft was probably three inches long.

As Flora's face dropped back to the couch, and Richard's hands moved underneath her to stroke her stomach and tickle the sides of her waist, Pavin took advantage of her distraction to slide the head of the vibrator swiftly into her rectum.

Flora gasped. She thrust her buttocks upwards, but this only made the vibrator penetrate her more deeply. Then Pavin turned on the control in the base and Deborah, along with everyone else in the room, watched in a state of electrified excitement as Flora's upper body twisted and turned while Pavin held her lower body still, gripped between his long, hard fingers. Suddenly her neck went tense, her head lifted and she cried out as an orgasm swept through her.

Pavin immediately turned off the vibrator, but left it securely within her back entrance. As Richard stripped of his clothes, Pavin slid the gasping Flora around on the sofa until she was half-lying and half-sitting over the width of it, her buttocks just over the edge and the wicked plug-head still embedded within her. Then Richard knelt in front of her and lifted her legs over his shoulders but he left a good space between them so that Pavin could crouch in front of him and with one hand keeping the vibrator inside her rectum he proceeded to lick across her vaginal opening, refusing to let his tongue enter but occasionally swirling it just at the opening so that Flora thought he was going to and thrust upwards to welcome him.

As he teased and tantalised her, Deborah felt her whole body swelling with need. She needed to feel Pavin's tongue on her, and his hands. She needed fulfilment just as badly as Flora, and watching her lover adminstering to another woman was driving her mad.

She shifted frantically on Brian's knees and he braced his leg so that her pubic area received some stimulation, but not enough to let her climax because that was for later.

Flora was crying out now, begging for Pavin to finish her off, but he took his time, refusing to be rushed and instead he played her like a violin until every part of her felt so tight she thought she would snap.

When they'd started, Flora had simply wanted to show Deborah that Pavin was used to her body and knew how to satisfy her. All that had gone out of her head now. She was simply one burning mass of desire balanced on the edge of what she knew would be a mind-blowing climax.

Pavin twisted the anal vibrator a little, and Flora's body responded by jerking upwards again. Then he closed his mouth over her clitoris and sucked but so lightly that although the blood pounded in her ears and a warm glow began to suffuse her breasts and belly, the climax was still denied.

Flora was crying out now, begging the men to finish what they'd begun, and the air in the dungeon was heavy with sexual passion and mounting arousal. When Pavin removed his mouth from between her legs, Flora wanted to cry but as he moved away and went round behind her, Richard, his purple circumcised penis so tight it was paining him, slid into her. He began to glide smoothly in and out, judging his speed and rhythm by her responses while at the same time he tugged gently on her pubic hairs to move her clitoris around.

Everyone in the room knew that Flora's climax was about to engulf her, and some of them moved closer to the prone woman while others, including Deborah, stayed in their seats trying to quell their own rising desire.

For Flora the sensations were all bliss now. The fullness in her rectum, the smooth easy strokes of Richard's gratifyingly long penis and the exquisite tugs that were exciting her clitoris represented everything she loved about these abandoned holidays.

She sensed her release approaching, felt her toes curling upwards and her legs going rigid as the first waves of satisfaction began to sweep over her. 'Yes! Oh, yes!' she screamed, and as she twitched and spasmed in the throes of her climax, Pavin leant over her. Placing his throbbing organ between her breasts, he pushed the insides of the softly rounded globes together and rubbed them against the side of his shaft so that a few seconds after Flora's climax had ended he was spilling himself between her breasts while Richard's rhythm became rougher, more urgent until he too had his climax.

Carefully, Pavin moved Flora round and laid her on her side on the sofa so that she could rest while he and Richard disappeared to tidy themselves up, in order to watch the next part of the afternoon's filming – the part that was to involve Deborah and Sara, the maid, along with Brian and Celia's husband Martin.

For a moment after the scene had ended there was complete silence in the room. Deborah glanced around her and saw the same suppressed excitement in other people's eyes that she guessed was in hers. Tansy and Paul were openly fondling each other, their arms locked in a tight embrace, but no one else was touching, they were simply savouring the atmosphere.

Despite the heavy wall drapes, the roaring fire, and the lights needed for the filming, the dungeon was still a cold place. Deborah was surprised that Pavin hadn't had the floor covered, but when she suggested this to Brian he smiled knowlingly.

'Pavin didn't want to get rid of the flagstones because they remind people the place was a dungeon. Sometimes it adds to the atmosphere, especially for bondage and games like that. Surprisingly enough, once you're involved in anything you get pretty warm. It's only when you first come into the room that you really notice the cold.'

'I thought Flora must have been chilly,' commented Deborah.

'She looked warm to me! Right then, it's your turn now. We're just waiting for Sara and then we can set things up.'

Deborah's stomach lurched and her throat tightened. 'What have I got to do?' she asked hesitantly.

Brian shrugged. 'No idea; it's up to Pavin. He likes to control everything, as you doubtless know.'

Deborah mistakenly took comfort from this. She was quite sure Pavin wouldn't expect her to do anything she couldn't cope with on her first time.

'That was great!' enthused Pavin when he returned. 'Okay, Brian, set up the cross-beam and get the equipment ready. Debbie, come over here, sweetheart. I want to talk to you.'

She left Brian's lap and moved to the centre of the room, totally unaware that the film scene had already begun. Once in front of Pavin she looked up at him with a questioning smile.

He didn't smile back. Instead his face was cold and his voice sounded annoyed. 'When I invite people onto my island, Debbie, I expect certain courtesies from them. That's not unreasonable, is it?'

She didn't understand him. 'What's wrong? I thought the whole place belonged to you, but if I trespassed somewhere on my walk, then I'm sorry. It was ignorance, that's all.'

'You can walk where you like and do what you like, but you must never, ever lie to me,' he said softly.

Deborah's eyes could no longer meet his hard blue gaze and she lowered her head. 'You mean about Tansy,' she whispered.

Pavin put a hand beneath her chin and forced her head up again. 'Yes, I mean about Tansy and Richard. You said you hadn't seen them, but you had. You'd even indulged in sex play with Tansy. Why didn't you tell us? We don't have secrets on Pavinsay.'

'But Celia said. . .'

'Celia's already being punished. She can't take part in the filming today. As a born extrovert in front of the camera that's hurt her, but you're not like that, are you? You don't really want to do this, which is why your punishment is going to take place in front of the camera. We can keep it as a perpetual reminder of what happens when you break one of the very few rules we have here.'

'This isn't fair!' protested Deborah, taking a step backwards. 'I didn't know about any rules.'

'I think telling lies at any time is bad manners.'

'Yes, of course it is, but I didn't want to get Tansy into trouble.'

'She wouldn't have been in trouble. She can do what she likes, as long as we all know about it. Anyway, that's enough talk. I'm afraid Sara's behaved badly as well, so you and she will be punished together. Bring her in, Martin.'

Deborah wanted to run from the room, get away before this punishment, whatever it was, began. But as she took a step towards the door she saw Flora, now dressed in a blouse and skirt, smiling to herself in the shadows and she stopped. No, she wouldn't go. Pavin would never let her be hurt, it was another of his sexual games and she would go along with it and hopefully find enjoyment along the way.

Sara, wearing black stockings with a seam up the back, a tiny frilly white apron and a low-cut white blouse, was led into the room by Martin, who was scarcely able to keep his hands off her as he guided her towards Pavin.

'Brian found Sara pleasuring Elizabeth in the bath,' said Pavin shortly. 'As you all know, the domestic staff are not permitted to take part in sexual acts unless permission is obtained from two guests. In this case it was only Elizabeth who had consented. Sara knew it was wrong and accepts that she has to be punished if she wants to keep working here. Isn't that right, Sara?'

The girl nodded, but she seemed unable to speak and Deborah could see that she was trembling slightly.

'Excellent. Brian, are you ready?'

'Everything's in place,' responded Brian. Pavin and Martin turned the two young women round. While Pavin had been talking to them, a beam had been lowered from the ceiling until it was about six and a half feet from the floor, supported at both ends by heavy chains.

Instinctively Deborah took a step backwards, but

104

bumped against Pavin's solid form and felt his hands tighten on her elbows as he pushed her forward. Brian then seized her hands in his slim but wiry fingers and pushed them upwards until her arms were fully stretched. Pavin gripped her round the waist and lifted her into the air while Brian stood on a wooden block behind her and locked her wrists into the padded handcuffs that were fastened to the beam. Pavin immediately released her and for one agonising second her whole body weight was taken by her shoulders, but then wooden blocks were quickly pushed beneath her feet, and adjusted until she was able to take most of her weight on them but only by standing on tiptoe, which stretched her long legs into a tight line.

As she was manhandled into position, Deborah was vaguely aware that the same thing was happening to Sara, but Sara was protesting quite vigorously until Pavin went and murmured something into her ear at which point she fell silent.

Now Pavin, after one final look at the two suspended women stretched tightly from the beam and struggling to keep their balance on the wooden blocks, went back to the wall and sat down in one of the chairs to watch the scene that was about to unfold.

Deborah, her breasts rising and falling rapidly, realised that Brian was standing on a block behind her while Martin was behind Sara. All at once, a black blindfold was placed over her eyes and then fastened at the back of her head. She shouted out and her body swung painfully from the cuffs.

'Keep still, Debs,' murmured Brian, his voice softer than usual as he tried to calm her. 'This is to enhance the whole experience for you.'

Sara, who had also been blindfolded, kept silent. She'd been through this kind of thing before, and after her first time, when she'd thought she'd die of shame and humiliation, she'd become addicted to this particular form of pleasure. She knew that she could never go back to the mainland and settle down into ordinary domestic work again. Her body enjoyed these bizarre erotic episodes too much.

For Deborah it was terrifying not being able to see, and when she heard the sound of something heavy being moved over the flagstones she swallowed hard against her fear, but as Brian spoke to her from the front she realised that it was only another block to enable him to attend to her from both front and behind. For the next minute or so nothing happened, and as Deborah held her breath in anguished anticipation, the watchers around the room leant forward in their chairs, waiting eagerly for what was to come.

Brian and Martin glanced at each other and then in perfect unison reached forward and tore the clothing from the women suspended in front of them. Deborah's dress, carefully chosen by Pavin for this very purpose, opened easily, the press studs snapping apart and the material falling away leaving her exposed down the centre of her body. After that, all Brian had to do was unfasten the tie shoulder straps and the dress dropped to the floor so that she was entirely naked except for her suspender belt and stockings. Sara's uniform had also been torn from her, and her black-stockinged legs shook with mounting excitement while Deborah's trembled with fear of the unknown.

Without the two women's knowledge, Elizabeth and Flora had moved to help Brian and Martin. They both carried ice buckets from which the men removed cubes and then, working from behind the imprisoned women, positioned them just over their navels, fastening them there with wide, webbed strapping which fastened at the back.

The sudden cold touch on her overstretched skin made Deborah's body leap like a salmon from the water and for a moment her feet left the block and she was suspended in the air again. Hastily she scrabbled for a foothold, and then she realised that the heat of her skin was making the ice cube melt so that tiny rivulets of cold liquid were making their way across her lower abdomen and down through her pubic hair. She wanted to move, but couldn't because of her position. Instead she had to stay stock still and endure the cold invasion that slipped stealthily along her skin.

Next, a wide strip of soft velvet was passed between both women's legs from the front to the back; Brian and Elizabeth working it slowly against Deborah's labia, moving in a slow sensual rubbing motion while Martin and Flora did the same for Sara.

Deborah's body responded instantly. The material was so sensuous, the movement so carefully calculated to arouse with the minimum of pressure, and she began to thrust her hips forward with growing desire. Gradually both the ice cubes melted and the liquid soaked into the two strips of velvet while the women moaned quietly at their increasing excitement.

Lulled by the gentleness of it all, and even more easily aroused than normal because of the physical tension of their bodies' positions, neither Sara nor Deborah were ready for what happened next.

Without any warning, Martin and Brian suddenly started to slap the undersides of their victims' breasts with their fingers. The slaps were firm and evenly spaced, and the onlookers watched the way Sara's and Deborah's breasts jiggled and swung and saw the red marks slowly appearing on the white flesh.

Deborah cried out in shock and Flora smiled to herself while Pavin leant forward in his chair, his elbows on his knees and his hands cupping his chin. He was surprised to find that despite his recent session with Flora he was slowly being aroused again by the sight of Deborah naked in front of them all, and helpless beneath Brian's expert ministrations.

Deborah bit her lip to prevent herself crying out again as the firm, rhythmic slapping continued, but beside her she could hear Sara gasping in obvious arousal at the same stimulation. Then Brian stopped and cupped her swollen, burning breasts in his hands, lowering his mouth and applying strong suction to one nipple while his left hand fondled the other with vividly contrasting gentleness.

Deborah's breasts felt larger than ever before and she heard her breath rasping in her throat as he skilfully switched from one breast to the other, taking it in turns to gently manhandle them. The contrast was unspeakably stimulating and she too began to gasp with pleasure.

Once she was thoroughly aroused, Brian let Elizabeth take over Deborah's breasts, pinching the nipples and then sucking as much of the surrounding areolae as she could into her mouth.

In the meantime he went round behind the suspended blonde and she felt his hands cupping her buttocks, tracing their outlines and lifting them as though weighing or assessing their worth. Despite Elizabeth's expert ministrations on her breasts she began to tense, and when she felt her buttocks parted and some jelly spread around her rear entrance her terror increased, especially when Sara suddenly cried out: 'No! Not that, please!'

'It won't hurt if you bear down,' Elizabeth whispered in a low voice as Sara continued to cry out. 'Sara's only worried she'll come too soon. The first one to come isn't thought to have been sufficiently punished you see.'

'I don't want this!' protested Deborah violently.

At once Brian stopped what he was doing and Pavin rose from his chair. He walked across to stand in front of Deborah. 'Did I hear you right, Debbie? Do you want to stop now and leave?' Her naked and exposed body trembled before him as he waited for her answer.

Deborah didn't know what to say. Now that all the manipulations had stopped her body felt strangely neglected, and she realised that her level of arousal had been far higher than she'd realised; there had been great pleasure alongside the slight pain and her body had adored it. Now, left alone and with the prospect of never again seeing Pavin, making love with him or indeed with anyone else on the island, she felt her mind clear.

'No, of course not. I'm sorry, Pavin, I just panicked. I want to go on. I need to go on,' she admitted, dropping her voice in shame so that only he could hear.

Satisfied, Pavin stepped away from her again. 'Carry on,' he instructed the men. 'And girls, the idea is not to get too much satisfaction from what's happening, this is meant to be a punishment. The first to climax may have to be punished further.'

Deborah knew then that Elizabeth had told the truth, and that she at least was a real friend.

Brian returned his attention to the entrance between Deborah's tight buttocks and remembering what Elizabeth had said, Deborah bore down. This opened her up to him, but it also meant that her clitoris became more prominent and as Brian slid a cold nozzle into her lubricated rectum and began to fill her back passage with whipped cream, Elizabeth took a piece of waxed cord and with agonising gentleness let it caress the highly sensitive tip of the exposed clitoris.

Deborah gasped, and Sara gave a cry of excitement too as the same thing was done to her. Hearing another woman in such a state of sexual ecstasy only added to Deborah's own excitement, and she tried to block out the whimpering noises of heightening pleasure coming from the young maid.

Brian slowly continued to squeeze the whipped cream into Deborah's tight opening, and soon she began to feel uncomfortably full there and her stomach was visibly distended, much to the excitement of the onlookers. The pressure created a deep ache in the pit of her stomach and her toes moved restlessly on the wooden block.

'Keep you buttocks clenched,' Brian instructed her firmly. 'Don't let the cream escape. Elizabeth, come round here and tell me if any starts to ooze out.'

Deborah heard them changing places, and then she felt Brian's hand on her already pressurised stomach, spread across the lowest part, just above her pubic hair. His fingers kneaded softly at the tight flesh so that her nerve endings screamed with the increased stimulation and hot sparks of desire pierced through her breasts and thighs and she longed for some touch between her legs where she was already swollen and damp.

Brian was an expert at this kind of manipulation, and he continued to apply pressure to her seemingly bursting flesh until she was moaning in a kind of mad delirium, straining to keep her buttocks closed despite the muscular spasms in her belly triggered by his wickedly knowing touch.

Finally he took pity on her, and lazily he let his tongue slide down her inner thighs to knees, calves and ankles, peeling her stockings down as he went, and then in a diabolically tender gesture he placed his tongue beneath each of her straining feet in turn and licked along the length of the overstretched arches.

She felt herself growing more and more damp between her thighs and when he started to move his head up again she could have cried out in gratitude. Pavin, seeing the way she was fighting against the contractions that were her natural reaction to such skilful arousal, longed to take Brian's place and wrench her climax from her himself but he knew that he couldn't. The game was never played like that. It was just that this was the first time he'd really wanted to interfere, and he was amazed at his depth of feeling for the blonde-haired young Englishwoman.

Brian sensed Pavin's desire and smiled to himself. It only made what he was doing all the sweeter. He knew that Deborah wouldn't be able to hold out much longer, and as his tongue started to slide smoothly up her moist inner channels towards her despairing clitoris he felt her push herself towards him and knew that she would precipitate her own downfall through inexperience.

In the meantime, Sara was groaning and gasping but using every trick she'd learnt over the past three years in order to keep her orgasm at bay. In any case, Flora wasn't working as hard as she could and even when a small dribble of cream escaped from between the maid's buttocks she didn't say anything because she wanted Sara to beat Deborah.

Brian's tongue started to circle the outer portion of Deborah's clitoris, and at once she forgot to keep her buttocks tightly closed.

'There's cream coming out,' said Elizabeth, her voice sympathetic.

'Naughty!' said Brian, and nipped lightly at the inflamed bud.

To Deborah's horror this merely seemed to bring her climax closer and she felt her entire body gather itself together, every inch of skin pulling tight over the flesh beneath as a slow pulse began to beat behind her clitoris.

Nearing its peak of arousal the clitoris started to slip beneath the fold of protective flesh, but Elizabeth had played this game with her husband many times before and knew exactly what she had to do. Just as the bud began to disappear from view she put her tiny hand sideways across the top of Deborah's pubic bone and moved it up towards the middle of her stomach so that the pulling of the skin forced the hood away from the clitoris.

111

Now it was totally exposed and Deborah was making tiny mewing noises mixed with deep guttural groans of desire that she didn't recognise as coming from herself. Brian took the waxed cord from his wife, drew it delicately up the middle of the suspended blonde's parted sex lips and then with one quick flick of his wrist he struck the red, engorged nub of her pleasure a sharp stinging and totally unexpected blow that proved the final death knell to her self-control.

As the red-hot blaze of pleasure-pain lanced through her, Deborah felt a flood of moisure flow from her front passage and then it seemed as though every single muscle in her body was convulsing with the huge waves of blissful release that tore through her. For the onlookers, the sight of her taut, shackled body heaving and twisting as the muscles of her thighs and belly rippled and shook and her vaginal juices flowed down between her thighs while the last of the cream escaped from between her buttocks and down the backs of her legs, was one of the most arousing they'd ever seen.

Her blonde hair flew around her face as her head twisted from side to side and her cries of pleasure were so loud that they toppled Sara over the edge and for a brief instant both of the tethered women were racked by their orgasm at the same time, although it was Deborah who was the first to become still.

As Brian removed her blindfold and released the handcuffs, he pinched her still swollen and erect nipples. 'I can't wait until we get a chance to be alone together,' he said softly. 'Since you lost, although admittedly by a very short head, I think I'll suggest that's what happens next. The winner chooses her partner you see, the loser gets it chosen for her.'

Deborah hardly heard him, all that she was aware of was Pavin coming across the room towards her, wrapping her in a huge rug and then he was carrying her from the room holding her tightly against his chest and murmuring endearments that made everything she'd endured worthwhile.

As he laid her on their bed he asked: 'Did you enjoy it, really enjoy it, or was it just for me, Debbie?' and his eyes were worried.

She knew she had to be completely honest. 'I enjoyed it,' she confessed, and then she slept.

Chapter Seven

When she awoke she could hear Pavin moving about in the dressing room and assumed it must be dinner time. It was hard to tell from the amount of light coming in through their window. At this time of year it stayed light until eleven o'clock at night on Pavinsay.

She was just reaching for her watch when he came into the room, already dressed in his dinner jacket. Hastily Deborah started to climb out of bed. 'Why didn't you wake me?' she demanded as she padded naked towards him.

'Hey, what's the rush?' He sounded amused. 'Dinner's over, honey. I did try to wake you but you just groaned and kept your eyes shut! I guess the excitement of the afternoon tired you out.'

'What's the time then?'

'Nine-thirty. Do you want some food sent up?'

Deborah looked about for something to put on and found one of Pavin's shirts. It was so large she felt like a child dressing up in adult's clothing.

Pavin smiled. 'Very fetching! Tell you what, honey. How about us taking a stroll for half an hour, that will help wake you up, and you can eat when we get back.'

Deborah liked the thought of him showing her round his island. Hastily she pulled on a black leisure suit with white diagonal stripes across the back of the jacket and white circular bands round the arms. She knew it suited her and saw desire in the American's eyes even though he didn't say a word.

They left the castle grounds by a small wicket gate at the rear of the building. This path led them across the island where the strange goat-like sheep, said to be descendants of an earlier primitive breed, wandered.

'Cute, don't you think?' asked Pavin proudly. 'They live on seaweed! Not at lambing time, then the ewes use the grassland such as it is, but the rest of the year it's just seaweed.'

Deborah smiled. 'You're really into all the culture of these islands, aren't you?'

'Sure; *when in Rome*, as they say.'

'First you come and steal our publishing industry; now you're stealing our heritage as well. America must be a very unsatisfying place to live!'

She heard Pavin's quick intake of breath and knew she'd irritated him, but she didn't care. Even here, where she was supposed to be forgetting herself in an erotic holiday of the senses, the hurt of her lost job occasionally resurfaced.

Pavin put his hand in his pockets and left a distance between them as they continued walking. 'I didn't steal your heritage, Debbie. No one wanted it. The young need bright lights and work, while the elderly don't want to be as cut off as they would be here in winter. Where's the harm in buying something no one else wants?'

'I didn't say it was wrong.'

'You sure as hell sounded as though it was.'

'I just think it's a pity that dollars can buy anything.'

115

He stopped and turned to face her. 'They can't. I've got two broken marriages and countless unsuccessful love affairs behind me. I'm rich enough to indulge my every desire, but sometimes I can't find enough people to share them with me. Added to which, how do I ever know that it isn't my dollars rather than my personality the brings me these wives, lovers and friends?'

Deborah considered for a moment. 'I suppose you don't, but if it's any comfort to you, I had no idea you were rich and famous when I met you at the party!'

'Then why did you let me take you home?'

'Because I fancied you, I suppose. You were easily the most attractive person in the room, and money can't do that for anyone.'

At last he grinned. 'I guess that's a compliment! Well, at least I was right about you, you're fitting in here exactly as I'd imagined, even if you are still suspicious of us Yankees!'

Deborah slipped an arm through his. 'Tell me about the others,' she suggested as they walked across the scrubland and down towards the pebbly shoreline.

'What do you want to know?'

'The kind of people they are, and why you chose them for your holiday island.'

Pavin sat down on a boulder and wrapped an arm around her so that she was leaning against his shoulder. 'It was a case of trial and error. Some of the people who came for the first couple of years didn't really take to it and they just drifted away. Brian's been coming ever since I bought the island. He used to bring girlfriends, and then last year he married Elizabeth and brought her. I didn't think she'd fit in, she seemed far too docile and shy, but an attractive masochist could hardly fail to add something to the overall pleasures on offer.'

'Brian's pretty intelligent, right?' asked Deborah.

'Yes, and a very good organiser. If I'm in America and there's some kind of crisis on one of the North Sea

116

rigs and they call us, he's more than capable of getting the right people out there with the minimum of fuss. Engineers, divers, firefighters, we've got a huge pool of expertise to draw on and he'll find the best in the shortest possible time. He likes to control, you see, which is why little Elizabeth suits him so well.'

'What about the Woolcotts? Tansy seems more outgoing than him.'

Pavin laughed. 'She is! She and I had a fling a while back and I brought her here for an early summer break. Paul was here working on a complicated job that meant he wanted peace. Instead, Tansy decided she wanted him. He had no chance at all!'

'Won't she tire of him? He seems so quiet compared with her.'

Pavin shrugged. 'She might, but nothing is forever, honey, remember? Now, Celia's Welsh you know, very in tune with the island and all things pagan. I suspect she fell for Martin's English style of good looks; the fair hair and marvellous diction. She probably needs these holidays more than he does because she likes variety and that's what we aim to offer people here.'

'And Flora's here because she's in love with you,' said Deborah slowly.

Pavin stared out to sea. 'Is that a fact? We sure get on pretty well at work and even between the sheets now and then, but small brunettes aren't my style. I have a fatal weakness for leggy blondes!'

Deborah snuggled closer to him. 'I'm glad to hear it. How about Richard?'

'He has a fatal weakness for Flora! They work together and play together but so far there's no sign that she's been bowled over by his manly charms. There must be some sexual chemistry missing for her.'

The breeze off the sea was cool and Deborah stood up. 'Can we walk some more? I'm cold.'

'Sure.'

117

Hand-in-hand they walked along the top of of the low cliff. 'How long have you been into this kind of experimental sex?' Deborah enquired softly.

Pavin looked at her in surprise. 'Ever since I can remember. I think most of us are if we're honest. It's just that society condemns it, or shall we say frowns on it. You get married and either stay married and have secret affairs or end up bored and divorced a few years later. This way everyone knows that at least once a year they can enjoy a different kind of sex from their usual daily couplings, and that probably keeps them going through the boring times.'

'But what about when the holiday ends?' asked Deborah as they slowly retraced their steps to the castle. 'Isn't it possible that a break like this could make things worse for some people?'

Pavin tipped her face up to his. 'Like you for instance?'

She blushed furiously and tried to pull away from him. 'No, not me! Anyone! Celia, Tansy, Richard, any of them might feel discontented once things got back to normal.'

'It hasn't happened yet, sweetheart. But I think you might be another story, because you're only just coming to terms with your sexuality, which means you've got to rethink the kind of life you want when you go back to London.'

'Just because I'm enjoying the holiday it doesn't mean this is the way I want to live my life!' she protested.

'No, but somehow I can't imagine you settling for another Mick after your film debut, can you? He forced you into a nurturing role. You're a far more sexual being than you ever allowed yourself to admit before.'

They were back at the castle now, and as they crossed the courtyard they could hear sounds of laughter and splashing coming through the open door that led to the recreation area.

'Fancy a group swim?' asked Pavin.

Deborah shook her head. 'I want to be alone with you tonight.'

His blue eyes darkened until they were the colour of the night sky. 'I think that's a pretty good idea. What shall I have the kitchen send up? You must eat something to maintain your strength!'

'Make it something light, I'm not that hungry.'

He disappeared for a moment and then together they went up the beautiful staircase, past the first floor dining room and on up to their Elizabethan-style bedroom, where at last Deborah would be alone with him again.

She went to bath and change, and by the time she'd finished one of the servants had brought up a plate of smoked salmon sandwiches, together with a mixed salad and a crème brûlée, all of which she devoured hungrily without even putting on a robe.

Pavin watched her lack of self-consciousness as she sat on the side of the bed nude, now and then licking the tips of her fingers, and he remembered the way she'd looked when she'd first met him. She'd been beautiful, that was what had caught his eye, but so tightly coiled and withdrawn that he'd wondered if it was worth trying to get to know her better.

Even he, used as he was to easy conquests, had been surprised when she'd made love with him that same night, and now he knew that it would be easy to expand her horizons even further because she trusted him and her body was made for sex.

'While your food goes down, why don't we watch a movie?' he suggested, pulling her back against his bare chest.

'I don't want to watch myself,' she said quickly, not yet willing to face up to how she must have appeared that afternoon.

'I was thinking of something from last summer;

119

before you were here. Wouldn't you like to see Tansy, Paul and Brian enjoying themselves?'

Deborah remembered Tansy's curvaceous body in the cove that morning, and especially the clitoris standing erect like a miniature penis without its usual covering hood. She felt the first faint stirring of excitement deep within her. 'Why not?' she said as casually as she could.

Pavin disappeared into the dressing room and reappeared with a video which he inserted into the console. 'Right, let's lie back on the pillows and make ourselves comfortable while they do the hard work!'

As the picture appeared on the screen the first thing that struck Deborah was the high quality of the film. This was no normal cheap, home movie effort, it could have been done by professionals and she wondered how much Pavin had spent on the equipment in order to get such good results. Whatever it was, it was worth it because almost immediately she forgot anything but what was happening on the screen.

It began with Tansy, nude apart from a bra with openings through which her nipples were visible, walking over the flagstones to where Paul was sitting on a high stool. His torso was bare but he was wearing jeans.

When Tansy reached him she knelt down and carefully unzipped the jeans then sat on her husband's lap facing him and, with her feet just touching the floor, slowly moved herself back and forth on his thighs.

Paul put his hand on each side of her waist and every time she moved towards him he would kiss her neck and the top of her breasts, just above the line of the bra, while her exposed nipples would rub against him.

Gradually her nipples began to expand and she pulled back a little to release what was obviously a rapidly swelling erection from Paul's jeans.

Deborah expected Tansy to then raise herself up and lower her body onto the erection, but instead Brian came and stood behind her then taking hold of her beneath her armpits he lifted her off Paul's lap. The look of surprise on Tansy's face was clearly genuine and she struggled, but Brian was far stronger than she was and with Paul's help it was easy for the two men to keep Tansy suspended in the air.

Paul put his hands beneath the tops of her thighs and Brian kept a firm hold under her arms so that they could move her lightly across Paul's rigid penis, allowing it to keep sliding up between her outer sex lips and then over her permanently exposed clitoris.

Soon Tansy was making small begging sounds and trying to push downwards but the men continued to tease her with Paul's erection and at the same time Brian started to roll her nipples between his fingers.

Deborah watched as Tansy's mouth opened and her head went back. She was panting with excitement and seemed almost unaware of what was happening when the men suddenly carried her bodily to the centre of the room and laid her on a high wooden table, its surface covered by a satin cloth.

It was only when Paul fastened a strap just below her breasts and secured it to the table beneath, while Brian slid a metal spreader bar up between her knees, that she started to struggle and by then it was too late.

Pavin watched the unfolding scene and idly ran a hand down over Deborah's stomach. She turned to look at him and her eyes were bright. 'Did Tansy know what was going to happen?' she asked softly.

'Probably not, but she chose the men she wanted to play with so she knew the kind of things that could happen.'

Deborah looked back at the screen. Now Brian had placed a tiny round pillow beneath the cheeks of Tansy's bottom so that her entire vulva was pushed upwards, fully exposed because of the spreader bar between her legs. It was easy to see that she was excited because she had glistening beads of moisture on her lower pubic hairs and when Paul bent his head and drew one of the thrusting nipples into his mouth in a long pulling motion, Tansy's outer sex lips flattened away from the centre, revealing her moist pink inner lips.

Brian was busy at the side of the table and when he came fully into the camera's view he had a small bowl in one hand and a tiny artist's paint brush in the other. 'I think you'll enjoy this, Tansy,' he said quietly, a small smile playing around his lips. 'It will be interesting to see if your reactions are more intense since that interesting piece of surgery you've had done.'

'What have you got there?' demanded Tansy, lifting her head to look.

'It's the heat gel,' he said shortly, and Tansy's eyes went wide which shock.

'Normally that's something everyone likes,' explained Pavin, his eyes still on the now squirming Tansy as the camera closed in on her. 'But it was the first time Tansy would have tried it after her particular brand of circumcision and I think she felt a bit anxious!'

Deborah could understand that. Watching the American woman being serviced by two men was highly arousing, but she knew that the edge of danger that Brian's presence seemed to bring was an extra aphrodisiac. The longer she watched, the more she wanted Pavin.

After dipping the pointed brush into the mixture, Brian kept it suspended above the woman's vulva for a moment and then moved round the table and instead swirled it over her nipples where they protruded through the open-fronted bra.

As he moved the sable filaments firmly over her tender tissue the heat began to course through her and Deborah saw the way the entire areola swelled so that her nipples and surrounding flesh were forced even more tightly through the hole until the edge of the opening was cutting into her breast.

Once she was painted to Brian's satisfaction he left Paul to keep massaging it, making sure the blood continued to course through the veins of the breasts while he returned to stand to the side of her hips. This meant that he could reach the vital spot and not obscure the camera's view of her reaction.

Tansy's head was moving around and she was moaning with the throbbing of her firm breasts. Her nipples stood out larger than any Deborah had ever seen. Paul seemed to take great delight in stimulating his wife as soon as the liquid began to cool, and his fingers scarcely left her alone even though, after a while, she begged him to stop.

In the meantime, Brian was drawing the brush delicately along the inside of her inner lips, spreading the lotion thinly and evenly and then he drew the brush back down again to make sure it took effect. Within a few seconds Tansy was screaming out as a hot throbbing began deep within the centre of her sexuality and she tried to reach down to touch herself but Paul pinned her arms to her sides and she groaned in disappointment.

It was clear from the picture on the screen in front of Deborah that Tansy's unprotected clitoris, although not yet touched by the lotion, was being affected by the general sensation of spreading heat. It was filling with blood, darkening in colour and standing out proudly providing Brian with an easy target.

Deborah wondered what Tansy had wanted at that moment. Had she wanted the lotion to be put on the tip of such a sensitive organ or had she been hoping Brian would only go around it? There was no way of knowing, but once the brush began to glide with careful precision upwards and Tansy knew beyond any doubt that he was going to touch her there, the American woman started to protest.

'No! Paul, stop him. It will be too much! This isn't fair! I'm burning up, for God's sake. I want a man inside me, not more lotion.'

'You should have thought of that before you had the operation done,' said Brian. 'As for wanting a man inside you, I thought women all wanted more foreplay. You should be grateful to us!'

As he finished speaking he finally flicked the tip of the brush over the nub and twirled it around in the lotion.

At once Tansy began to writhe on the table-top, her back squirming against the satin. Her face was contorted as a blazing heat seemed to fill every part of her with a frantic, despairing need for more stimulation, satisfaction and an easing of the pulsations she could feel in her breasts, belly and between her legs.

She was nothing but a mass of overstimulated nerve endings, and when Paul massaged her already bursting nipples once more and Brian slid the brush up and down the stem of her clitoris, she at last felt her body convulse with the incredible sensations and her 'Yes! I'm coming!' echoed round the room and Deborah felt an answering throbbing heat between her own thighs.

'Watch this next part,' said Pavin softly, well aware of Deborah's sexual excitement.

Deborah watched, and as Tansy's body began to go slack after her climax it suddenly tightened again and the muscles of her abdomen could clearly been seen bunching together as the continuing heat on her exposed clitoris, triggered afresh by the most delicate of touches on the tip by Brian's brush, forced her into yet another tearing spasm of release. This time the waves of the climax seemed to go on and on and Tansy's cries became cries for help not of bliss.

'How long would that go on for?' whispered Deborah, unable to stop watching the woman in the throes of multiple orgasms.

'Quite some time I imagine, but don't worry, they let her stop now!'

As Tansy moaned and screamed, Paul and Brian each took a damp cloth from a nearby ice bucket and even as she twitched and spasmed in front of them they began to wipe the lotion from her protruding nipples and between her thighs.

When Brian wiped her clitoris Tansy screamed again, but this time is was with pleasure, both at the release from the burning heat that had so overexcited her and from the touch of the cloth on her still aroused and exposed button.

'She's insatiable!' laughed Brian as Tansy squirmed and moaned while a small climax made her judder against the table top.

'Is the lotion all off?' asked Paul. Brian nodded, and then Paul was walking round the table. He unfastened the spreader bar, climbed up on the table, pushed down his jeans and within seconds was thrusting smoothly into his wife.

Because of the cushion beneath her hips and the stimulation her clitoris had already received, she was more than receptive to his movements and without its protective hood it was easier for him to make contact with the throbbing tissue as he thrust, so that very quickly Tansy was gasping in ecstasy while Paul's long, slim penis plunged deep inside her. He rode her well, withdrawing sometimes to circle just inside her vaginal opening, stimulating the nerve endings there, and then thrusting back inside again and as he worked her towards her peak Brian was holding her head firmly between his hands while crouching over her breasts. Tansy opened her mouth to receive him there until finally Paul climaxed within her, Brian came inside her mouth and Tansy bucked violently as her body was suffused with her final orgasm of the session.

As the bodies of the three participants went slack the screen went black and Deborah was left with a final image of Tansy, exhausted, tousled but undeniably totally sated while her own body was now on fire with desire for Pavin.

He turned towards her in the vast bed and drew her head into the hollow at the base of his solid, muscular neck. She reached across and softly played with one of his nipples, running her fingers through the wiry hair that covered his chest. Very soon the nipple was hard and pointed and so she did the same to the other one and Pavin signed with pleasure.

Encouraged by this – Mick had not really liked her to take the initiative – Deborah wriggled until her body was on top of the American's and then she slid slowly down his body nibbling at tiny portions of flesh as she went. When she reached his navel she let her tongue dip inside it to curl around the hollow and she felt his growing erection start to nudge against her thigh.

As Pavin lay back with his eyes closed, Deborah knelt between his parted thighs and carefully grasped his testicles in one hand. Then, as her other hand rubbed the shaft of his penis she increased the tension within it by holding the testicles firmly downwards.

Pavin gave a tiny moan and Deborah thrilled to the sound of this obvious sign of pleasure she was giving him. For a few minutes she continued to stroke his shaft while keeping the testicles down. Then, when she sensed that he was becoming too aroused, she released them and instead lowered her head and took them in her mouth with exquisite gentleness, letting her tongue caress the crinked flesh.

Pavin's hands came down and gripped Deborah's hair as she continued to use her mouth and tongue on him. She licked along the underside of the shaft, let her tongue flick lightly at the highly sensitive perineum behind the base of his penis and then drew the swollen glans into her soft mouth and ran her tongue around the ridge just beneath it until his hands were clutching at her hair almost frantically.

He was now so hard that he didn't want her to do any more for him. Instead he pulled her back up the bed and ran his hands along the sides of her body, then when they travelled across her stomach and the undersides of her breasts he used the tips of his nails to scratch lightly on her skin, not enough to mark it but sufficiently hard to cause a new and highly pleasing sensation to course through her.

Next he laid her on her back and cupped her sex in his hand, pressing slowly up and down against it until she felt she'd scream if he didn't part her sex lips and touch her more intimately, but he didn't. Instead he simply massaged her above her pubic bone, his hand rotating in quite heavy circles so that she began to feel full and tight inside and again she felt an ache deep inside her.

She was beginning to whimper with desire for him now, and so he allowed three fingers to slide across her pubic hair and then he pushed down on the clitoral hood, indirectly stimulating it as he went, before taking her outer sex lips between the fingers and pulling them even more tightly together which had the effect of rubbing all the sensitive inner tissue against itself and increasing Deborah's desire even further.

She was frantic for him now and he knew it. He moved back up the bed, leant against the pillows and grasping her by the hips helped manoeuvre her until she could lower herself onto his erection while sitting facing him. Then he pulled her legs out in front of her and as Deborah began to move they were both startled by the intensity of the sensations the position caused.

Pavin's hands now grasped Deborah's breasts

roughly. His fingers were no longer soft but hard and his grip painful, but she didn't care because she wanted him this way, no longer thinking just of her but instead caught up in the power of his own passion. She wanted to bind him to her in every possible way, including the best sex he'd ever had.

She could feel her climax slowly building, and when one of Pavin's hands left a breast and began to stroke the base of her taut belly she knew that it was very close.

'Lean back slowly,' said Pavin, his voice tight with passion. 'Move gently until your head's on the bed, that way I'll be pressing on the inside of your vagina. You like that, don't you?'

She knew that she did, that her G-spot was highly sensitive with this man, and carefully she did as he said until they were both lying with their heads at the opposite ends of the bed and Pavin could move steadily against the most sensitive spot in her love channel.

Almost at once she felt herself becoming very damp, and the sensations were entirely different from those of normal intercourse. Pavin waited as long as he could before reaching down and carefully bringing her back up into a sitting position again. He then used his powerful arms and hands to lift her up and down vigorously as his own climax built to a glorious crescendo that he could no longer hold back and he felt himself losing control as his body was shaken from head to foot and his face twisted up in a grimace of delighted ecstasy.

As his breathing slowed and he regained more sense of what was happening, he realised that Deborah still hadn't finished. Remaining inside her he reached beneath the pile of pillows and took out a pencil slim vibrator then, before Deborah realised what he was doing, he was trailing its silky vibrating head down from her stomach button and through the pubic hairs,

128

to where the inner lips joined and then onto the clitoral area itself, where he let it play all around the yearning flesh as she cried out and trembled above him until he could feel the forceful contractions of her internal walls as she at last climaxed with him inside her.

She opened her eyes and smiled down at him. Pavin smiled back, then switched the vibrator back on and let it play over her still throbbing inner lips again.

'No!' gasped Deborah. 'I've finished, don't!'

'Wait,' he said softly. 'You might get a surprise.'

He was wrong, she thought to herself, there was nothing she wanted more than to rest. But then, within a few seconds, that glorious pleasure-ache was returning and her whole stomach and vulva was tightening as thrills of excitement darted along her nerves and she knew that he was right and that this time her climax was going to be even bigger.

By this time Pavin was no longer inside her, but he slipped a finger into her vagina instead and it closed around him tightly, hungrily as the inner walls began their second series of muscular contractions and as she spasmed at the peak of her pleasure he let the tip of his middle finger just touch her cervix and Deborah screamed at the almost painfully intense feeling that seemed to go right through her body, piercing even the normal waves of climactic pleasure. Now, finally, she slumped down against him, utterly spent.

Chapter Eight

*A*t some time during the night, Deborah heard Pavin's phone go and he muttered a few words before she slid back into sleep. When she woke in the morning she was surprised to find he was already bathed and in the process of getting dressed.

'What's happened to your usual lie-in?' she asked with a smile.

'Brian called during the night. Elizabeth has asked that Richard and I keep her company for the day, so I had to put duty before pleasure!'

Deborah felt a surge of jealousy that she quickly tried to suppress. After all, as Pavin had explained to her on their walk, this was what the holiday was for. She tried to keep her expression neutral.

'What about the rest of us?' she asked.

'You can either watch, Elizabeth never minds an audience, or you can find your own entertainment for the day. At some time you should try a few hours with Martin and Celia. They're very experienced at giving pleasure.'

'I'll see,' said Deborah, privately deciding that she'd

130

watch at least some of Elizabeth's time with Pavin and his personal assistant, Richard.

Her second surprise of the morning came when she and Pavin entered the huge dining room. Beyond the silver-covered breakfast dishes, Elizabeth was standing entirely nude, her back towards the room. When she saw Pavin enter she leant forward from the waist and rested her forehead on her hands which were placed palm down on the top of the sideboard.

Pavin's mouth lifted at one corner in the lopsided smile that Deborah recalled from their first meeting, and before helping himself to any food he walked and ran the palm of his hand the length of her back before slipping it beneath her and up her stomach until he could reach her tiny gold nipple rings. These he tweaked softly and her back arched outwards, then he walked away from her and piled his plate high with food.

Elizabeth stayed bent submissively face downwards, but everyone else in the room ignored her. Deborah, finding that she wasn't in the least hungry, simply took a large cup of coffee and some scrambled eggs back to her place.

Flora was sitting opposite her and she smiled at the newest addition to their holiday group. 'Does the sight of Elizabeth like that disturb you?'

Deborah decided to honest. 'Yes, a little.'

'Because you know she's going to be in Pavin's hands all day? Or because you want to touch her yourself?'

'Just because it's bizarre,' retorted Deborah, refusing to admit to her possessiveness of Pavin.

'Why come here if you don't like the bizarre? You can lead a mundane life back in London, I imagine.'

'I didn't say I didn't like it, simply that it disturbs me.'

Flora nodded, then pushing back her chair walked round behind Deborah on her way to collect more

131

coffee. 'You know why Pavin likes you, don't you?' she said softly in her ear.

Deborah looked up at her. 'For the usual reasons I imagine.'

'It's because you're the image of Angela. That's why we were all so shocked when you arrived; we thought he'd made it up with her. Pavin adored Angela really; and although he divorced her it was because that was what she wanted. He was heartbroken to lose her. They made the perfect couple. If only she'd enjoyed the island as much as he does then they'd still be together.'

Deborah stood up, pushing her half-eaten eggs away from her. 'Well, she didn't, did she? And it isn't surprising if I look a bit like her because men usually have a particular type they find physically attractive. Pavin's already told me he favours leggy blondes,' she added and was pleased to see a flicker of irritation cross the petite brunette's face.

'Where's Richard?' Pavin called down the table. 'Has he eaten?'

'He's setting up his bedroom ready for the three of you,' explained Brian with a glance towards his wife's bare back. 'I think he had quite a lot to do. You know the kind of involved games my wife enjoys playing!'

Pavin seemed to deliberately take as long as possible over his food, and at one point Elizabeth shifted her position slightly. 'Keep still!' he said sharply, and at once she froze.

'Personally I can't think why she enjoys being dominated all the time,' murmured Tansy as she left the table. 'I think I'll go and have a swim once I've digested breakfast. If anyone wants to join me they're welcome.'

'I might,' said Celia and Martin nodded too.

'How about you, honey?' Pavin asked Deborah.

'I'd rather watch Elizabeth,' she said coolly.

Brian laughed. 'That should broaden your horizons,

Debs! I think I'll be there too. I can always explain anything you don't understand.'

Eventually even Pavin decided Elizabeth had waited long enough and he rose from the table, went over to the girl and ran his hands down the outside of her legs so that she quivered beneath his touch.

'Let's go and find Richard, Lizzie. He should be ready for us by now.'

The room that Richard and Flora shared during these holidays was quite small compared to some, but again dominated by a vast canopied bed whose covers and hanging curtains, along with the canopy itself, were all made of the finest Chinese silk, shot through with riotous colours, while on the floor a crimson and yellow carpet covered a square in the middle, around which were polished dark boards.

Chinese silk screens that matched the bed coverings were placed on each side of the bedhead and there were three comfortable armed chairs in which onlookers could sit.

The first thing Deborah saw when she came into the room was a small, relatively modern table just in front of one of the screens and on it was a range of objects; jars, scarves and strips of leather and cord that made her wonder what lay ahead for Brian's wife.

He, Deborah and Flora were the only spectators, everyone else having decided to find their pleasure elsewhere, but when Elizabeth stood at the foot of the bed facing the three watchers she dropped her eyes to the floor and a delicate hint of colour suffused her cheeks.

'Now, now, Elizabeth! This is no time to be shy,' said Pavin with a laugh. 'I thought you enjoyed spectator sports. Right, Richard, how do you want her?'

Richard emerged from behind one of the screens. He was entirely nude apart from a small posing pouch which only emphasised his already burgeoning manhood, and the dark mat of curly hair that ran up from the pouch in a thick line through the middle of his stomach and then covered his slim but well-muscled chest added to his attraction.

Deborah thought that if she wasn't so besotted with Pavin she could very easily fancy Richard, and from the way Flora was staring at him it seemed that she did too.

'First we oil her,' he said to Pavin, and taking a bottle from the table he poured a few drops into Pavin's outstretched hands and some into his own. 'Remember, Elizabeth, you can only have your orgasms when we tell you, but if you have them at any other time the game stops. It that clear?'

Elizabeth nodded.

'Good,' continued Richard. 'Obviously we don't expect you to have one while we're oiling you, but to make quite sure a small one doesn't escape our notice the spectators will keep a close eye on you!'

Elizabeth was pushed towards the onlookers and then the two men started oiling her body, Richard working down her back and over her buttocks while Pavin's large hands spread across the width of her breasts and he tenderly massaged the scented oil into her small firm breasts with their suprisingly long, dark nipples and wide areolae that seemed to cover most of the surface of the breasts.

Deborah, who was watching Pavin more closely than Elizabeth, noticed that despite the tenderness of his touch, every time he glided across the surface of her breasts he would let his little fingers catch in her nipple rings and the resulting tugs would pull the long nipples sharply to the sides, stretching them to the limit before his hand began the return journey and they slowly eased back into position before being extended sharply to the opposite sides.

From the widening of Elizabeth's dark eyes, it was clear that this pain-edged pressure was highly stimulating for her, and when he finally left her breasts alone and moved across her abdomen her breasts were rounded and plump, the internal tissue straining against the enclosing flesh.

He oiled her belly and the sides of her waist as Richard worked down between the cleft of her buttocks, and at one point Richard slipped a well-lubricated finger into Elizabeth's tightly closed second opening. Once again her flesh responded, her nipple rings swung in the air and she had trouble keeping her toes still on the carpet beneath her feet.

'If she's not careful she'll climax now and put an end to her morning's pleasure,' said Flora, her voice excited. 'Pavin's really skilful at playing her body. Last summer he spent hours with her. It drove Angela mad.'

It was driving Deborah mad too, but not with rage. She wanted to feel him oiling her just as he was oiling Elizabeth. She watched from the edge of her seat as his hands moved down to the other woman's lower belly and now his fingers pressed tightly against the flesh.

A fleeting expression of discomfort crossed Elizabeth's features, quickly followed by the blush of arousal this caused her. 'How tight you feel,' murmured Pavin. 'I love it when your body's swollen with desire and need. We must fill it even more.'

Then his oiled fingers glided briefly between her thighs to linger for a few moments around her outer sex lips, pushing them together and downwards, creating pressure on the trapped clitoris and then turning the visible section of her clitoral ring between finger and thumb. Her eyes widened and she tried to withdraw her clitoris a little. Pavin tugged more firmly on the ring and this time she squirmed with discomfort and it was plain from the way her breathing grew more rapid and her head went back that this was highly stimulating for her.

Finally she was totally oiled, her body gleaming like

135

a statue, and Deborah realised that Elizabeth was a beautiful young woman. Her figure was small but perfect and her colouring combined with what seemed like a submissive shyness made her highly desirable. She could quite understand why Brian had married her.

'Well done!' laughed Richard and he came round to study her from the front. 'Now lie on your side in the middle of the bed and pull your knees up to your chin. As Pavin said, we want to fill you until every part of you is tight as a drum.'

Obediently Elizabeth lay down gracefully, and then Richard was reaching for a piece of tubing with a tiny flat sac at the end of it. He covered the sac in oil, rolled it into a tube and very gently eased it into Elizabeth's rectum while Pavin continued to play with her breasts from the other side of the bed, again stretching the nipples out and then releasing them like pieces of elastic.

The young woman's mouth was open with the sensations he was causing and because of this her muscles were relaxed and Richard found it comparatively easy to insert the roll of rubber inside her. Once it was fully in he fitted a rubber bulb attachment to the protruding end and squeezed it with slow steady movements.

'Now the sac inside her will inflate,' explained Brian. 'Eventually it will be touching the walls of her rectum and she'll feel as though it's pushing through her vagina.'

Deborah swallowed hard, and watched Elizabeth start to squirm as the device did as her husband had described and expanded until it was filling her to capacity. At one point her body was shaking with sexual excitement and they thought for a moment she was about to come there and then. Finally, just when Elizabeth felt certain that she could take no more, Richard stopped, and with a deft movement removed the inflating bulb and fitted a seal to prevent any air escaping.

Pavin swiftly pushed Elizabeth onto her stomach and slid a hand beneath her, again pushing and probing downwards across where her abdomen was lying against the bed, and this had the effect of accentuating the pressure within her so that she wriggled and squirmed against his hand, gasping in reaction to what was happening to her. She had never felt so many different sensations of pain and pleasure-tightness, and darts that coursed through her like electric currents as over stimulated nerve endings shouted messages to her brain.

Pavin pressed steadily until she began to moan, and then he pulled her to her feet so that the spectators could see the rubber tube protroding from between her tight buttocks. He patted them lightly and Elizabeth gasped as the swollen sac within her pressed against her rectal walls and almost precipitated an orgasm.

Richard laughed. 'Not yet, Lizzie. Now, turn and face everyone.'

Slowly she turned again, and it was clear from her distended stomach, swollen upthrusting breasts and trembling thighs that she was aroused almost to the point of no return.

Pavin slipped a leather collar over her head and then fastened two leather straps that dangled from it round her swollen breasts, the better to accentuate her large protruding nipples and trembling tender tissue.

This done he bent and put his tongue inside one of her nipple rings, then licked around the areole before taking the ring between his teeth and moving his head back with a swift tug. He repeated the action twice on each of the breasts and the leather straps fitted more snugly on Elizabeth as her breasts expanded yet further.

For Elizabeth it was bliss and torment at the same time. She loved the way Pavin played on her weaknesses, using her need for domination to take her to the edge of pain and yet keeping the pleasure at a high level too. She adored the way he could make her entire body come alive, until it felt as though there wasn't a part of her that wasn't sexual, but at the same time she feared him because within him there was no love for her. With Brian there was love, and that meant that the danger was never total, with Pavin it was absent. This was why she needed the holiday, and yet now, at this moment when she was at Pavin's mercy, she wondered fearfully what he might do to her without the constraints that love provided.

She soon found out. As her body continued to swell beneath the men's manipulations, the confining straps and the wickedly air-filled sac within her rectum, Pavin suddenly produced a string of very large, transparent marbles. 'These are to fill your other opening,' he said with a thin smile. 'I want you more swollen that you've ever been before. Lie back on the end of the bed, I'll insert them.'

Elizabeth started to obey, and immediately the pressure on the highly sensitive walls of her rectum increased. She started to sit up again, but Richard caught hold of her nipple rings and pressed down on them. 'You heard what Pavin said, Lizzie. Lie back.'

Elizabeth had no choice but to obey and felt her stomach thrusting upwards with the pressure beneath her. Then Pavin was parting her oiled legs and Richard took hold of one while Pavin thrust a firm thigh in front of the other. He then carefully opened her outer sex lips with one hand while with the other he inserted the first of the cool, smooth glass marbles into her vagina.

She was very aroused and her own secretions made it slip easily inside. 'Now contract your vagina,' Pavin instructed her. 'Pull it deep inside you, and the others will follow.'

She knew that she had to obey him, despite the fact

that the marbles only served to expand her vaginal walls so that both her passages were full and her body felt as though it couldn't bear any more stimulation.

Deborah and Flora watched with increasing excitement as the marbles disappeared inside Elizabeth's frantically contracting vagina. All the time Richard was urging the young woman on while Pavin let his hands caress her stomach, knowing that this meant she had pressure from above and below her vagina and that the whole feeling of fullness would extend to her bladder so that every possible nerve ending would be alive with bitter-sweet pleasure.

Once the last marble was inside her, Pavin bent over Elizabeth. He tightened the leather straps beneath her breasts, flicked his fingers across the tender flesh under her arms and then pulled her to her feet and paraded her in front of the silent watchers.

'See the way she's rounded and swollen with need,' he said softly. 'Touch her, Flora. You know how much Elizabeth likes to be touched.'

Elizabeth turned to the American. 'If they touch me, can I come?' she begged him.

Deborah looked at Pavin and saw that his eyes were totally without feeling. 'No,' he said shortly. 'Not yet.'

Flora smiled, and as Elizabeth came towards her she stood up, then bent her head and drew her tongue across the other woman's rib cage. She used it to make tiny circles across the bird-like bones, then moved higher and tickled within the cleft of the armpit and all the time Elizabeth's rounded, painfully constrained body struggled to keep the marbles inside her, ignoring the mounting pressure between her buttocks and forcing back the spasms of pleasure that were coming closer and closer.

Then Elizabeth moved on to Deborah, who didn't quite know what to do. But then suddenly as she looked at the flesh over Elizabeth's straining stomach she had

139

an overwhelming desire to strain it still further. She let the fingers of her right hand reach into the dark curly pubic hair and then rubbed up and down in a firm motion that made the marbles move, the ring on the end of the engorged clitoris tremble, and caused Elizabeth to stare at her in terror. 'Please, don't!' she whispered.

'Why not?' Deborah whispered back, stroking the bronzed flesh tenderly for a moment.

'Because I can't hold back much longer and I don't want the day to end so soon.'

Deborah was shocked to find that she wanted to go on touching her. That she had a sudden urge to be the one to force the climax from her and end her pleasure for the whole day, but Pavin stopped her.

'Come back here, Elizabeth. You've done very well,' he said, and this time there was a note of amusement in his voice.

Now Richard crouched on the carpet on all fours, then Elizabeth was lowered across his back, face upwards, so that she was staring at the ceiling with her back across his and her feet on the ground. Then Pavin picked up a small whip with three strands of rope coming from an ivory handle. For a few seconds he trailed the handle around her trapped breasts, letting it slip through her nipple rings and tug at them, then moving it down her desperately thrusting pulsating belly.

Finally, he lifted the whip a few inches above her and whispered, 'Now you may come, Lizzie,' before bringing the stinging cords down across the despairing tautness of her body.

For Elizabeth it was a moment of almost indescribable pleasure. All the hideous tension, the softly innate cruelty of what they'd done to her earlier, the long-withheld relief of her mounting sexual excitement came together in an explosion that made her shriek and

Deborah felt her own internal muscles contract in a sudden, startling orgasm at the sight of Elizabeth's pleasure. She shuddered in her seat, and felt Brian's hand caress her knee as though he knew only too well what was happening to her.

Elizabeth's climax seemed to go on and on, and when Deborah looked more closely she saw that Pavin was now continually stimulating her clitoris by sliding its gold ring around, manipulating the moist, throbbing flesh so that it was impossible to tell where one climax ended and another began until eventually Elizabeth's cries turned to cries for respite and finally his hand was still.

'That was good,' said Brian, getting to his feet.

Deborah stared across the room to where Pavin and Richard were carefully helping Elizabeth onto the bed, then they lay one on each side of her and held her in a tender embrace.

'What happens now?' she asked.

'Who knows? I'm sure they've got something planned, but we're not invited to stay for the rest. Why don't we go and join the others in the pool? I think you need a cool swim!'

'Did you come?' asked Flora. 'I wouldn't have thought that was your scene, especially since Pavin so clearly enjoys Elizabeth's body.'

'I thought it was incredibly erotic,' confessed Deborah. 'I suppose I shouldn't but. . .'

'Why on earth not?' asked Brian, leading her down the winding stairwell and across the courtyard to the pool. 'You're perfectly entitled to enjoy anything you like while you're staying here. Don't take any notice of Flora. She just hoped you wouldn't like it because she's jealous of you. Isn't that right, Flora?'

'Why should I be jealous of her?' asked Flora. 'She's only a guest. The rest of us see Pavin all through the year. If she enjoys her two weeks on the island, fine.'

Brian watched her stalk away in the opposite direction. 'That's one less for the pool. Come on, let's see what the others are up to.'

Tansy, Martin and Celia had been swimming seriously for most of the time that Brian and Deborah had been watching Elizabeth receive her pleasure. For Tansy it was vital that she didn't let all her fitness training achieved while in America go to waste during the fortnight's holiday, mainly because she didn't want Paul to stop finding her attractive. Although not outstandingly handsome, his boyish type of looks drew many women, and she was horribly aware that he was two years younger than her; a fact he never considered.

'Hi!' Tansy called as the new couple entered the swimming area. 'Fun over?'

'The participation part is!' laughed Brian. 'Debbie and I thought we'd join you here.'

Martin and Celia could tell from Deborah's overbright gaze and still flushed cheeks that the scene she'd just witnessed had aroused her. They glanced at each other and nodded, then Martin called out to Brian. 'We've done our required number of laps. Has Deborah seen the water bed yet?'

Brian glanced enquiringly at Deborah who shook her head. Soon the other three were climbing out of the pool and wrapping towels around themselves before padding through a shallow footbath and into a room beyond.

'This is all totally modern,' explained Tansy. 'Pavin might like tradition, but he likes comfort as well. Whenever he swims he plays the sound of dolphins, whales and seagulls through the music system he's had installed, so that he's got the best of both worlds. The genuine feel of nature in the warmth of his own tropical pool!'

Celia opened a white wooden door and showed

Deborah the large box-shaped wooden surround that was filled by a strange, slightly lumpy looking blue mattress. 'That's the water bed. You can make it move by pushing the button at the side there, that way you get waves without moving, or you can move around a lot yourself and make your own waves! Poor Angela used to get seasick on it, so if you're bad on boats better give it a miss.'

'I'm fine. Celia, what was Angela like?' asked Deborah curiously.

Celia frowned. 'Hard to say really. She was typically American, all blonde hair, teeth and tits, like Tansy only younger and slimmer but she was rather hard. I mean, Pavin's a hard-headed businessman, but when he likes people he likes them and he's a good husband and lover. He gave her a lot, but she didn't give much back in return.'

'Did he love her?'

Celia smiled a catlike smile. 'You'd have to ask him that. Has Flora been telling you they were the perfect couple? If so that's rubbish. They rowed about everything from sex to money but I suppose he loved her. He must have done to have married her. You aren't falling in love with him I hope?'

'Why? Isn't that allowed here either? I thought it was how Tansy and Paul met up.'

'It's allowed, but with Pavin I don't think it's advisable. He just adores women, and I think two failed marriages are enough for him. In America divorce is an expensive business, especially when you're as rich as he is.'

'Stop nattering you two,' said Brian. 'Who's going to try this out first? Or are we all going to have some fun?'

Martin, being British himself, understood Deborah's reserve better than Brian. 'I think you and Celia should have first go, Brian. Tansy's already had her fun in the water.'

'That was nothing!' complained Tansy, but Brian was already stripping off his clothes and Celia dropped her towel and joined him on the bed. As they moved closer to each other the bed began to heave beneath them and Celia squealed with pleasure as she lay face down and let her breasts squash against the rolling undulations of the ribbed mattress.

Brian lay along her spine, his arms spread out on either side of her, and as Celia lifted her hips he slid three fingers beneath her and inside her vagina, palm uppermost, while at the same time bucking so that she was moving around against the pressure within.

Deborah watched them as they rolled and embraced on the water-bed and her own excitement began to rise again. She wanted to have a man make love to her, but suddenly she thought that one man wouldn't be enough, she'd like to have two as Elizabeth had done.

Martin, standing behind her, slipped his hands around her waist and started to caress her breasts while at the same time pressing forwards with his hips so that she couldn't fail to feel his erection beneath the towel.

Celia, who despite enjoying herself was watching Deborah closely, suddenly scrambled off the bed, leaving Brian looking somewhat surprised.

'I'm tired,' she said with a laugh. 'Deborah, why don't you and Martin join Brian? He still seems to have plenty of energy.'

Deborah hastily pulled off her blouse and skirt and then Martin was lifting her onto the bed and for the first time she felt it moving beneath her as she rolled onto the surface.

The men knew that she would be easy to bring to a climax and they both went to work quickly and efficiently. Martin stroked her upper arms, shoulders, neck and breasts while Brian concentrated on her feet, legs and the warm moistness between her thighs.

When he spread her legs and inserted some marbles,

144

similar to those used on Elizabeth, inside her she gasped a mild protest, but then as the bed moved beneath her and the marbles slid around, making her clench her pelvic muscles instinctively, she felt the first tingles of a climax shoot through her and her protests stopped.

Martin enjoyed playing with her breasts. They were so responsive, especially when he flicked at the tips of her nipples with his middle finger and then once they were hard he bent down and nipped them sharply between his teeth, making her throw back her head and setting the water bed moving even more strongly.

For Deborah it was a fantastic experience. She loved the gentle pulsations of the liquid below her, the attentions of Martin's lips and fingers on her breasts and the way Brian was playing with her clitoris and manipulating the marbles within her. When he started to slowly draw them out she wanted to protest, but then she realised that he was going to replace them with his tongue and he lapped at her in time to the lap of water below the surface of the bed so that she shuddered time and again as they brought her to several small but intense climaxes.

Finally they decided that it was time for the big one. Now the two women joined them on the bed, clinging to any part of Deborah that they could reach and she realised that hands and mouths were all over her, sucking and nipping at her most delicate places. Then, laughingly, they spreadeagled her and held on to her wrists and ankles while Brian carefully eased his way into her now empty vagina. Then he began to move in a forceful rhythm that made the bed surge around more violently than before. Every thrust that he made seemed magnified ten times to Deborah, because the movement of the bed meant that he touched parts of her that were never normally stimulated, and soon she was gasping and panting as she felt the warm liquid heat spreading throughout her body.

Martin kept her hands above her head while Tansy played with her breasts, first licking the nipples and areolae and the blowing on them so that they went from hot to cold and the breasts engorged with the thrill.

As Brian thrust, Celia gently caressed his tight testicles from behind and this was too much for him. With a loud shout he drove into Deborah as hard as he could and this combined with the undulations of the bed tipped her over the edge into a blissful climax at almost the same time as he finally achieved release.

When he withdrew and rolled off the bed, Martin took his place, only he decided to use his tongue on Deborah, determined to see her thrash around on the water bed, totally losing control. She felt him start to touch her with his delicate pointed tongue and reached down to stop him, but Tansy and Celia gripped her hands and Brian stood on the floor gripping her ankles so that she was helpless as Martin re-stimulated her hot, damp flesh and watched her clitoris retreat beneath this renewed assault.

Hastily he lifted a hand and pushed the skin at the top of her pubic mound upwards so that the hood retracted and now he could swirl his tongue around the bud itself, then down across the surrounding tissue and finally up to the entrance to her urethra.

Just as he got there the bed moved violently and the tip of his tongue skimmed the opening. Deborah, already startled by the speed with which her flesh was responding for a second time to the attention it was receiving, felt the muscles at the base of her pelvis contract into a giant wave that rolled up her until it engulfed her entire body in a blinding white flash of tearing satisfaction. The other four released her as she twisted away from them, her body gripped by muscular spasms that made her lose all control as she rolled around the water bed crying with ecstasy while her body continued to be rocked by the now decreasing movements of the water-filled mattress.

'Not bad, is it?' drawled Tansy when Deborah was at last motionless, her hair sticking to her head with perspiration. 'I'm trying to persuade Paul to have one put in our spare room at home!'

Suddenly, now that it was over, Deborah felt shy and she climbed from the bed only to find that her legs wouldn't support her. Brian grabbed her by the arm and led her to a stool where he helped her dress again.

'Remember to allow recovery time when you next use the bed! Just what you needed after watching Lizzie, wasn't it?'

'It was amazing,' admitted Deborah. 'I had no idea how much it would increase all the sensations.'

'Guess you're pretty senstive; it doesn't work that well for everyone.'

Deborah wondered what it would be like to have Pavin on the bed with her; just the two of them alone together, free to enjoy their lovemaking with all the sensations heightened by the swell of the water. She shivered at the prospect.

Celia and Martin were still on the bed, now joined together while Tansy crouched over Celia's head and let the other woman make love to her with her lips and tongue.

'They'll be a while,' said Brian. 'Why don't you and I have some lunch and then we can find something else to amuse us.'

Deborah hesitated. She found Brian attractive, but sensed that he was dangerous. At times she had seen him watching her with an almost predatory look, as though he wanted to hunt her down, but then she reminded herself that he wouldn't dare hurt her. He was as much Pavin's guest as she was, and whenever she wanted to call a halt to anything she could. Since

147

Pavin was going to be busy with Brian's wife all day it seemed only fair if she spent the time with him, and there was no doubt that he would be able to offer her increasingly hungry flesh new stimulation.

'Well?' He was watching her closely and his dark eyes had a strange light in them.

'That sounds like a very good idea,' she said with a smile.

'I hope you still think that by the end of the afternoon,' he responded, but his tone was light, his lips were curved upwards in a smile and she decided he was only anxious to assure her he'd try to satisfy her.

'It there anywhere special you'd like us to go?' he asked when they were eating.

'It's beautifully sunny,' she replied, glancing out of the nearest window. 'Is there anywhere secluded where we could enjoy ourselves out of doors?'

'Right away from prying eyes you mean?'

'Well, yes, and out of the wind!'

'I know just the place; we'll go to Puffin's Cove. Don't mention it to anyone though or they'll all come along. It's such a gorgeous spot but I think it's time we enjoyed ourselves without spectators, don't you?'

Deborah smiled at him. 'Sounds great!'

'Eat up then and we'll set off. It takes about twenty minutes on foot. If I wear you out, I'll carry you home.'

'You're on!' agreed Deborah. Neither of them realised that Sara, who was clearing away the plates from the sideboard behind them, had heard every word.

Chapter Nine

*I*t was mid-afternoon before Pavin, Richard and Elizabeth finally finished their day's activities and went into the small dining room for afternoon tea. Elizabeth, now wearing comfortable stretch pants and a sleeveless polo neck cotton top, looked calm and relaxed. Her beautiful dark eyes were sleepy and sighing with pleasure she took a bone china cup filled with Earl Grey tea from Pavin's outstretched hand.

He smiled at her with genuine affection. 'Happy now?'

'Blissfully! I hope Brian didn't mind having to leave, but it's much easier to get caught up in the more extreme things when he isn't around. If he's there I can't get totally carried away.'

'He knows that,' said Richard, helping himself to buttered scones and adding a liberal helping of home-made strawberry jam. 'After all, he was a founder member of these pleasure breaks.'

'I know. He looks forward to them as much as I do,' agreed Elizabeth. 'It's only that before we came he suggested that whilst we could both still go with anyone we wanted, the other one should always be there.

149

When I didn't agree he dropped it, but I had the feeling he wasn't happy.'

Pavin frowned. 'The whole point of this island holiday is that we do as we wish. Why should Brian try to change things?'

Elizabeth stretched sensuously, revealing tiny love-bites beneath her chin. 'Don't ask me. Perhaps watching is becoming his major turn-on.'

'In that case he can choose to watch for his own pleasure, not try to dictate yours,' said Pavin. 'I guess it's another symptom of this need to control that he has. If he's not around then he can't even pretend he's controlling you.'

'Perhaps he's possessive of you, Lizzie!' laughed Richard.

A shadow crossed the young woman's face. 'I hope not. That would really spoil things.'

Pavin shook his head. 'Brian isn't possessive, he simply can't bear not to be involved. Which reminds me, where is he now? Sara, do you know where Brian is?'

Sara, her eyes downcast, shook her head. 'No, sir.'

'How about the Woolcotts? Or Celia, Martin and Flora? Have you seen them?'

The maid hesitated. 'I served tea to Mr and Mrs Woolcott and Mr and Mrs Craig half an hour ago. I haven't seen Miss Stewart since breakfast.'

'What about my husband?' asked Elizabeth softly. 'You must have seen him at some time. He'd never miss his lunch!'

'He took lunch with Miss Woods,' admitted Sara, hastily collecting up the remaining scones and piling plates onto the silver tray.

Pavin blocked her way. 'Sara, did Brian mention where he was going to spend his afternoon?'

'I couldn't help overhearing,' the maid said hastily. 'I wasn't trying to eavesdrop, but I was right behind him.'

150

Pavin gave her one of his most reassuring smiles, although deep inside him he was beginning to feel the first premonition of something not being right. 'No one expects you to be deaf, Sara, merely to pretend to be deaf when it suits us! So, where was he planning to go?'

She looked apprehensively at him. 'He told Miss Woods he'd take her to Puffin's Cove, but that she wasn't to mention it to anyone else.'

'Why on earth not?' demanded Pavin.

'He said he didn't think they wanted spectators,' explained Sara quietly.

Pavin moved to one side and the maid quickly left the room. Richard glanced at his employer. 'Puffin's Cove's on the furthest side of the island. They're bound to be gone some time.'

'He didn't mention taking Deborah out for a private twosome. It is considered polite to mention it, as you well know.'

Elizabeth's eyes were troubled now. 'Perhaps it isn't a twosome,' she put in softly. 'Isn't it possible Flora's there as well? No one's seen her since she left us. Perhaps she and Brian set up a threesome but without mentioning it to Deborah.'

Richard sat back in his chair. 'That's all right then! I think I'll go and have a nap before dinner.'

Pavin picked up his jacket from the back of a chair. 'I think I'll take a walk to Puffin's Cove. After all, it is my island, and you're all my guests. Not even Brian is likely to have the nerve to tell me to go away because he doesn't want a spectator.'

'You sent him away,' Richard pointed out.

Pavin shook his head. 'Elizabeth sent him away, because that was part of how she wanted her day to be.'

'Suppose this is how Brian wants his afternoon to be?' suggested Richard.

'As long as Deborah and anyone else involved goes along with him, I'll leave. I just think I'd better check. Besides, it's a long time since I visited that side of the island. I'll take my binoculars and see what I can spot!'

Although he laughed, both Richard and Elizabeth could tell that he was concerned. After he'd gone Elizabeth turned to the American's PA. 'It looks as though he cares quite a lot for Deborah.'

Richard nodded. 'That was plain to most of us from the start, including Flora I'm afraid. She sees our fair-haired English rose as an obstacle to her chances of becoming the next Mrs John Pavin III.'

'She ought to become the first Mrs Richard Ford,' said Elizabeth lightly.

Richard pulled a face. 'I don't think there's much chance of that, unfortunately.'

As Pavin left the castle, Deborah was wishing fervently that she'd told someone where she and Brian were going that afternoon because right at that moment the fun was beginning to go out of things.

It had all started well enough. They'd chatted amiably as they'd crossed the island, Brian talking about his wife and the way her sexual needs complemented his desire to dominate, while Deborah told him about her first meeting with Pavin.

'How come he was so attractive to you?' Brian asked. 'Did the money add to his ample manly charms?'

'I didn't know he was rich! I suppose he was the complete opposite of Mick, who's slim, sensitive and rather moody. Pavin was so incredibly masculine and yet I had the feeling that he really liked and understood women. There was just something about him, a sort of involuntary chemical attraction, that made me feel we'd be good together. And I was right.'

'Yeah, but he's right with most women!'

Deborah shrugged. 'Of course he is. I don't expect him to have lived like a monk for forty-two years.'

'He'll never live like a monk.'

'Elizabeth will never live like a nun, but you still love her,' retorted Deborah. Brian fell silent.

When they reached Puffin's Cove, Deborah was glad they'd taken the trouble to walk the distance. On this side of the island the rock face was steeper, and in the many nooks and crannies formed by the various crumbling layers there were masses of seabirds. Down in the cove the white-crested waves broke on the outlying slate-grey rocks giving the island a far more raw beauty than that afforded by the sheltered cove where she and Celia had met up with Tansy.

'It's breathtaking!' she enthused, when they'd finally scrambled down to the bottom.

Brian watched her face as she stared out to sea. She had a tranquil beauty that was similar to his wife's but their colouring was totally different. Normally he wasn't drawn to blondes, but he definitely fancied Deborah. He also fancied getting his own back on Pavin for sending him away while he and Richard enjoyed themselves with Elizabeth.

Linking his arm through Deborah's he drew her back into the more sheltered part of the cove, then opened the beach bag he'd brought with him and spread a thick towel over one of the large, flat-topped pieces of grey rock.

'Strip off and lie on that. The sun's warm and we're out of the wind here.'

Deborah glanced at him. He looked relaxed, cheerful, and undeniably sexy in his tight jeans and white T-shirt. His slender but wiry arms were covered with fine dark hairs and there was an air of great energy about him which, combined with the hint of danger in his occasionally brooding brown eyes, excited her.

As she did as he suggested, Brian too stripped off and then when Deborah was naked he drew a dark red silk garment out of the beach bag. 'Here, slip this on. It will add to the excitement of the afternoon. Lizzie loves wearing silk next to her skin.'

'So do I,' confessed Deborah. 'Pavin bought me a fantastic silk dress. The one I wore to dinner that first night.'

'I remember it. Here, let me help you.' Brian drew the silk teddy up Deborah's long legs, sliding his smooth hands caressingly along them as he did so. Then he eased it up across her abdomen and to her surprise carefully drew her breasts through the gaps left in the top for that very purpose. He then slipped the straps over her shoulders and as she stood up to adjust it she realised that it was also crotchless and had a thong back that slid between the cheeks of her bottom. She felt more naked than when she'd been without clothes.

Brian stared at her approvingly. 'Great! Lie back on the towel then. I'm sure those inviting boobs would like some sun and attention!'

She lowered herself onto the covered rock and felt his mouth sucking gently on the outer sides of each of the breasts in turn, then he ran his tongue round the rim of them, making the edge of the silk openings damp. Deborah felt her breasts growing and her nipples hardening.

'You're beautifully responsive,' he murmured, and she wriggled with the pleasure of the warm sun and his mouth. She was grateful when he finally moved to her nipples and felt them spring to life when he took each in turn between his teeth, tugging softly and nibbling on the areolae.

Brian could feel her whole body beginning to tremble with arousal and when he slid a hand between her parted thighs he could feel through the opening at the crotch that she was already damp. As his hand carefully massaged her outer sex lips she pressed down against him, a small smile on her lips.

Brian waited until she was completely relaxed and then bit sharply on her left nipple. Deborah's eyes flew open. 'That hurt!'

'Lizzie loves it when I do that.'

'I'm not Lizzie.'

'You are for the next couple of hours,' he whispered. 'I'm going to pretend you're my wife and give you the time of your life.'

Deborah started to sit up. 'I didn't come here as a substitute for Elizabeth. I came here as me. If that isn't what you want then we'd better go back.'

Brian's eyes gleamed with excitement and he pushed her flat on the rock again. 'Don't be silly. It's only a fantasy. See, you did like it,' he added and he now softly licked the previously abused nipple and it stood out harder than ever before.

Deborah was shocked at her body's treacherous reaction, just as she was shocked by the growing dampness between her thighs and the strange, erotic feelings that were coming from the tightness of the thong between her buttocks.

'Lie on your stomach,' said Brian.

Deborah hesitated. 'I prefer it this way.'

'Too bad. Flora, help me turn Deborah onto her stomach,' he called. To Deborah's amazement, Flora emerged from a concealed opening to a small cave away to Brian's left. She was carrying a long strip of seaweed in her hand. Walking over to where Deborah was prone on the rock she drew it across her exposed breasts. Deborah's breath caught in her throat at the feel of the cool, damp strip covering her burning nipples and swollen breasts.

'She says she wants to go, but her body says otherwise,' laughed Brian, watching the flush of arousal spread up Deborah's neck as the seaweed continued to snake backwards and forwards over her exposed flesh.

'I've been waiting ages for you,' complained Flora.

155

'Sorry, but it took a while to persuade Debbie here to come with me. Now, help me turn her over.'

Although Deborah struggled, the two of them found it easy to overpower her and within seconds she was lying face downwards, her arms stretched above her head and the wrists held together by Flora.

When Brian's hand reached between her buttocks and slipped the thong of the caressing teddy to one side, Deborah kicked out with her legs but he easily caught hold of her ankle, slapping her lightly on the back of her thigh. 'Don't be naughty, Debbie, or I'll have to get rough. Just enjoy yourself. Flora and I have had a lot of fun over the years in Puffin's Cove. You're in good hands.'

Once the thong had been pushed aside Brian drew a jelly-like double headed vibrator out of the bag, lubricated it with some gel and then carefully slid the smallest head in between Deborah's tightly clenched buttocks. He had to hold them apart with one hand while inserting the vibrator into her puckered opening with the other and her initial resistance made it difficult for him. He ran his tongue along the top of her spine, swirling it on each of the sensitive upper vertebrae in turn until she automatically started to relax. Then, with one swift movement, the soft jelly-like thing was inside her.

Deobrah lifted her head and her mouth opened in a strangled gasp as she felt the strange, almost liquid coldness invading her rectum. Then Brian turned the vibrator on and it began to squirm within her, its cool pulsating sides brushing against the paper-thin walls of her back passage and arousing every vulnerable nerve ending while at the same time she felt her stomach swelling and tightening as her body recognised this as a prelude to a climax and began to prepare itself.

'You see, you like it!' Brian laughed, but there was no humour in the laugh, rather a note of triumph and

Deborah wished that her flesh hadn't responded so rapidly.

'Clench your buttocks and keep it there,' he continued. 'Now, turn onto your back and we'll make you into a very sexy mermaid.'

Flora laughed and then Deborah was turning onto her back again while the softly insinuating pressure of the incredibly flexible vibrator continued its stimulation between her firmly clenched buttocks.

When Flora released her hands, Deborah decided to keep still. There was no point in trying to get away from these two, and in any case her body was now starting to take over from her mind and her flesh, already more responsive than ever before because of all she'd done since coming to Pavinsay, was craving satisfaction.

Flora walked down to the edge of the sea and filled a large shell with salt water, then walked back to where Deborah lay outspread like some pagan sacrifice. She smiled to herself as she saw Brian cover the young woman's eyes with two dark pads. This meant that Deborah was quite unprepared when Flora held the shell aloft and then tipped it gently so that the salt water fell in a slow trickle over the outthrust bare breasts.

Deborah, her body warm from the sun, shouted in shock as the ice-cold water hit her and then, as it continued to dribble down in a relentless trickle, her nipples rose, the flesh burgeoning after its initial shrinking and Brian spread her thighs wider. Carefully he ran his fingers along her moist inner channels, sliding them up and down, always to the very base of the stem of the clitoris but never further.

Deborah thought she'd go mad with the conflicting sensations. Her breasts had gone from hot to cold, in her tender back passage the jelly continued to move and touch her inner heat with its alien coldness and between her thighs her body screamed for those clever fingers to rise higher and touch her on the one spot that would bring the various sensations together into a climax.

When the shell was finally empty, Flora dried off the other woman's breasts and then massaged in some of the heat lotion so that now the tissue was warm and Deborah groaned, pressing down in an attempt to let her clitoris make contact with Brian's torturing fingers.

'Not yet, Debs,' he said firmly. 'You aren't quite at one with nature. We want to make a proper mermaid out of you, don't we Flora?'

Flora laughed in agreement. Now the dark pads were removed from Deborah's eyes and she watched as Flora pressed two small shells carefully over the blonde's aroused nipples. The heat lotion worked as a glue for them and they stayed in place, their slightly rough insides tickling against the suffused flesh they were covering.

Next Brian pushed a rolled-up towel beneath her hips to raise her pubic area more and then spread her legs wide. 'I think Flora has something for you. Isn't that right, Flora?'

Flora smiled, and picked up a different piece of seaweed; it was long and thin with tiny rounded bubbles on the surface and she drew this down Deborah's body until it came to rest between her outspread thighs.

Flora laughed at the half-despairing, half-yearning look on Deborah's face, then seated herself on the rock by their captive's feet and stared at the upraised, unprotected sex mound. 'You look very moist,' she said gently, and the seaweed trailed across the outer lips.

It was exquisite and Deborah couldn't help her groan of delight. Her outer lips parted of their own accord and the inner lips swelled so that Flora could draw the long strand of seaweed back down across them and watch for herself as Deborah's clitoris swelled and stood

158

up proudly erect, pulsating with need. For one brief instant she let the seaweed touch it, but although it triggered sparks of bliss it didn't precipitate a climax, it merely left Deborah straining all the more and as her muscles tightened the cool jelly vibe in her back passage stimulated her even more.

'You'd like to be filled, wouldn't you?' asked Flora. 'I know what it's like to ache deep inside. Well, don't worry, I'm going to ease that ache for you.'

Deborah stared down at the other woman, and then Brian's clever fingers were opening her inner lips wide, and she felt the cool breeze off the sea touch her most sensitive opening. Suddenly she cried out in disbelief as Flora, with a skill born of practice, teased Deborah's vaginal opening with the end of the seaweed before, with diabolical slowness, gradually letting it feed into the writhing young woman's vagina so that the raised bubbles on the moist walls of the seaweed touched her vaginal walls. As more of the seaweed was fed into Deborah it felt as though there was something alive inside her and when she had taken as much as she could, Flora stood up and twirled the seaweed ribbon in slow circles so that Deborah felt she would go out of her mind, so full and aroused was she in both passages, while her nipples remained tightly imprisoned in the shells.

Deborah squirmed, writhed, tried to thrust her pelvis upwards, cried out for release, for cessation from the stimulation and the bliss of a climax but no one listened and all she could hear was the sound of the waves and the birds calling to each other while Brian and Flora continued to torment her body.

She closed her eyes, the blood pounded in her ears and she felt as if she would pass out from their stimulation, but she knew that they weren't going to let her come. They were going to make her wait and wait, arousing her to such heights that she knew she'd end up begging for them to help her and that this was why

159

they'd brought her here. To reduce her to nothing more than a mass of screaming desire, and although she hated the thought of it she was aware that very soon she'd start to beg.

Brian knew it too. He let his fingers massage the heat cream into her swollen breasts, then drew the same fingers along the insides of her outer sex lips so that they too were consumed by heat, and all the time the seaweed continued to play inside her vagina, touching spots she hadn't even known were sensitive before.

'Finish me!' she screamed at last. 'Brian, Flora, do something! Help me, please. I need . . .'

Brian never even heard Pavin approaching him from behind. The first he knew of his arrival was when he was pushed to one side and then Pavin's hand was between Deborah's thighs and he eased a finger up her throbbing, damp inner channels until he found the stem of her clitoris. Then he carefully let his finger slide up and down the side in two quick movements that immediately had the desired effect and Deborah's voice screamed louder than the gulls as her body was at last allowed to spasm in release.

When the final shattering paroxysms of her climax had died away, Deborah became aware of the cool vibrator still pulsating between her buttocks. 'Please, take the vibrator out,' she begged, her eyes closed against the glare of the sun.

'What vibrator, sweetheart?' asked a familiar voice, and Deborah sat upright in amazement. 'Pavin!'

He smiled at her. 'Having a good time?'

A momentary shadow touched her face and he took note of it without her even realising what she'd revealed. 'In a way,' she murmured.

'Sure sounded like it!'

This time she did smile. 'I know I was noisy, but it was partly relief. I thought they were going to keep me waiting forever.'

160

'They probably were. Luckily I came along and ended the game.'

'You were the one who touched me just now?'

Pavin nodded. 'Where's this vibrator then?' Deborah turned over and he removed Brian's jelly-vibe, then removed the shells that were covering her rosy pink nipples and lovingly drew the silk teddy from her soft, pliant, post-climactic body.

'Where are the other two?' Deborah asked as Pavin handed her back her clothes.

'Gone back to the castle. Did the game get out of hand?' he added casually.

'It just wasn't what I expected. I came here with Brian, thinking it was going to be the two of us, although he knew Flora was here. She stayed hidden until we were well under way.'

'But you weren't hurt? Nothing happened that you didn't want to happen?'

'No, I wasn't hurt.'

Pavin nodded thoughtfully. 'Sometimes it's possible for people to get carried away. We always take precautions where possible. Going in for threesomes more than pairs; ensuring that someone always knows where you're going and with whom; but if you want to live like this you can't take away every element of risk.'

Deborah stood up and slipped her hand into his. 'If you did, wouldn't that be defeating the object of the holiday?'

He laughed. 'I guess it would! So, what did this teach you?'

'That I'm becoming more and more insatiable as the days go by! You know, Pavin, Mick wouldn't know me now. When I was lying there earlier, listening to the waves on the rocks and hearing the blood pounding in my ears, I suddenly remembered the way I used to be and it was as though that person no longer existed.'

'Tonight, I want to watch all you women together,'

said Pavin, his voice husky. 'After dinner I want you to give us men a floor show and when it's over I'll carry you off to our room and we can do anything you like. How does that sound?'

Deborah thought of Celia's brooding sensuality, of Tansy's overt sexuality and Elizabeth's contrasting subdued but highly individual taste in eroticism. She also thought of Flora, and what it would be like to have the opportunity to keep her waiting as she'd been kept waiting in the cove. 'I think that sounds a wonderful idea!' she enthused.

Pavin threw the few remaining things in the beach bag and then they set off back to the castle. 'I never did see a puffin!' complained Deborah.

'You will before the holiday's over. We must have a barbecue on the beach soon, while the nights are still long. They're always great fun. Dress is optional, in both senses of the word!'

'Pavin, did you love Angela?' asked Deborah abruptly.

His stride never faltered. 'Did you love Mick?'

She nodded. 'Of course I did, in the beginning.'

'Same here. I don't marry people I'm not in love with. Sex is great with lots of women, and you don't have to love them all as long as there's a mutual attraction, but love is a definite prerequisite for marriage.'

'Then you must have been very hurt when she wanted a divorce.'

This time he stopped in his tracks. 'Who told you Angie wanted a divorce? I had the devil's own job getting rid of her. It cost me plenty too.'

'Yet you brought her here for a holiday only a year ago. How could it have gone wrong so quickly?'

Pavin took hold of Deborah by the shoulders. 'Look, sweetheart, this is not my favourite subject. Let's just say that Angela used to like her extra-marital thrills to come from illicit affairs rather than a group holiday like this, where everyone knows what's going on. There was no fun in it for her if I knew what she was doing. Her pleasure came from making a fool out of me, or trying to.'

'So it wasn't that she was jealous of sharing you?'

'She wanted me to get rid of Brian, because she claimed he didn't play the kind of games she wanted. Maybe he didn't, but the truth is I didn't like the kind of games she played back in Texas when I was busy working, so I got rid of her instead! Okay?'

'I'm sorry,' Deborah apologised. 'It's only that someone said I looked like her and . . .'

'You're both blonde, and that's as far as the resemblance goes. She was one hard-boiled lady, Debs, and she never had your style. Now, can we drop the subject. This holiday is meant to be light-hearted you know.'

'Sure,' agreed Deborah quickly. Inside, she was delighted with what she'd learnt. Pavin hadn't adored Angela, it had never been a perfect marriage and she was beginning to think that he cared for her just as she cared for him.

She was definitely sure of one thing now. By the end of the holiday she'd know whether they had any kind of future together at all, or if when the helicopter took her away from Pavinsay it would be taking her away from the owner as well. When they arrived at castle she told Pavin she needed a bath.

'Sure, and take a nap first. There's plenty of time before dinner. Don't mention my idea for the evening's entertainment to anyone. I'll surprise them during the meal.'

'I can't wait,' she said, and she meant it. The prospect of the excitement she and the other women would arouse in the men was a powerful aphrodisiac, and she was anxious to try out some of her newly discovered sexuality in an exhibition of this kind.

Chapter Ten

When Deborah stepped out of the bath, Pavin was standing watching her, his massive figure entirely filling the doorway. His eyes roamed over her appreciatively and she felt a flutter of desire deep within her.

'Let me wash your hair for you,' he said, moving towards where the shower head was fastened to the wall. She stepped out of the bath and then bent, still wet and naked, over the side of the tub, her long hair spilling down across her face.

Pavin let the spray play across the golden strands, his fingers massaging her scalp in firm circular movements. Then he added some shampoo and soon the top of her head was a mass of bubbles.

His fingers kneaded strongly at her hair and she felt like purring. All his movements were sure and certain. She had never felt so sexually alive before she met him. Finally he rinsed the shampoo away. Then he wrapped a towel round her head and pulled her back a little, parting her legs before letting the jets of water from the shower head spray between her thighs. She felt the jets hitting the tip of her clitoris and groaned with delight.

'Pull back the hood,' he murmured huskily. 'Keep yourself exposed for me. I want to watch you come.'

His words excited her even more and she pressed her hand to the top join of her outer sex lips and then moved it upwards, just as she'd learnt from Pavin, so that the centre of her sexuality was entirely unprotected and the warm water continued to bombard it.

The towel on which she was standing was soaking wet, but neither of them cared. Deborah was whimpering now as the sensations grew too intense and her clitoris tried frantically to retract.

'Bear down,' said Pavin roughly. 'Keep it there, where I can see it.'

Breathing heavily, Deborah obeyed and suddenly the raw nerve endings could take no more and she was shuddering violently as an orgasm rippled through her.

Pavin turned off the spray but kept Deborah standing the same way, roughly pushing her hand back upwards when she tried to release the tight skin to cover the aching nub.

Now he was licking at it, nibbling with his teeth so that she actually screamed out at the intensity of feeling he was causing her, but Pavin didn't seem to care any more. He wanted to take her still further, to show her what was possible if she let him take over her body. When he drew her clitoris into his mouth and sucked steadily, another climax wracked her, and this time she let her hand fall to her side and the little nub was hidden from his view.

Pavin picked her up, carried her to the bedroom and threw her onto their bed. For the first time she realised that his size could be used against her, and yet this only increased her strange, dark excitement. Without a word he reached down, pulled on her trembling hands and then stood her at the foot of the bed, tying her hands to the posts with soft scarves. Next he moved onto the bed behind her and took a nearby candle from its holder. He covered it with oil from a small bottle and with a rapid twisting movement inserted it between the rounded cheeks of her bottom, pushing steadily upwards at the same time until Deborah cried out because she felt she couldn't take it any deeper.

'Hold it there,' Pavin said curtly. 'Don't let it slip out.'

'I can't,' she said frantically. 'It's too well oiled, it won't stay in.'

He moved to the front of her and watched her straining muscles. 'Sure it will, if you want it to. It should improve your muscle tone. Keep clenching and whatever I do, remember to keep it in.'

Deborah had never seen him like this before. He wasn't smiling and there was a hungry passion on his face that both flattered and frightened her. She didn't dare to disobey even though no punishment had been mentioned.

Now he was kneeling between her feet and his hands were tenderly parting her outer sex lips. Then he slid the tip of his ring finger into her opening and circled the rim. 'Use your muscles on my finger too,' he ordered. 'Remember, keep in the candle and hold my finger tight.'

As Deborah clenched all the muscles needed, the pressure caused by the contractions themselves, the thick, oiled candle and his still moving finger brought her to an orgasm in seconds and as it swept over her she forgot what she was meant to be doing, and her muscles went limp.

Pavin, who had known very well what would happen, smiled to himself as the candle fell to the bed behind Deborah while his finger was released from her internal clutching.

He slapped her lightly low on her belly and she jumped, her wrists pulling against the silk restraints. 'You forgot to keep the candle in,' he reproved her. Now he was slapping harder and the skin on her stomach turned a rosy pink while deep within the pit of her belly the treacherous ache of need began again.

'Will you do better this time?' he asked, staring directly at her.

'Yes,' whispered Deborah, who knew that she had to if she wanted that ache satisfied.

Pavin again inserted the candle, this time less well lubricated to make retention easier, and then he stood in front of her and started to lick her ears and the sides of her neck. He knew she was sensitive there and she wriggled within her bonds.

'Remember the candle,' he cautioned her, and quickly she tightened the muscles that had started to relax.

He licked beneath her arms, in the hollows of her armpits, down the sides of her body and along the inward curve of her waist and she felt as though he was stripping a layer of skin from her as he went, so sensitive did she become.

When he reached the area above her pubic hair he nipped lightly along the straight line and then sucked and tongued along the folds of skin at the tops of her thighs while all the time the candle seemed to Deborah to grow more and more heavy as she struggled to keep it in.

Pavin could see that it was as much as Deborah could do to control herself and now he decided to introduce her to something new. He took a tiny phial out of the pocket of his slacks and Deborah watched him, her eyes wide.

'What's that?'

'It's something to increase your pleasure. I get it when I'm travelling in the East. You'll like it, Debbie, I promise you, but remember the candle now.'

Deborah swallowed hard. Her whole body was tingling from his expert kisses and touch and she was so moist between her thighs she was almost ashamed. When he parted her sex lips he laughed. 'That's good, you're certainly ready for this. Now, where's the wand?'

Like a sexual conjuror he produced from his other pocket a long-stemmed rod with a tiny sponge tip, like a large eye shadow applicator, which he dipped into the pot until it was covered in the strange-smelling lotion.

Deborah felt herself going limp with desire and the candle begin to slip. 'If it falls, Debbie you can't try this,' he cautioned her. She strained to hold the soft wax object inside her while he fingered her warm moistness, testing it as though wanting to be quite sure he had everything right.

All at once he pressed the length of the wand handle right down the middle of her inner sex lips, and the head was set at such an angle that when he closed her outer lips and held them firmly together, the sponge tip was pressed exactly against her clitoris.

Once he was sure he had it correctly placed, Pavin simply cupped her sex in the palm of his hand and kept up a relentless pressure against the stem of the wand, and indirectly the tip.

At first she felt nothing apart from an arousing pressure against her inner sex lips but then, very slowly at first, the lotion began to take effect. It started as nothing more than a very mild heat, but this increased until her whole bud was tingling with desire, a desire that grew and grew until it felt to Deborah as though the clitoris itself was growing with her need. It felt huge, swollen to three times its normal size and yet unable to expand because Pavin had it trapped within her outer sex lips.

She moaned with desire, pulling against the scarves and thrusting her pelvis forward but all the time remembering to keep in the insidious candle.

The hot tingling sparks of desire expanded until they lanced through her whole body. They shot down her legs to the soles of her feet and up through her stomach and breasts right to the top of her head. She was consumed by need and just when she thought she could bear no more, Pavin cruelly tapped on the outside of her vulva, right over the spot where he knew the sponge tip was driving her pulsating clitoris insane. Now she began screaming at him to enter her, to fill her up and satisfy her.

Pavin stood back from her. He looked at her straining legs, her bursting breasts and upthrusting nipples and watched the frantic movements of her hips and knew that for the first time he had truly taken her beyond anything she had known before and that she was utterly consumed with her need for him.

He stepped towards her, parted her labia, removed the wand and then thrust fiercely into her, regardless of the fact that he'd intended to wait for the night, regardless of anything but the need her arousal had sparked in him.

For Deborah, half-crazed by the aphrodisiac cream from the Orient and by the earlier way he'd aroused her, the feeling of him sliding into her, filling her and ending that terrible aching void was close to heaven.

As he thrust in and out of her he used his left hand to caress her still swollen and desperate clitoris and almost at once she tightened around him in a huge climax so that his own release came quicker than he'd anticipated and his soft sigh mingled with Deborah's cries as he wrapped his arms around her still fastened body and held her close. Neither of them noticed the candle falling gently to the bed.

When Pavin and Deborah went down to dinner, Deborah was feeling totally exhausted. It had been an incredibly erotic and sexually intriguing twelve hours. First she'd watched Elizabeth, then been made love to on the water bed, experienced genuine fear at Puffin's Cove and finally a strange half-fear along with truly astonishing sex with Pavin. Knowing what she did about his plans for the evening, she wished he'd left her alone in the bedroom. However, he'd confessed as they dressed for dinner that once he'd seen her nude, climbing out of the bath, he'd been totally overwhelmed by desire and she found this highly flattering, especially considering he'd spent most of the day with Elizabeth.

Tonight the damask tablecloth was a soft shade of pink, the napkins a darker pink and in the standing candelabras dotted along the walls, pink candles gave off the scent of summer roses.

Deborah wondered if this particular night often involved something exotic after dinner because all the women seemed to have taken particular care with their clothes. Elizabeth was in a flame-coloured satin shift that emphasised her olive skin, while Tansy was wearing an ankle-length gown of midnight blue silk with tiny silver shoulder straps. Celia too was looking very striking in a dramatic grey and purple low-cut dress that was floor length but had hip-high slits on both sides of the skirt. Flora, like Deborah, was wearing black, but whereas Deborah's dress was Empire line and extremely demure, enlivened only by the thousands of multicoloured sequins that fringed the sleeves, bodice and hem, Flora's clung to every curve, and was so low at the back that you could clearly see the cleft at the base of her spine.

Pavin smiled broadly as he sat down. 'You ladies all look extremely beautiful tonight,' he said warmly. 'You must have guessed what was on my mind.'

The women never moved, they remained sitting straight-backed in their chairs, looking slightly aloof but the men shifted forward eagerly. 'What's that then?' asked Richard. 'Has someone designed a board game for the girls?'

Pavin shook his head. 'Not a board game tonight,

170

something more conventional – a floor show.' There was a low murmure of disappointment and he raised his eyebrows at Deborah in amusement. They both knew there would be no disappointment once the details were explained.

'It isn't an ordinary floor show,' he continued as two maids served French onion soup. 'I thought the ladies could give us an erotic display. Show us how they'd like us to pleasure them by using each other as models. They'll start right from the beginning, fully dressed, and work in pairs or as a group, whichever they prefer.'

'What's the point?' asked Brian. 'Do you expect them to make us feel inadequate or something?'

Pavin threw back his head and laughed heartily. 'It's difficult to imagine you feeling inadequate, Brian! No, the point is this. Before the ladies begin, we gentlemen take off our clothes and sit on chairs around the floor space. The women can touch us, but not with their hands, and they can talk to us but we can't answer them.

'The idea is to see which of us manages to control ourselves the best. In other words, he who comes last comes first!'

Paul Woolcott grinned at Tansy. 'That sounds great, honey, don't you think?'

She smiled at him. 'It certainly does; but I doubt if you'll win.'

The smile faded from her husband's face and Pavin frowned. 'Personal remarks like that are not appreciated, Tansy. He might surprise you yet. Perhaps with an audience he'll outlast us all.'

It was only now that Pavin had revealed the full details of the night that Deborah realised how useful their session earlier had been to him. Unless the other men had been similarly engaged with their partners just before dinner, it would obviously be easier to arouse

171

them sexually than someone who'd only had a climax two hours earlier.

The soup bowls were removed, rare roast beef placed in front of them, and animated chatter broke out as they all discussed Pavin's idea. 'What do you think, Debbie?' Richard asked, leaning across the table towards her.

'I'm looking forward to it.'

'Have you ever done anything like it before?'

She laughed. 'Hardly! It isn't usual at publishing parties in London!'

'But you were living with an actor; he must have taken you to some pretty wild parties.'

'Not that wild,' she assured him. 'Mick liked to be the centre of attention himself. He'd never have sat back and watched women performing with each other.'

'He's missed a lot; it's a great turn on.'

'Only for you men,' complained Celia, who looked less happy than the rest of them at the prospect. 'I'd rather make love to a man any day.'

'I'm sure you would, Celia,' said Pavin calmly. 'The point is though, this gives you a chance to show us all exactly what you'd like us to do to you, and I have a feeling that once you get involved you'll enjoy yourself. You've never minded threesomes with another woman.'

'No, and I don't mind this, I simply prefer to have a man somewhere in the scene.'

Pavin grinned. 'You'll have five of us very heavily involved, Celia. Just think what you can do to us when trying to make us lose!'

Celia looked directly at her husband's boss. 'You expect to win this, don't you? After all, your control is legendary.'

Deborah was surprised to hear it; he seemed to get carried away when he was with her.

'It's up to you to make sure I don't then, isn't it?' he

responded, but it was plain from the look in his eyes that he didn't care for Celia's direct attack on him.

'She's annoyed because Martin didn't get the job in Texas that she wanted for him,' Richard explained to Deborah in a low voice. 'Pavin said he needed Martin here on the mainland but she sees it as a demotion and won't shut up about it. I feel quite sorry for Martin because he's perfectly happy.'

Brian turned to Tansy who was sitting on his left. 'I think you should be able to make Elizabeth very happy, especially if you combine your talents with Flora.'

'I'll choose my own partners thank you,' responded Tansy. 'If I'm any judge of things, Flora will want to be involved with Pavin's nubile blonde most of the time. She'd love to show him she can excite her more than he can.'

'I should think she'd drop dead in the process!' laughed Brian. 'The delightful Deborah looks like one very satisfied young woman tonight.'

When the small pots of dark chocolate mousse had finally been eaten and the last of the liqueurs drunk, everyone rose reluctantly from the table to walk the short distance to the smaller room where the game was to be played.

'It's not that I'm not looking forward to this, because I am,' confessed Martin. 'It's just that the food tonight was superb and the whole atmosphere more inducive to sleep than sex.'

'It was designed to relax you and bring your sensuality to the fore,' said Pavin with a grin. 'Only an Englishman would confuse that with a programme designed to send him to sleep! Come along, let's get the show underway.'

In the room where Deborah had first been introduced to Pavin's idea of evening 'games' the chairs had been pushed back to the sides of the room and the women immediately stepped into the square in the middle, then turned to Pavin for guidance.

His eyes gleamed with amused anticipation and Flora literally went weak at the knees when he caught her eye and winked in a conspiratorial manner. She wanted him so badly, not just for a day or a night, but for the rest of her life. Yet no sooner had Angela gone than this English girl had appeared, to come between her and the man she wanted. She was determined to show him in some way before the two weeks were up that it was she, not Deborah, who was most suited to becoming his next wife. The fact that he'd marry again was taken for granted by all who knew him. He never stayed single for more than a year.

At that moment soft music began to fill the room, coming through four speakers concealed in the corners. It was mostly reed pipes and sounds of the sea, conjuring up images of tropical shores and warm sunshine. The women felt their muscles relaxing and grew languid.

'Begin when you like, ladies,' said Pavin as soon as all the men had removed their clothes. 'I think there should be at least a ten-minute show before you approach any of us though.'

Deborah felt awkward. Elizabeth was already reaching up behind her and unzipping her flame-coloured dress so that it fell into a soft heap at her feet, while Tansy was elegantly shrugging off her shoulder straps.

For the first time, Deborah wished she'd worn something that was easier to unfasten, but then Celia came round behind her and very slowly slid each of the buttons out of its loop of material until the dress was open right down to the base of her spine.

'Bend forward,' Celia whispered, and Deborah did as she suggested, letting her arms hang down so that the dress slipped off her torso, revealing her half-cup satin bra trimmed with French lace. Then she wriggled out of the rest of it and threw the dress over to where Pavin was sitting.

Now all the women were down to their underwear, but it was Flora who was the first to remove her G-string and black lace bra and the men gave her a round of applause. Deborah looked at where they were sitting and saw that already Martin and Richard had partial erections, and this encouraged her to remove her own matching panties and bra and very soon none of the women had any clothing left on.

The music continued to play, and Deborah found that, like the others, she was swaying in time to the reed pipes. It felt good when her breasts moved gently and her stomach arched as her hips undulated sensuously.

It wasn't long before Tansy was stroking Celia's breasts, running her fingers round the outline of the areolae and then skimming them across the top of the nipples in a way that had Celia sighing with contentment.

Deborah continued to dance and watch, but then Elizabeth approached her. 'Lie down, Debbie,' she said quietly. 'I'd like to give you a massage.' Deborah lay face down on the carpet, and felt the small but surprisingly strong fingers kneading at her trapezius muscles, loosening small pockets of tightness between her shoulder blades and then tenderly flowing up the sinews of her neck and into her scalp so that she moved her head around to increase the contact.

'Turn over,' Elizabeth murmured in her ear, and Deborah willingly obeyed. Now Elizabeth could use her mouth on the tall blonde's breasts and belly, not licking in the way that Deborah was used to but instead using her tongue like a knife and stabbing at highly sensitive nerve points, moving so quickly from place to place that Deborah never knew where the next sensation would come from.

Without realising it, Deborah had parted her legs, and while Elizabeth continued to work her upper body with her mouth, Tansy sat between the outstretched thighs and let her fingers explore the warm moist tissue of the young woman's inner sex lips. She was surprised at first to find that Debortah's clitoris was reluctant to swell, but then she guessed that Pavin must have made love to her just before dinner and she wasn't really ready for full rearousal.

Tansy glanced across to the other women, and they quickly came and joined her so that soon it was only Deborah who was spreadeagled on the carpet, while all the other women set to work on this newcomer in their midst.

All that Deborah knew was that there were hands everywhere. Fingers caressed her inner knees and thighs, others massaged her breasts and belly while soft tongues swirled around her ears and beneath her armpits.

She felt totally relaxed and when one of the women inserted a small finger into her rectum she welcomed it, because after her earlier experience with Pavin and the candle she now had a need to be filled there as well. In the meantime Flora was sliding two fingers rapidly in and out of Deborah's front passage, feeling the other woman's juices surrounding her and knowing that this was what Pavin enjoyed.

Deep within Flora an anger grew and her movements increased in vigour. She added a third finger so that Deborah was now as full as she wanted to be. She moaned a little and tried to shift her hips, but Tansy was sitting astride her, letting her rigid, permanently exposed clitoris rub the soft fair skin of Deborah's abdomen, gripping her waist with her thighs to increase the pressure.

The men watched in rising excitement. They were all fully erect now because the women made sure that

176

whatever they did there was always a gap through which the men could see what was happening.

What was particularly arousing about the scene was the fact that it was Deborah who had become so abandoned. She was the one whose eyes were closed, whose breathing was rapid and audible and whose twitching legs, twisting head and frantic attempts at hip movements signified her state of high arousal.

To most of them she always seemed cool and controlled, and yet now she was as abandoned as any of the women if not more so. And when Flora continued thrusting with three fingers but used her thumb to rotate the now aroused and visible clitoris, Deborah climaxed immediately, giving a long drawn-out moan of satisfaction as the ripples of orgasm washed over her. The women seemed to take this as a signal to turn their attention elsewhere, and leaving Deborah sprawled on the carpet they approached the watching men.

Elizabeth went to Paul. After swaying in front of him for a few seconds she went down onto her knees and then licked the tops of his toes before letting her tongue travel up the length of his leg until she reached the creases at the tops of his thighs.

His erection was huge; his glans purple and apparently shining with a drop of clear pre-ejaculatory fluid which was balanced in the slit at the top of the head. He swallowed hard. Knowing that he found Elizabeth tremendously attractive, he couldn't imagine how he was going to last very long if she kept letting her breasts brush against him while using her mouth on his most sensitive parts.

As Paul struggled, Martin had to endure Tansy sitting astride his legs and moving herself back and forth so that her whole vulva was stimulated, and her permanently exposed clitoris gradually slid more and more easily over him as his legs became moistened by her secretions.

He could feel that tiny fleshy button expanding with every move she made, and saw in her eyes that she was approaching a climax. This was so incredibly exciting that she didn't need to touch him at all and he was desperately afraid of coming first. He bit on his lower lip and prayed that someone would have less self-control than he had.

Celia was working on Pavin. She was determined to make sure that he didn't win the competition, not because she didn't like him – she did – but because he was always so good at everything that just for once she wanted to see him lose.

Pavin knew what she was about and since the sight of Deborah, only just beginning to pull herself upright after her orgasm, her hair rumpled and her face flushed, had aroused him far more than he'd expected at this stage, he thought that Celia's chance of success was greater than she perhaps anticipated. Nevertheless, since he hated to lose, he would oppose her as much as his flesh would allow.

Celia knew that it was the sight of Deborah that was the greatest aphrodisiac for the American this evening, so she wisely moved behind him and, leaning over the back of his chair, let her breasts rub up and down his spine and over the massive breadth of his shoulders while he remained watching the young Englishwoman. 'Isn't she lovely?' she purred. 'Don't you wish you could take her here and now? She was so moist to touch, Pavin, so very moist.'

Then, as Deborah got unsteadily to her feet and began to make her way towards Richard, Celia let her tongue caress the outside of Pavin's earlobes before drawing it lazily round his inner ear and then down the side of his neck.

It was subtle but arousing and her words had only inflamed him more. Pavin felt his testicles tighten and draw up towards his body despite his earlier climax. It was the sight of Deborah lying on the floor at Richard's feet, her legs stretched upwards round his waist so that he could look down on her open, still damply excited flesh that was adding to his difficulties, and yet when he looked away he found that he wanted to look back to see exactly what she was doing now, and how Richard was coping with such abandoned behaviour from the least likely member of the group.

Richard wasn't coping at all well. From the moment Flora had stripped naked he'd been consumed with lust for her; and then when this beautiful blonde, still bright-eyed and sated from her climax with the other women, proceeded to lie down at his feet and wrap her legs around him, tilting her pubic mound upwards and then clenching and unclenching her internal muscles so that he could see the entrance to her vagina contracting, it was too much for him. With a groan he felt his semen rising up along the shaft of his tight penis, tried vainly to distract himself with thoughts of other things and then as Deborah sighed with the genuine bliss of an orgasm induced by her own muscular efforts, he was forced to concede defeat and his sperm shot from him, up across the front of his stomach where it dribbled warmly down again into the dip of his navel.

The sound of Richard's climax proved too much for Martin. Tansy had now manipulated herself to two orgasms on his legs and her breasts had been continually thrust into his mouth, whereupon he'd found himself licking at their proud firmness without thinking about the consequences, unable to resist the perfection of their shape.

His legs were trembling, his scrotum aching and his foreskin tight and once he knew that someone had already come he allowed himself to lose control and as he spurted, Tansy bent her torso so that his shaft was caught between those delicious round globes and his own stomach. This increased pressure gave him one of

179

the longest orgasms he'd ever had and he heard himself shout with the joy of it.

As Elizabeth continued to work on Paul, Flora was busy with Brian. She had used her knowledge of his darker streak to good effect, teasing him cruelly by nipping at his most tender flesh, even just below the tip of the glans, so that Brian had nearly been driven to distraction by the swings between pain and pleasure that her teeth and tongue caused him. When she sat on his naked lap, pressed her hard pubic bone against the root of his shaft and then bent forward and bit on each of his nipples in turn he too was lost. Flora then had the satisfaction of feeling him spurt warmly between their bellies while he cursed her softly under his breath.

Now it was only Pavin and Paul left in. The other women, their work finished, moved to the centre of the room and Tansy lay down on the floor, her legs supported on Celia's shoulders while they got Deborah, whom they knew Pavin was watching, to work on Tansy's still eager clitoris with her tongue.

Deborah found that it was very rewarding to let her tongue glide over the erect little organ, moist with Tansy's copious juices, and to feel it jump and judder beneath her as it rushed towards a climax.

'I'm coming!' Tansy shouted suddenly, and then she was shaking with the force of the orgasm but because there was no hood there her clitoris remained upright and Deborah found that she couldn't stop stimulating it.

Despite Tansy's panicked cries for a moment's respite, Deborah continued to work away remorselessly at her. She could feel the debased flesh trying to shrink away, but the other women were caught up in the excitement too, and they held Tansy still while the clitoris was licked and flicked and then Deborah took it into her mouth and suckled on it like a tiny kitten.

The searing moment of agony passed in seconds, and

then Tansy was precipitated headlong into a shattering climax that made her lose consciousness for a few brief seconds while her body continued to shake and heave with uncontrollable contractions. At last Deborah left the shattered woman alone.

Both Pavin and Paul had seen it all, but because Elizabeth was so excited by sado-masochism she forgot to work on Paul during Tansy's final moments of pain-filled bliss. Celia though continued relentlessly to stimulate Pavin, whispering how Deborah looked and finally moving to the front of him and drawing his huge glans into her mouth she sucked on it just as Deborah was sucking on Tansy.

Even for Pavin it was too much. He gave what sounded like a bellow of rage and then he was spending himself straight into Celia's mouth, thrusting fiercely into her soft lips as though it was her sex lips he was invading and Celia swallowed it all with silent satisfaction. When he'd finished Pavin was breathing heavily but he had to smile at her. 'Well done, Celia! You really worked for that. Paul, I think that makes you the winner. You were quite wrong about him, Tansy.'

'And I'm the only one fit to do anything but sleep when we retire!' laughed Paul, thankful that he and Tansy could still go on to the sauna room as they'd planned, before going to their bedroom.

Slowly everyone came back to earth again, although Deborah found it hard to shake off the almost overwhelming feeling of permanent sensuality that had filled her ever since she'd entered the carefully prepared dining room.

Pavin put an arm round her. 'It was your fault I lost! You were far too good at the game. And you looked fantastic.'

'It was great,' she said, smiling up at him. 'What happens tomorrow?'

The rest of the group turned to hear what he had to

say. Pavin considered for a moment. 'I think after this, tomorrow should be Deprivation Day for the women.'

Brian laughed. 'Excellent! My favourite day of the holiday!' But the women said nothing.

As they climbed into their bed, Deborah turned to Pavin and wrapped her arms round his back. 'What is Deprivation Day? Does that mean we women all have to sit around knitting or doing flower arrangements, something non-sexual?'

He chuckled. 'Hardly! It simply means that although you're all kept sexually aroused, none of you can have fulfilment until five o'clock in the afternoon.'

'I don't see how you can stop us,' murmured Deborah.

'Believe me, we've had plenty of practice at that,' Pavin assured her. 'You should find it a very stimulating day!'

Chapter Eleven

Deborah was awoken the next morning by the feel of Pavin's hands cupping her breasts from behind as he lay curled against her back. She gave a sleepy murmur of contentment and felt her nipples hardening against the slightly rough skin of his fingers.

He blew lightly against the nape of her neck and she wriggled with sensuous joy, knowing that now his hands would roam further down her body and as she pressed back against his morning hardness his arms moved and he carefully pulled her top leg back at a slight angle so that his hand could wander more freely between her thighs.

She found this kind of coupling delicious. Sometimes he would wake her in the night and was always slow and considerate then. She adored the feeling of being only half-awake while he brought her to a tender, caring climax. Her body responded quickly now to this familiar ritual and she was soon moist between her thighs and felt the slight tension within her abdomen, the tightening of nerve endings behind her pelvic bone that meant she was approaching a climax.

Then, as she savoured the sensations, Pavin's hands

stopped moving and he rolled away from her. 'Guess it's time we got up, honey. They'll all be down to breakfast promptly this morning.'

Deborah rolled onto her back and reached out for his hand. 'Hey, what about me?'

Pavin chuckled. 'Didn't you enjoy that?'

She rolled on top of him. 'Very much, but it wasn't enough!'

He looked up at her, his blue eyes glinting with amusement. 'It'll have to be, Debbie. Remember, today's Deprivation Day!'

Deborah didn't care if it was Abstinence Day, she had no intention of being left feeling the way she was now, aroused, tense and dissatisfied. She placed a hand between their bodies and moved herself up and down on him, letting her own fingers rearouse her.

Pavin watched her, smiling, but when he saw her eyes start to widen and her lips to part he caught hold of her by her waist and deftly twisted her off him, at the same time bringing her hands round behind her back and tying them together with a pair of padded leather handcuffs that he'd already concealed beneath his pillow before he woke her with his lovemaking.

'You're not the first young lady to think of that way out of it!' he chuckled. 'Right, time to get you washed and dressed.' Deborah couldn't believe it when he carefully helped her out of the vast bed, waited until she'd used the bathroom and then joined her so that he could wash and dry her without releasing her hands.

'Bath, shower or strip wash?' he asked.

Deborah thought quickly. The erotic possibilities of the first two were far too great under the circumstances. 'A strip wash will do for now,' she said sulkily.

He traced a line beneath her naked breasts and she shivered with sexual tension. 'Don't get cross, Debs. The day will be something really special, I promise. Right then, a strip wash it is.'

As he got to work on her, the same kind of scene was being played out in all the bedrooms, except that Elizabeth was already far more sexually tense and sensitive than any of the other women.

Brian had awoken her early. He'd fastened her hands before he began and then played for what seemed like hours with her nipple rings, watching her face by candlelight as he twisted and pulled on them. The painfully intense feelings that Elizabeth always experienced when he did this were reflected on her face, and he could bring her so close to an orgasm by this means alone that several times she was sure he'd gone too far and then just as her legs started to go rigid and her body to suffuse with warmth he would stop moving the rings and press the palms of his hands flat over the tops of her breasts until the glorious feelings died away and she was left shifting restlessly on the satin sheets.

Once or twice he'd let her fall into an early morning doze for a short time, but then he'd woken her and played with her body again, using his fingers to touch on delicate spots inside her elbows and knees, increasing the pressure until pain started to shoot through her, at the same time licking around her clitoral ring with his tongue, but always stopping at the very last moment.

By the time he came to take her to the bathroom she felt stretched to the limit and exhausted by thwarted need. Her eyelids drooped heavily. Of all the men it was Brian who was best at this game and she was grateful that he wouldn't spend the whole day with her.

Flora hated this game. Normally it started quietly for her because Richard wasn't very good at it, but this year he seemed to have changed and to her amazement he'd woken her at six and spent some time sponging her down with warm water and soap suds before massaging in body lotion. As a result, although she hadn't come

185

close to climaxing she was more than ready for sexual satisfaction on the one day of the holiday when it was guaranteed she wouldn't get it until the end of the afternoon.

Tansy and Celia, together with Paul and Martin, were the first into the dining room. Tansy was wearing a cream satin chemise with a plunging neckline and lace covered breast panel that hid her breasts but dipped into a small V-shape between them. Beneath it she had matching lace-trimmed satin French knickers and cream hold-up stockings.

Celia had been dressed by Martin in a red stretch bodypiece with a ruched front panel that was fastened by a concealed zip which ran the whole length of the front, down under the crotch and up between her buttocks at the back. Round her neck she had a small thin gold necklace and a matching bracelet adorned her wrist.

'Very sexy!' commented Pavin when he and Deborah entered the room. The two women glanced quickly at him. They knew very well that they'd been dressed in this way for two reasons; to heighten their sex appeal and to make them easily accessible for the men to arouse during the day. The trouble was that the clothes were sexy to wear as well, and this meant that their senses were permanently heightened.

Pavin had chosen Deborah's outfit on the same basis, but of all of them she was the most aroused, because her clinging playsuit was made of black rubber. It had a halter neck and plunging neckline while two small silver chains crossed the V-shaped opening between her concealed breasts. The back of the suit was thonged and between her legs the rubber left a gap for her sex lips. Again tiny chains covered this opening. Her entire body was tightly enclosed, subtly pressurised and designed to continue the arousal Pavin had begun earlier.

When Flora and Richard joined them, Flora was in a

green two-piece with high-cut briefs and a short-bodied teddy that left her entire stomach temptingly exposed. The top of the teddy was fastened with press studs so that it could easily be opened for access and as she crossed the room in black silk stockings and high heels she looked as sexually arousing as the other women.

Elizabeth and Brian were the last to join them. Deborah had expected Elizabeth to be in some highly complex leather costume but to her surprise she was wearing a multicoloured soft flowing kaftan with long, wide sleeves, a high collar and hanging almost to the floor. As she crossed the room to where the breakfast dishes were kept the sun shone in through the window and it was clear that beneath the kaftan she wore nothing at all.

What everyone gradually realised as they watched her was that with every movement she made, the material of the kaftan caressed her nipple and clitoral rings, brushing against them, occassionally snagging on the slight roughness of the join of the rings and generally making sure she was stimulated the whole time.

The only thing all the women had in common was that their hands were fastened behind their backs.

They were spoon-fed by their partners whilst sitting at the table, and Deborah found the pressure of the black rubber suit uncomfortable, especially when she tipped back her head to let Pavin tip scrambled egg into her mouth and her upthrust nipples rubbed against the covering. With his free hand he reached casually down into the plunging neckline and eased the rubber away from her nipples for a moment, rolling them each in turn between two fingers. When he released the suit she was actually more aroused than when he'd started and because of this her stomach and vulva swelled slightly and again the rubber constrained her.

'There's one thing about this day,' Tansy called down the table as she watched Deborah struggling to come to

187

terms with what was happening to her. 'We certainly don't get neglected!'

'I like it,' admitted Celia. 'At least, I like the idea. In practice it becomes a bit overwhelming, but remember you won't be the only one reduced to screaming pitch before the day's over.'

None of the women ate much, and they settled for only one cup of coffee knowing that natural breaks would be few and far between. Once the men had eaten, the entire group went down to the swimming pool area and there the women were stretched out on poolside loungers while the men enjoyed a swim and threw a ball around in a game of water polo.

Every so often one of the men would leave the water and attend to one of the prone women. Deborah didn't want to know what was happening to anyone else. She knew that it would be as much as she could do to cope with what happened to her, and since other people's arousal seemed to be such an aphrodisiac for her, she thought it wiser to remain in ignorance. Nevertheless, she couldn't help but hear the half-muffled groans and soft sighs that these visits elicited from their victims.

It was Martin who finally came to see to Deborah. Being British himself he was less attracted to her than the other men were; she was a type with which he was familiar, but he could quite understand her fascination for a man like Pavin. He was also becoming intrigued by her blossoming sexuality.

'Spread your legs, Debbie,' he said quietly. 'You're going to enjoy this I promise you.' She didn't even open her eyes, but simply did as he said and waited for what was to come.

Martin covered his erection with a soft, pliant ripple sheath. Once pulled on it squeezed at the base of his shaft and so enabled him to maintain an erection for as long as he wanted while the deeply etched ripples on

188

the surface ensured that the recipient enjoyed quite a different experience from normal.

Deborah felt Martin's hands pulling at the fastening to the chains that covered her protruding vulva and within seconds she was fully exposed to him. He found the effect of the tight rubber surrounding her sex lips highly erotic because it made her seem swollen and excited before he'd even begun.

The cool, soft head of the ripple sheath moved between Deborah's outer sex lips and she drew in her breath in surprise. It wasn't like anything she'd felt before. Slowly Martin moved his hips back and forth, and as he did so, Deborah's rubber suit gripped her burgeoning flesh more fiercely so that she was pushed out towards him even more and he had to part her outer lips with his hands in order to let himself slide along her moist channels, while the cool ribbing teased the inner walls of those outstretched sex lips.

Now it was Deborah's turn to give a soft groan of excitement and she lifted her hips on the lounger to give Martin easier access to her. He saw her opening, and could almost sense the hunger within her, a hunger which he knew would increase as the day went on.

'Hey, don't take all day!' called Richard from the pool.

Quickly, Martin let the head of the ripple sheath slide into that needy, aching opening and as he slid back and forth the ripples rubbed against her vaginal walls. Deborah's breasts strained upwards and sharp flashes of pleasure darted through her pelvic area. Without realising it she began to move in the same rhythm, and immediately Martin stopped and withdrew. Carefully he refastened the chains over the damp, frustrated tissue of her outthrust sex, whispered 'Until later,' and then slid back into the pool.

Deborah lay on her back, her hands fastened to the sides of the lounger, and tried to slow her breathing. It had been a delicious sensation and with a few more thrusts and just a fraction more stimulation of breasts or clitoris she could have come so easily, but she knew it wasn't to be. When her body refused to settle back into any kind of stillness she realised just how long a day it was going to prove for her hungry body.

When the men had finished in the pool they got dressed and then led the women through into the room where the water bed was kept. Pavin decided to turn his attention to Flora. He knew her well, knew what particular kind of stimulation could drive her to the edge of insanity and he decided to use that knowledge now.

As he stepped towards his secretary she felt her mouth go dry. At last Deborah was going to see for herself the kind of sex Flora and Pavin enjoyed together, and although Flora knew it wouldn't end in total satisfaction she still longed for his skilful manipulations.

Very gently, Pavin drew her towards the water bed. 'Bend forward from the waist,' he said quietly and she complied instantly. She had her back to the rest of the group and when Pavin pulled down her high-cut briefs her tight little buttocks aroused all the men.

Reaching in front of her, Pavin unfastened the top half of her outfit so that her breasts hung free and then pushed her face down onto the water bed, at the same time pressing the button that caused it to vibrate more intensely.

'Lean forward on your arms, rest your head down and keep your buttocks raised,' he said softly. 'I'm going to make sure you're very clean, Flora; very clean indeed.'

Excitement gripped Flora like a vice and she squirmed against the undulations of the bed. This had always been their secret, something never before shared, but she didn't mind Deborah knowing because it would show the Englishwoman exactly how far Pavin liked

190

some of his games to go, and what kind of sex she could expect to be introduced to if she stayed with him.

As the other four women watched, each with a man behind her casually fondling and caressing her body in the way each individual responded to best, Pavin opened a small box and took out a strange-looking item, rather like a small candle holder, from which protruded what Deborah at first thought to be a long, thin piece of wax.

He held it up for them all to see more clearly. 'This is one of Flora's favourite toys,' he explained. 'It's merely a soap stick, made from remnants of various bars, then moulded together into this candy-shaped twist. Not only does it arouse her; as its soapy qualities make themselves felt it causes other feelings too, that I'm sure you can imagine very well for yourselves. This, combined with other stimulation, is Flora's idea of bliss.'

Even Elizabeth looked surprised, and Celia shivered, but Tansy felt a spark of excitement. She could imagine very well what Flora would soon be feeling, and wondered if she might try it herself some time.

Flora heard him talking and longed for him to begin as her breasts filled with extra blood due to the massaging movement of the water bed. When Pavin's finger spread lubricating jelly around the flesh between the cheeks of her bottom she tensed in anticipation and then as he pulled her nearer to the foot of the heaving bed and carefully twisted and turned the soap stick until it was deep inside her rectum she gasped at the heavy, tingling sparks of arousal already beginning within her.

With one hand, Pavin continued to twist the soap stick, making sure that it touched every part of those paper-thin rectal walls, and every time he increased the pressure, Flora's belly cramped as her bowels, irritated by the sensation, started to heave and writhe.

Pavin slid his free hand beneath her belly and mas-

191

saged it firmly for a few minutes, hearing her groans of pleasure beginning to mix with sounds of increased discomfort.

Now his hand moved lower and he massaged her pubic hair, then slid the whole of his palm down between the join of her thighs and pressed up against her vulva, so that the contractions within her back passage and bowels were increased by the stimulation of all the nerve endings within her heavily lubricated vulva.

As the soap stick turned and the hand on her sex pressed harder it all became too much for Flora. She'd never before done this on the water bed and the increase in every sensation meant that she was feeling the pain as well as the pleasure more acutely.

'That's enough!' she gasped. 'Please, stop the soaping now. I can't control myself.'

'Of course you can,' whispered Pavin. 'Surely you want to show the others how skilful you are at this little game?'

She did, but she wasn't sure she could bear it. Then as Pavin, in total defiance of what she'd said, rotated the soap stick more swiftly within her rectum while parting her sex lips and carefully inserting one finger into her vagina, pressing down hard against the swollen little gland that identified her G-spot, she felt the pain and discomfort being overwhelmed by the ecstasy of the tortured nerve endings gathering together for their moment of release and her head went back in readiness.

She had forgotten what day it was. Pavin swiftly pulled her from the arousing bed, removed the soap stick and turned her to face the rest of the group, holding her arms tightly to her sides and keeping her absolutely still so that the delicious gathering sensation was halted in its tracks and all Flora could do was stand there, her breasts heaving, her eyes frantic and wait as very slowly the sensations died away and she was left with nothing more than a heavy ache at the base of her tight abdomen.

All the watching women were flushed and breathing almost as heavily as Flora. Even Deborah, who knew very well that Flora disliked her, felt pity for the other woman. She'd been so close to what they could clearly see would have been a shattering climax only to have it snatched away from her in the closing seconds. Now her hands were being tied behind her back again, her briefs were put back on and she was once more simply one of the crowd.

Beneath her kaftan, Elizabeth's nipples were standing out painfully hard, the rings brushing constantly against the material. She was shivering with excitement and need and felt as though she could climax simply by thinking about what she'd witnessed as long as the kaftan continued to caress her.

Pavin's eyes swept over the women and he saw how the scene had affected Elizabeth. 'I think we should all get some air now,' he said casually. 'It's a lovely sunny day, I don't think Lizzie needs that long gown on while we're out there. I'm sure she'd rather feel the warmth on her flesh.'

Brian, guessing what must be happening to his wife, carefully removed the kaftan, making sure it didn't stimulate her further as it was taken off. 'We must try that some time,' he whispered in her ear and she swallowed hard against the knot of desire in her throat.

Up on the balustrade of the castle it was like a suntrap and Deborah was grateful for the change of atmosphere. She'd found the scene with Flora so incredible that she couldn't get it out of her mind and it had left her own body longing for some kind of exotic stimulation too.

As they wandered along the balustrade, Richard came up to Deborah and quite unexpectedly tugged hard on the back of the chains between her legs. They split her outer sex lips neatly in half and were immediately pressing on the soft tissue beneath and she felt her clitoris begin to swell as part of the chain pressed against the covering hood.

Richard tugged again, and this time sparks of pleasure shot up through her pubic mound and the clitoris engorged further, revelling in the pressure of the chain. Still standing behind her, Richard moved his hands to the front of the increasingly tight rubber suit and pressed them firmly across her waist and stomach so that she could feel herself expanding with the resulting increase in pressure on every part of her that was encased within the garment.

Deborah's breasts had never felt so full nor longed so much for some kind of touch. She heard herself whimper with frustration when Richard moved away and Celia looked at her with a sympathetic smile. 'Gets pretty stressful, doesn't it? Still, no one can say we get left out of things while our men have fun! I often think these holidays are better for us than for them.'

'I need more,' Deborah said through clenched teeth. 'This suit just keeps on and on arousing me but it isn't enough to make me come.'

'Of course it isn't. Pavin's very good at choosing clothes for days like this. Don't worry, it will be worth it in the end. Actually I think it's fantastic to be permanently aroused. Think of all those women wishing their husbands would give them more foreplay at night!'

'There must be a middle path,' moaned Deborah.

Brian came over to the two women. 'Can I help, ladies?'

Celia knew he was possibly enjoying this day more than anyone; it appealed to the sadistic streak in him, and she had no intention of giving him more pleasure. 'I doubt it,' she said coolly.

'Pavin wants us all to play ball,' Brian announced as

194

he turned away. 'Form a ring, girls, and we'll tell you all about it.'

Paul Woolcott waited until the young women were in a circle and then produced a large latex ball, white in colour, but in shape rather like a child's space hopper. He threw it up and down in the air a few times so that they could all see the size and width of it.

'Right, everyone, I'm sure you've seen things like this before. They're usually used for children, but this time they're for your delights. The idea is that you take it in turns to have a ride. You sit astride it, grip it between your thighs and then bounce around the inside of the circle until one of the men calls a halt. Then it's the next person's turn. There's one other thing I should mention. Each of you will be given one of these.'

He then held out his right hand and between his finger and thumb there was a seven-inch latex tube, shaped exactly like a penis with an imitation glans on the end. At the base of this extension was a small pad, clearly designed to sit against the clitoris and add further stimulation during the ride.

'I think Celia should try it first,' continued Paul, reaching for the small Welsh girl. He easily located the concealed zip of her red bodysuit, and with a swift motion unfastened it right down to her crotch and then bent his knees and continued to release it until it was fully unfastened.

Celia's small breasts showed through the parting and as she spread her legs to sit astride the inflated ball, she took the imitation penis from Paul's outstretched hand, fastened it to the screw valve on the top and then gently lowered herself onto its head. Everyone watched in total silence as the full, curved length of it slid inside her and Celia's breasts thrust through the opening of her bodysuit while she adjusted her position.

Pavin crouched down to check on her. 'Not quite, Celia, but a nice try! I don't think that little stimulator

195

at the base is quite in line with your centre of pleasure, do you?' He lifted her hips a fraction and tilted her forward more, and this time when she was sitting on the ball it was clear from her expression that the pad was definitely in place.

Brian sighed with appreciation and Paul told Celia to start on her 'ride of pleasure'.

All the other women watched to see how quickly the movement of the imitation phallus in her, combined with the pressure against her entire vulva caused by the tight grip of her thighs on the ball and the soft, insidious caress of the pad would affect her. It didn't take long.

For Celia it was something totally new, and at first she thought that although agreeable enough it wasn't particularly mind-blowing. However, before she had bounced halfway round the circle she was beginning to feel a deep throbbing inside her vagina and as her thighs were forced to grip tighter in order to keep her balance all the nerve endings contained along her soft, inner sex lips were aroused too and she longed to run her hands over her bouncing breasts but they were still bound behind her and she couldn't. Even so, the movement itself was exciting and soon her head was back, her eyes closed and she was lost in the sensations.

Martin watched his wife closely. As her husband he was expected to be able to judge better than anyone else when she was about to climax and he had to stop the ride just before that glorious second of release. He waited and waited, thrilled as they all were by the sight of her with parted lips and swollen swinging breasts bouncing away in front of them.

Then he noticed a coiling of her abdominal flesh, saw her naval draw inwards as the first tightenings of her climax began and he knew that she was very close. Celia knew it too, and she was determined to get there. Her body was revelling in the sensations, her clitoris had never felt so huge or so sensitive and she just knew

196

that it was going to be one of the biggest orgasms she'd ever had.

Her feet suddenly stiffened and her back curved inwards, and at that very moment, just as the shooting darts of pre-climactic pleasure lanced through her, Pavin lifted her off the ball.

For the first time ever in such a game, Celia wailed in frustration. She twisted and turned in the large man's grip, certain that somehow she could still manage to finish off what the ride had begun, attempting to rub her aching, throbbing breasts against his heavy plaid shirt, but Pavin kept her suspended in the air well away from his body and they all watched her twisting and crying in the summer air as those wonderful feelings ebbed away to nothing.

Once she was still, Celia was put back on her feet and silently took her place in the circle again. She couldn't bear to think about what had happened, about how close she'd come, and nor did she want to look any of the other women in the eye. Let them find out for themselves what it was like.

In fact, it didn't affect all the women the same way. For Elizabeth it was pleasant enough, but she was never in danger of an orgasm, the arousal was too gentle. Flora, still exhausted by Pavin's attentions earlier, managed quite a long ride before there was any suggestion of a climax and she wasn't as distraught as Celia when she was stopped, while Tansy found it all a great game and controlled her arousal level herself by the clever use of thigh pressure.

Finally it was Deborah's turn. She fastened on her own personal probe and waited while Paul released her chains. Then, already very damp after watching Celia's painful frustration, she bent her knees and heard a collective intake of breath from the men at the sight of her pushed out sex lips parting over the head of the probe.

197

Because she was both nervous and aroused, Deborah's knees couldn't support her very well and she almost collapsed onto the ball, so that the probe thrust hard into her vagina, filling the entire length of it and her clitoris, which had throbbed intermittently for most of the morning, shrank away from the sudden violent stimulation of the pad at the base.

'Start riding, Debs,' said Pavin with a hint of amusement in his voice. 'It's lunch after you've finished and we're all starving.'

She wished that her rubber suit wasn't so tight. It meant that as she bounced around the flagstones her breasts rubbed hard against the material and since they couldn't protrude they were flattened. This meant the whole area was continuously stimulated.

There was such a need in her now for sexual release that she could hardly bear to keep bouncing. Like Celia, this particular type of penetration and stimulation suited her and within a few minutes her whole body was tingling while she longed to stop bouncing and instead to simply wriggle around on the gadget so that all her screaming tissue could be stimulated beyond the point of no return.

Her breathing was so harsh it was audible to them all, and even through the rubber suit they could see her hard nipples trying to protrude. Pavin watched her closely and when a gentle rosy flush started to spread over her neck and in the V of her exposed chest he called for her to stop.

Like Celia it was too much for Deborah and when Paul lifted her off the ball she too gave a cry of anguish. 'I wanted to come!' she shouted furiously at Pavin but he turned away as though it was of no interest to him.

Paul could feel how close to the edge she still was and he made Brian assist in holding her totally immobile for a good five minutes until every sexual spark that had been alight in her body had finally dampened

198

down. Only then was she released and allowed to join the others for lunch.

Because the dining room became cooler as the day went on, all of the women except for Elizabeth had cotton wraps put over their outfits before lunch, and this time their hands were freed while they ate, although they were never left unwatched.

Pavin sat on a dining chair opposite Deborah's so that their knees touched and as she nibbled on a smoked salmon sandwich he lightly stroked one of her bare knees.

'Enjoying yourself?' he asked.

'A few minutes ago I could happily have killed you, but it's certainly an extraordinarily erotic day. Quite apart from feeling totally desperate for you all the time, I must admit it's incredibly exciting to watch other women on the brink of an orgasm.'

He smiled at her. 'So, you continue to surprise yourself, honey?'

'I certainly do! Is it just you, the island, or was it in me all the time?'

'In you all the time. Believe me, I wouldn't have made a mistake. You can't afford to bring a genuine shrinking violet here!'

'But I'd never have known,' said Deborah, watching out of the corner of her eye as Richard moved Elizabeth slowly up and down against his body while her dark eyes grew heavy.

'I guess not.'

'The only thing is . . .' She hesitated.

'Tell me,' urged Pavin.

'I'm beginning to wonder how far I'd be willing to go. It frightens me.'

'Why should it frighten you? As long as what you do doesn't cause unwanted suffering to anyone else, you can go as far as you like.'

'But away from here, back in London, what will I do then?'

'Perhaps you won't go back to London. Maybe after your holiday you'll choose a different sort of life,' he said enigmatically. 'I wouldn't let it inhibit you, sweetheart. The more I see of you the more certain I am we're two of a kind.'

At that moment Richard came up to Deborah and began talking about the morning and Pavin disappeared to chat with Tansy. Deborah had been waiting ever since they met to hear him say something like that, and now she wanted him to explain himself further. Did he mean they might stay together for a while? Might he take her back to the States with him even? And if asked, would she actually want to go? Suddenly she didn't know, and she wondered if such prolonged abandonment to sensuality had dulled her brain.

After a forty-five-minute break for lunch, they all went down to the steam room. It was the first time Deborah had been there, and she was surprised at the size of it. Pavin had asked for it to be constructed along the lines of a Turkish steam room and so there were large stone slabs covered with towels down the centre while heavily-muscled young men wearing only the briefest of pants waited with various lotions and oils. This afternoon though they were, much to their disappointment, dismissed, with the exception of one particularly well-built lad who remained behind.

All the women went into the actual steam cubicle first and then came out to lie on one of the slabs, where they were massaged by their partners. Only then did they each receive the attention of the remaining attendant.

His touch was quite different from that of the men. As soon as Deborah felt his fingers moving along the sides of her spine, pressing deep down into her tissue she knew that this was a fresh experience. He kneaded away at the knots of frustration deep in her belly and breasts, firmly running his hands over her straining globes and letting them rub the oil deep into the areolae and nipples while small trickles ran into her armpits.

Some of the ache of frustration eased, but he aroused fresh sensations in her. She'd heard the other women sighing when he tended to them, and soon she knew why because he even massaged the tops of her inner thighs, and now and again his outspread fingers would accidentally brush against her pubic hair and her flesh would leap and pulsate only to be left alone as he again concentrated on the soft tissue of her limbs. Eventually she was placed back on her stomach, and now he was kneading her buttocks hard, pressing down on them so that her pelvis pressed against the hardness of the shelf and she wriggled.

'Lie still!' snapped Pavin unexpectedly. Deborah hadn't even realised he was still there. Her buttocks were parted, oil was dripped into the gap and then the masseur's finger was easing into her tight rectum, circling round and thrusting in, flicking against the walls, withdrawing and then beginning the whole cycle again until her legs started to twitch and her hips were unable to keep still.

'Enough!' said Pavin, and again it was Deborah's turn to groan. She felt like hitting him, so great was her frustration, but before she could do anything she was being wrapped in a long sheet of muslin, her arms pinned to her sides beneath it and then a sticky mud-like substance was spread over the material and she was left lying on her back, her pores opening with the heat of the treatment and her body seeming to turn to liquid, so soothing and yet sensual was the whole experience.

All the women were left like that for half an hour, then the wrappings were taken off and the men led them to the far end of the room. Now Tansy and Celia tried to run because they knew what was coming, but they were pushed back again and suddenly jets of ice cold water sprayed down on them and their warm, contented flesh was shocked by the icy contrast. They all screamed aloud.

When the water stopped each woman was taken by a man and rubbed down vigorously with rough cotton mittens that both dried and stimulated the flesh. By the time it was all over every one of them was pink and glowing, their blood racing and their tissue firm.

Pavin smiled at them. 'And now, I think, it's time for your deprivation to end. We'll pair off for this. Brian, you and Lizzie come with Deborah and me, the rest of you can sort yourselves out.'

Brian picked up Elizabeth, Pavin swept Deborah into his arms and the two women were carried out of the steam room, away from the rest of the group and up the stairs to Pavin's bedroom, where Lizzie and Deborah were finally to be allowed to reach satisfaction.

Chapter Twelve

'We'll take the ladies one at a time,' said Pavin, kicking the bedroom door shut behind him. 'Deborah, you won't mind waiting a little longer will you, sweetheart? It should add to the final moment for you!'

Deborah did mind, but as he was sitting her on the top of a tall three-legged stool that had been placed there during the course of the day and her ankles were tied to the legs before she even realised what was happening, there wasn't much she could do about it. Then he tied her hands behind her back again.

For a moment he stood in front of her, letting his eyes roam over her delicate, fair skin, then he drew a line tenderly round each of her breasts with one finger before turning back to the bed where Elizabeth was waiting.

'Fasten her to the bedposts,' Pavin said curtly. Brian used leather straps, rather than the silk scarves that had been used on Deborah the previous day. Again it was only Elizabeth's hands that were fastened, leaving her legs free for the men to move as they wished.

'Shall I take off the jewellery?' suggested Brian.

'No!' protested Elizabeth, her eyes nervous.

Pavin smiled. 'A good idea. It has to come off sometime, Lizzie. Even sleepers need to be sterilised, and I'm sure it doesn't hurt.'

Deborah watched as Brian put his hands on one of his wife's breasts, massaging it firmly until it was swollen and the nipple firm, then he twisted the tiny gold ring round until he located the small join which he had to separate with his fingernails. As he worked the nipple was stretched and tugged and when it was finally pulled through the hole and out of the pierced opening she bit on her bottom lip.

'I'll do the other one,' said Pavin. Elizabeth shivered. Brian had taken off the rings before, but he was a smaller man than the American and his touch more delicate. When Pavin's large fingers began to manipulate the remaining ring it moved roughly against her delicate tissue and he found it difficult to separate the opening so that her whole breast swung from side to side. It was more than uncomfortable, it caused her pain, and for Elizabeth this was highly arousing. Despite herself she began to tremble with sexual tension, and both the men knew she was taking pleasure from all that was happening.

When the second nipple ring was free, Brian looked at his employer. 'Do you want to take off the other ring?'

'I think so. I'm always afraid it might damage me! Part your legs wider, Elizabeth. We want you free of all these encumbrances before we begin our work in earnest.'

She was slow to respond, and almost casually Brian flicked her lightly across her already painful nipples with a silk cord. She groaned and her legs moved, enabling Pavin to spread her outer sex lips, massage the damp tissue for a few seconds and then start to open the clitoral ring as her little nub of pleasure slowly emerged.

This was a genuinely difficult ring to remove and during his efforts, Elizabeth's clitoris was stretched to its fullest extent as well as rubbed and pushed until at last he slid the smooth gold band off the end of the pierced clitoris and held it up in the air.

'There, definitely in need of sterilisation! Now, I think we can safely proceed. I hope you remembered to make that detour through the garden area earlier, Brian.'

Brian nodded. 'I certainly did.'

Sitting on the hard wooden stool, Deborah shifted restlessly at the sight of the other young woman's outstretched body so clearly sexually in need with the swollen red buds of nipples and the upthrust hips. Within herself too, desire grew.

Then, as she saw what Brian was picking up, Deborah almost stopped breathing. She nearly cried out a warning to Elizabeth, but then remembering the other woman's sexual preferences she kept silent. Even Elizabeth looked alarmed at what Brian held in his hand. Pavin's eyes were cool and amused. 'Come now, Lizzie. You enjoy saunas and the subsequent beating with twigs. I fail to see the difference between that and what we have planned for you here.'

Elizabeth didn't answer him. Already her whole body was shaking with spasms of delirious anticipation at the thought of the torment that lay ahead. It was diabolical, but it was what her flesh craved and for once it would be an entirely new experience. Even so, she was afraid.

Very slowly, Brian drew the bunch of greenery that he was holding in a gloved hand across his wife's upper belly. For a moment she was silent, and then as the effect of the nettles began to make itself felt she cried out and started to writhe while the small red marks of the sting rose on her olive skin.

'Wait!' Pavin commanded Brian. 'Let's see how she reacts.'

Elizabeth continued to writhe and drew her stomach backwards, away from the torment of the plant but all the time her breasts were swelling and when Pavin slipped a hand between her thighs she was very damp. He let his fingers slide up and down her inner channels and could feel the moisture spilling from her vaginal opening.

'She's enjoying it,' he said in a low voice. 'Aim them higher this time.'

As soon as Elizabeth stopped moving and her breathing became more regular, Brian looked into her dark, sensual eyes and enjoyed the confused mixture of fear and violent desire that he saw there as he trailed the plant along the undersides of her breasts, then up through the valley between them and down round the outsides of the heaving globes until the whole area was encircled by a trail of red dots.

The hot, stinging fire screamed through Elizabeth's flesh and she felt as though she was burning up with need for sexual release. Coils of excitement moved heavily deep inside her belly while her pelvis moved in sharp, spasmodic jerks towards the watching men. Just as the burning began to abate it seemed to recharge itself and all the time her breasts, still untouched by the plant, lusted for some kind of touch or stimulation.

Pavin had the perfect contrast ready. He went into the ante-room, removed a tub of raspberry ice cream from the freezer there and spooned some into his mouth. Then he went back into the bedroom and standing in front of Elizabeth licked all over the surface of her breasts, spreading the ice-cold mixture as he went. Her nipples rose even higher in frozen rigidity and the areolae darkened while blue veins showed through the thin skin.

Elizabeth shuddered and cried out with pleasure. The

nettle rash was still burning her while the ice cream chilled her breasts like snow and as she cried and thrashed, straining against her wrist bonds, Brian drew the nettles lovingly up the backs of her legs and over the paper-thin skin of the backs of her knees. Now her legs began to jerk and thrash as well and yet the men left her genitals untouched so that despite the glorious torture she couldn't climax.

Deborah felt as though she would burst. She had never imagined Pavin being capable of devising such torment for anyone, let alone seeing a woman like Elizabeth lost in the bliss of the apparently ecstatic results. Watching Elizabeth's rising need only increased Deborah's, and although she wasn't being stimulated in any way she gripped the sides of the stool more firmly with her legs and pressed down on the seat so that she could allow her aching flesh some kind of ease.

Now Elizabeth was untied and as she half-fell into Brian's arms, a naked Pavin moved back up the bed until his upper torso was reclining against a pile of pillows. Brian fastened a blindfold round his wife's eyes and then lowered her until she was lying with her back along the length of Pavin's naked front. After that, Brian drew up her legs on each side bending them back from the knees and Pavin, gripping her firmly just below her breasts, lifted the upper half of her body into the air arching her back so that, with her legs positioned in the way they were, her pelvis was also thrust higher and her sex lips stretched open. Deborah could see the glistening, excited inner tissue beneath the dense dark triangle of pubic hair.

For Elizabeth, being unable to see meant that she was tense with nervous anticipation of what the men might have in store for her, while at the same time her desire grew and grew because without that fear her climax when it came wouldn't be intense enough to satisfy her after a whole day's deprivation.

207

Looking at her, so arched and defenceless, Brian was consumed with desire for his young wife. They were so perfectly suited that he could no longer imagine a life without her, and seeing her on top of Pavin, being manhandled by him, even knowing she would be entered by him, but aware that she was his wife gave Brian intense satisfaction. These holidays only increased the depth of his feelings for her.

As Pavin instructed Elizabeth to keep herself arched so that he could adequately protect himself for what was to come, Brian took the opportunity to further tease the outstretched, waiting body in front of him.

He took a spray of dried flowers from a vase and with the lightest of touches drew it across the opening between Elizabeth's outer sex lips. Elizabeth's whole body contracted with fear because she was certain that it was still the nettle he was using and for once she wasn't sure that she could cope with the pain that would follow.

She waited and waited, trembling with fear and then felt the stroking motion again, only this time it actually twirled around her front opening and she gasped a protest. Brian stopped, and watched as she clenched every muscle against the expected burning pain. It was several seconds before she realised that it wasn't going to come, and then a sheen of perspiration broke out all over her body in relief and she started to relax back against Pavin, only to feel his huge erection, now protected and lubricated, forcing its way between her buttocks.

By any standard the American was a large man, and Elizabeth made the mistake of tensing against the invasion. As a result when he pulled her body down hard against him he thrust into her with unexpected violence and Deborah heard Elizabeth's cry of pain as he filled her in that always tight, but incredibly sensitive place.

Her cry seemed to encourage Pavin, who used his hands to move her up and down on him, and the resulting friction against the nerve endings in the walls of her rectum started to ignite the red-hot flames of desire again and her head went back until the nape of her neck was just above his mouth.

Pavin blew softly against the tender skin. He moved his head a little and let his tongue thrust into her ear just as he was thrusting into her tight little back passage. 'Tell us what you feel like!' he urged her. 'Talk to Brian and Deborah, explain how I feel inside you at this moment.'

Deborah wanted to tear herself free from the stool and join the couple on the bed. She wanted to be part of it all, to touch Lizzie's straining breasts or caress Pavin's testicles, now tightly drawn up against the base of his shaft. She needed to be involved.

'You're hurting me!' Elizabeth whispered.

'Louder!'

'You're hurting me!' she cried out. 'You're large, and I feel tight and too full, but it's incredible. I feel as though I'm going to explode I'm so hot and heavy, but I can't,' she added, her voice dropping again. 'I still can't come.'

By this stage, Brian had stripped off all his clothes and at last he too climbed onto the bed. He knelt between Pavin's legs and his wife's stretched thighs and using both hands began to massage her rippling stomach with circular motions, spreading his fingers out to include the skin over her hip bones, and all the time Pavin was still deep inside her back passage.

Elizabeth groaned and cried out, the violent streaks of blissful arousal were shooting through her body and she was almost out of her mind with the mixture of pain and pleasure the men were giving her.

At last Brian decided to enter her and then she was filled by the two men front and back and as they moved

209

together she was pushed from one erect penis to the other without pause while all her internal membranes were aroused to the very limit. Then Brian's hand drew back the soft fold of flesh covering her clitoris and despite the pain to himself he reached down to the bed and picked up a tiny strand of nettle left lying there for just this moment.

Deborah, wriggling and gasping on the stool, watched in shocked disbelief as he waited until Elizabeth was arched at exactly the right angle and then he lightly touched the unprotected mass of excruciatingly sensitive nerve endings with the tip of the nettle.

As Elizabeth's body went into a convulsion of dark pain-streaked delirium the two men thrust in and out of her, feeling the way every one of her muscles was contracting fiercely around them while she screamed and wailed in the throes of the most intense orgasm she'd ever experienced.

When her abused but blissfully sated body was finally still the men were still thrusting into her and she was forced to let them continue despite her desire for sleep. At last they both climaxed within seconds of each other and she was finally allowed to fall backwards onto Pavin while her husband collapsed on top of her, his skin brushing against her gloriously tortured flesh. It was the best end to a day of deprivation that Elizabeth could ever have imagined.

To Deborah's amazement, once the trio on the bed had finally recovered sufficiently to untangle their limbs and get back onto their feet, Brian and Elizabeth left the room with scarcely a glance in her direction.

'Off to have a cuddle I expect!' laughed Pavin, enchanted by Deborah's high colour and inability to sit still while he talked to her. 'Don't worry though. I shall have some help while I give you total pleasure. Sara is going to join us. She knows very well how to assist me at times like this.'

210

'I only need you,' said Deborah, straining her top half towards him. 'Just make love to me, Pavin. That's all I want.'

'No, this has to be special, honey. That's the whole point of the holiday. Don't worry, it won't be extreme like it was for Lizzie. We tailor the treatment to the recipient, and I know that isn't a turn-on for you, although watching it sure seems to be!'

Just then, there was a light tap at the door and Sara entered. She waited for Pavin's nod, then crossing to where Deborah was still fastened to the stool, bent and untied her legs. Together Pavin and his maid helped Deborah to her feet, Pavin massaging her aching calves as she struggled to stay upright.

In the meantime, Sara had fetched a bolster from the bed and with Deborah's hands still behind her she slipped it down her back, between her spine and her wrists which meant that when Pavin picked her up and placed her on the bed she was stretched round the down-filled bolster, her skin tighter than usual.

'I want to be untied,' she said.

Pavin shook his head. 'Believe me, you don't sweetie. This way it will be fantastic. Now, Sara, fetch the bowls.'

The maid went into the bathroom and returned carrying two bowls of water on a tray. Deborah turned her head but couldn't see what was in them, only that there were also two large sable brushes each about three inches wide.

Pavin dipped one brush into the first bowl and then drew it across his lover's bursting breasts. Deborah was startled by the touch of ice-cold water on her over-heated skin and her nipples and areolae contracted with the shock. He ignored her cry of protest and brushed the other breast just as carefully, only this time Deborah was tensed in readiness for the cold liquid. Tiny trickles ran down the undersides of her breasts and along her ribcage before running off down the sides of her waist.

No sooner had he finished than Sara dipped the second brush in the other bowl, and this time piping hot water was swept over the sensitive breast tissue, and the contrast was so amazing that Deborah actually whimpered and struggled against the bolster but again she was ignored.

Slowly Pavin and Sara continued the treatment across the whole of Deborah's body, working down her stomach to her pubic hair and then starting at her feet and working up her legs to the join at the top of her thighs so that they had covered all of her except for her actual genitals.

The sensation was extraordinary, and as they progressed relentlessly, Deborah found that her body actually hungered for the two contrasts. That her nerve endings gloried in the difference and her body tingled, feeling more alive than ever before. When they had finished, they dabbed her dry with soft squares of towelling, again only working on small areas at a time and she realised that the areas which were being neglected were straining with anticipation for their turn.

She was squirming now and her whole body was flushed. Pavin smiled at the sight. 'Now we must clean you between your thighs. Sara, push the soles of her feet together and then you must flatten your knees back as far as you can, Debs. That way we can see to every tiny crevice.'

His words fuelled her rising excitement and she did as he said without any hesitation, although it left her totally exposed to the maid's gaze as well as his. Now Pavin fetched a tiny brush and dipped this into a small bowl of baby bath solution, so as not to inflame the more delicate tissue. He teased the tip of the brush around her outer sex lips first, despite the fact that she was blatantly trying to push her inner mound towards him.

As her need for satisfaction grew, the outer lips flattened so much that he could no longer avoid the part Deborah longed to have him touch and he drew the pointed tip of the bristles up one damp, pink channel and down the other. Then he stopped, and Deborah groaned her need aloud.

For the next few minutes he teased her by brushing briefly at a tiny segment of that pulsating flesh before stopping, moving the brush and then flicking elsewhere just long enough to send the flashing jolts of bliss searing through her before stopping again.

Now Deborah's fastened body was leaping around on the bolster, her hips never still for a second but he refused to let the brush touch her clitoris or its stem and she was frantic for contact there. When Sara put a finger against Deborah's lips to silence her cries, Deborah sucked on it like a baby, drawing it inside her mouth and trying to pretend she was drawing Pavin inside her. He saw what she was doing and gloried in her blatant sexuality.

Her clitoris was very swollen now, visibly engorging with the increased blood supply but all he did was turn to Sara. 'I'm going to clean her opening here. When the brush moves, swirl your tongue inside her navel in time with my movements. Don't stop until I do.'

Hearing what he was about to do drove Deborah mad. 'Pavin, don't do this! Please, hurry up and let me come! I shall explode if you don't.'

'Nonsense! Ready, Sara?' The maid nodded. She had done this before, although Angela hadn't enjoyed it like Deborah was, and as his hand twirled the brush around the needy entrance, Sara's tongue plunged into the small dip of the hapless Deborah's belly button and she screamed with pleasure. Her legs, bent out at the knees, trembled violently but still she didn't come.

213

At last, Pavin took pity on her. He signalled for Sara to lick the swollen, red nipples standing out so despairingly and as she obeyed he at last let the moist tip of the brush swirl around the base of the clitoris and Deborah's climax was triggered.

She arched off the bolster, the soles of her feet parted and her legs jerked wildly while the long-suppressed tremors finally drew together into what felt like a tidal wave of release and her whole body was engulfed by the hot, jagged tearing sensations of her orgasm.

Pavin remained sitting where he was, holding her legs apart so that he could watch her sex pulsing as she came and when the climax was ebbing he grabbed her ankles, pushed the soles of her feet back together again so that she was in the same vulnerable position and then let the very tips of the fine sable actually slide into her almost unbearably sensitive and never before entered urethral opening.

Deborah didn't know what was happening to her. One moment the huge climax was slowing down, leaving her spent and relaxed and the next her whole body felt as though it had been shot through with an electric current and an incredible sensation of pressure grew in her bladder until she was afraid she was going to lose control of herself. Then that sensation spread out and down through her whole pelvic area and it seemed as though a giant hand was picking her up and shaking her as every possible part of her took on a life of its own. She was grateful when Pavin threw himself across her heaving body and then his mouth was on her breasts, greedily sucking at first one nipple and then the other while his teeth grazed the flesh around it and still the intense sharp-edged sensations coursed through her and she heard herself gibbering, crying out meaningless words as both her mind and body were completely taken over by the pleasures of the flesh that Pavin had triggered.

Even Pavin was taken aback by her response. When she was finally still she was sobbing with the intensity of it all, and he wrapped himself around her, calming and soothing her, assuring her that she was safe, no harm had come to her.

For Deborah it had been a mind-blowing experience, and to come down from such incredible heights of ecstasy to find herself being held tenderly and lovingly by this huge, sexual connoisseur of a man who seemed to represent everything that she desired was, if anything, the best part of it all.

Pavin wiped her forehead gently, while Sara discreetly collected up all the bowls and brushes and left them alone together. 'I take it you weren't dissatisfied with the end of your Deprivation Day?' he asked with a small smile.

Deborah gazed into his eyes and felt her heart beating against his chest. 'If it hadn't happened to me I'd never have believed it possible,' she said. 'It was out of this world.'

'It's the waiting that does it. A whole day spent in a state of sexual tension can have some pretty impressive results, but yours was one of the most impressive I've ever seen!'

'What happens now?' she murmured.

'Now,' said Pavin firmly, 'we both sleep.'

That night at dinner, all the women bore the expression of sleepy, contented cats. Even Flora seemed to have forgotten her grudge against Deborah and flashed her a brief smile as they passed.

'I hope the evening's entertainment's quiet,' Richard said to Deborah during dessert. 'Frankly, I'm exhausted.'

'I rather think we all are!'

Pavin looked down the table and tapped on the cloth with the handle of his spoon to get everyone's attention.

'I hope everyone's had a memorable day,' he said with a smile at the women sitting closest to him. 'Tonight we'll just watch a film, unless some of you want an early night. Tomorrow is a pretty free day, to enable us all to recover, but in the evening since the forecast's good, we'll have the annual beach barbecue.'

There was a general buzz of approval from the group and Deborah assumed that it would be a more exciting barbecue than others she'd attended.

'Unfortunately,' continued Pavin. 'I've had a rather important telephone call in the last half hour and it looks as though my stay on the island will have to be curtailed. I'm needed back in the States in three days time!'

Deborah stared at him in astonishment. He hadn't mentioned a word of this to her, and although she'd heard him on the telephone while she was in the bath, this was quite normal at that time of the day and he hadn't seemed perturbed when she'd rejoined him. She felt a small lump in her throat at the realisation that they might only have another forty-eight hours together.

'Does that mean we all have to leave?' asked Tansy. 'I sure as hell hope not!'

'I hadn't expected any of you to leave with me,' said Pavin quickly. 'After all, I make you men work hard so you're damned well entitled to play hard! Naturally Deborah would have to leave with me, but the rest of you are more than welcome to stay on. In my absence Richard would be in charge.'

'What about me?' asked Brian. 'I take over at work when you're away.'

'Sure you do,' said Pavin smoothly. 'The truth is, Brian, I don't trust you to keep yourself under control, let alone the whole party!'

For a moment it looked as though Brian was about to argue, but then he shrugged, turning his attention back

216

to his food. He knew that the American was right. He was qualified to run the business, but not this kind of holiday where his own sexual excesses could well ruin it for some of the other participants.

'Why didn't you tell me?' asked Deborah when the meal was over and they were making their way to the study where the film was to be shown.

'We'd been having such a good time, Debbie, I didn't want to ruin it before I had to. I was going to tell you when you came out of the bath, but you looked so happy and gave me one of those heartstopping smiles of yours and I couldn't bring myself to say a word.'

'So you told me in front of everyone else instead!'

He put an arm round her waist. 'I can't change it, honey. This is what my life's like. Sure, I usually manage to get a couple of weeks without interruption but this year it hasn't worked out that way and there's not a damned thing I can do about it. I'm not leaving you here without me, it's too risky. Anyway, I don't want to, so it means both our breaks are screwed up. Angela always said I was never content with spoiling just one life!'

'I don't want it to end,' said Deborah quietly. 'I'm having such a great time and . . .'

He put a finger to her lips. 'What is it they say about a game never being over 'til the last ball's bowled?'

'I've no idea; I'm not a cricket fan. Pavin . . .'

He squeezed her tightly. 'Let it go, Debs. We'll talk more later.'

'Come on,' said Tansy as she and Paul pushed their way past the couple. 'We want to watch the film. Is it something good, Pavin? Something new, never before seen by human eye?'

'You could say that,' he agreed.

'Pity about you having to go early,' added Tansy. 'Still, it's the first time it's happened.'

'Is that supposed to be a comfort?' asked Deborah.

217

Tansy looked at her in surprise. 'Hey, don't take on so. I'm sure Pavin will invite you back next year. She's fitted in well, hasn't she Pavin?'

'One of the best. Paul, is everything set up?'

'Yes; look, Pavin, about those figures you'll need when you go. I can always get them done during the night and . . .'

'You'll do no such thing; Tansy would kill me! Forget it, Paul. I can just about remember how to balance books and estimate forecasts.'

Inside the study stood a large white screen and at the back of the room a small projector had been set up on a retractable shelf.

When everyone was seated in comfortable armchairs, Flora stood up. As she turned to look at the assembled group, her eyes sought out Deborah.

'The film you're about to see,' she said with a grin, 'is not considered suitable for viewing until after ten o'clock at night. It was made on the first morning of the holiday here and it stars Pavin and me. We hope you enjoy it!'

As the rest of the group clapped and laughed, Deborah turned to Pavin who was sitting at her side.

'When did you make it?' she whispered.

'The morning you went for a stroll, honey. It didn't take long!'

Deborah tried not to show how little she wanted to watch what was about to be screened, knowing that she had no right to mind but very aware that she did. She couldn't help thinking that since she was beginning to care so much for Pavin perhaps it was a good job they were leaving early. Sharing him with all the other women for another week would have been extremely difficult, despite the compensations of the kind of sex she herself was having.

'Lights out,' called Pavin. 'Let the film begin!'

Chapter Thirteen

When the film opened, Pavin and Flora were walking hand in hand towards the bed Flora usually shared with Richard. They slowly undressed each other, until Pavin was entirely nude and Flora had on only hold-up stockings and a black lace bra.

Then, to Deborah's amazement, Pavin stretched himself down on his back with his arms and legs extended in an X-shape and allowed Flora to tie his wrists and ankles to the bedposts. She had never even considered that Pavin might be willing to surrender control in such a way and found it immediately arousing. He had always seemed such a dominant personality, but if she could have him at her mercy she knew that there were countless things she could do to tease and inflame him, just as she'd been teased during the holiday.

Unfortunately for her it was Flora who was in this position on the film, and when he was securely fastened, Flora opened a second door into the room and the young maid Sara joined the couple.

She was already naked, but stood in front of Flora for an examination of her body. Flora ran her hands assessingly over the large, full-nippled breasts, squeezing them together and running the tip of her tongue across the nipples, then releasing them she spread the maid's legs apart and felt between her thighs.

'You're still quite dry,' she said approvingly. 'That means Pavin will have to work all the harder for his satisfaction. Well done.'

Sara remained silent, seemingly aware that her role was a strictly passive one. She was to be used by Flora on Pavin, but quite how Deborah couldn't make out. The rest of the group seemed to have some inkling, and there was already a sense of sexual excitement in the air. On Deborah's left she was aware of Brian slipping his hand up beneath the hem of Elizabeth's skirt.

On the screen, Pavin lifted his head to look over at the maid and immediately his large but flaccid penis stirred slightly. Flora flicked at it with a finger and his stomach jerked. 'You've a long way to go yet, Pavin,' she cautioned him. 'Better keep that as still as possible.'

She then signalled for Sara to step forward, and the maid hesitated at the outstretched feet of her employer. 'He has to bring you to three climaxes with his mouth before he's allowed his own,' explained Flora with a lazy smile. 'Obviously that wouldn't normally pose too much of a problem for him, but I shall be trying to add a little extra excitement as he works on you. That should test his self-control to the limit.'

'I may take a long time, Miss Stewart,' confessed Sara softly. 'I'm very tired today.'

'All the better. Pavin likes to extend his endurance time every summer. We'll start as soon as you're ready.'

With obvious apprehension the maid climbed onto the bed, and the sight of her sex mound exposed as she clambered over Pavin's naked body made all the men in the room feel definite stirrings of desire despite their exhausting day.

Within a few seconds, Sara had positioned her naked vulva over Pavin's face and she crouched a few inches above him for several seconds so that he could see her intimately without being able to touch her in any way.

Immediately his penis sprang into full erection and Flora carefully poured a few drops of baby oil into the palm of her hand and then spread them around his shaft. Pavin gave a soft 'Aaah!' of appreciation, mixed with reluctance to allow himself to dwell too soon on the pleasures of his own flesh when he had to satisfy Sara three times.

'Lower yourself,' Flora told the maid, and Sara gratefully settled so that she was squatting within reach of his tongue. Pavin stretched upwards, the cords on his neck tight as he ran the very tip not on her sex lips but through the tender folds of skin at the joins of her thighs.

This seemed to please Sara who soon altered her position so that he was forced to allow his tongue to slide along the gradually widening gap between her outer sex lips and then skimmed it over her still pressed together inner lips, trying to tease them apart by running it upwards from the vaginal opening.

Sara, despite her earlier plea of exhaustion, responded quite quickly to this and her inner lips parted speedily so that now Pavin could flick at the inner walls of her damp love channels until the maid was bouncing above him, her excitement visibly mounting.

Just as visible was Pavin's excitement. His testicles were swollen and when Flora let the baby oil trickle across their surface his whole body tensed in an effort to subdue the pace of his rising climax.

Seeing the man she adored lying there excited almost to breaking point by two other women was almost more than Deborah could stand. Whilst everyone else simply enjoyed the sexuality of the scene, she felt stabs of jealousy that were just as piercing as the stabs of sexual arousal also growing within her.

Once Pavin could feel Sara's juices flowing, he located

her tiny clitoris and drew it carefully into his mouth, then sucked on it with one long steady drawing motion that caused Sara to gasp and throw her head backwards in shock.

'Try and slow down,' called Flora, but it was too late. Even from the back view it was quite plain to the watchers that Sara promptly had her first climax as she shuddered and ground herself downwards onto Pavin's clever lips and tongue.

When she'd finished, Pavin's erection looked cruelly swollen and his testicles were now drawn right up to his body. Flora ignored this and let her own mouth slip over the head of his glans, sucking softly just as he had sucked on Sara, only without the prolonged intensity that had finished the maid.

Pavin struggled against his bonds and tried to distract himself from the sensations by causing discomfort in wrists or ankles, but the bindings were soft and it was impossible. Instead he had to strain against every natural inclination, trying to subdue his excited flesh despite the warm moistness of the maidservant that was now resting on his chest.

'Turn around, Sara,' Flora ordered her. 'I want to see your face this time, and tilt your upper torso forward a little.'

This pleased the group watching the film because it meant they would be able to see Sara's growing excitement and her face at the moment of climax, as well as Pavin's struggle to control himself, but Deborah didn't want to see the maid taking her pleasure from Pavin. She half-rose from her seat, only to feel the American's hand pulling her down again.

'You can't leave,' he hissed. 'Everyone will think you're jealous, and that's the last thing we want on these holidays.'

'I'm tired,' she protested feebly.

'Then close your eyes, only I'd rather you didn't. I

want you to watch,' he added, his hand going round her to cup one quiescent breast. 'I enjoy having you here with me while this is on. It makes me want you again.'

She knew that he was right and she had to stay, but felt a flicker of distress that he could so happily let her watch him with another woman. She began to appreciate that the depth of his feelings for her were not perhaps the same as hers for him.

On the film, Sara's new positioning was helpful to Pavin. It meant that by moving his head back and forth he could use the bridge of his nose to keep her inner lips apart and stimulate her clitoris again. Even the fact that it was once more protected by its little hood of flesh didn't matter because he could nudge this aside with each movement, and as the feelings this caused were so delightful, Sara didn't try and move out of his way.

On the contrary, she was clearly having the time of her life. Now that she was facing the camera they could see her wide, excited eyes and the flush on her cheeks while her breasts had filled out until they were firm, almost hard, and the nipples fully extended, long and surprisingly dark in colour.

Deborah looked away from the maid and back to between Pavin's legs. Flora was watching Sara as well, and she knew that the girl's unconstrained joy in what was being done to her must be arousing Pavin more than he was letting on.

As Sara slowly approached her second orgasm some clear fluid appeared in the slit at the top of Pavin's glans and Flora took a small strip of silk and drew it across the fluid, so that the moisture was absorbed. She then rolled the end of the silk into a thin line and as Sara cried out with excitement and Pavin inserted his tongue into the maid's vaginal opening, curling it upwards to try to find her G-spot, Flora inserted the point of the silk into the now clear dry slit. Pavin gasped aloud and

Deborah distinctly heard him give a muffled exclamation.

Pavin's stomach heaved violently and he exhaled sharply so that his warm breath covered Sara's frantic, throbbing clitoris just as his tongue managed to find the spot it was looking for, and this precipitated her second climax.

Watching the maid come was extremely erotic. Her head went back so that they could all see her taut, creamy neck with a heavily beating pulse in the soft dip at the base, while her breasts rose and her thighs, gripped on each side of Pavin's chest, shook violently with the intensity of her orgasm. When she slumped forward everyone watching exhaled with her.

All around Deborah there were soft murmurings and the sound of rustling material and sliding hands, but she was only aware of the fact that Pavin's grip on her breast had tightened and that her flesh was responding despite her own exhaustion and her mixed emotions at the scene on the screen.

She began to feel the heavy ache inside her stomach that meant she would eventually need sexual release, and when she shifted uneasily on her seat she realised that she was moist between her thighs.

Trying to ignore her physical reactions she looked back at the screen.

'You're coming rather quickly, Sara,' said Flora reprovingly.

'I can't help it!' protested the maid. 'He's so clever the way he . . .'

'Well, try and hold this last one back a little longer.'

The maid nodded, and then repositioned herself so that it was harder for Pavin to reach her. By making him stretch further she hoped to slow him down.

In the meantime, Flora was gliding a well-oiled finger along the American's highly sensitive perineum. Deborah could tell from the way his leg muscles clenched and his fingers curled into the palms of his hands that this was affecting him, and he worked all the harder on the girl above his head.

He was at a disadvantage now because Sara had tired and her body wasn't anxious to be rearoused. Despite licking and sucking as he had before, she merely wriggled a little but there was no sign of pre-orgasmic tension. It looked from his straining penis as though he was going to come before the maid did.

Flora clearly thought so too, but just in case she was wrong she decided to make it impossible even for Pavin to control himself. As her finger moved back along the perineum she let it brush briefly against the opening between his buttocks and he strained to lift himself away from her but his bonds meant the relief was very temporary.

Deborah knew that Pavin hated to lose at anything, and she could tell that he immediately began to increase his attentions on the maid. From small wriggles, Sara's movements began to quicken in tempo as Pavin changed tactics and used his tongue more as a rod than a feather. He kept it rigid and thrust it in and out of her vagina, then spread the resulting milky fluid up along her inner lips so that she was well lubricated for him. This meant that her clitoris at last began to swell again, and her stomach grew round and hard with the added tension.

Flora realised that Pavin was doing better and so she let her finger glide up and down the underside of his shaft three times, then slid it back to the testicles, circled them with a feather-light touch and finally allowed it to go right beneath him, up between his clenched buttocks and into the opening that he was straining to keep closed against her invading finger.

The baby oil meant it was impossible for him to keep her out, and once Flora's finger was inside, softly moving in tiny circles as it prepared to massage his prostate gland, Pavin knew that he had to make Sara come before it actually reached the gland or he'd be lost.

Still keeping his tongue rigid, he stopped all movement for a moment. Sara's stimulated body didn't know what was happening and she froze in surprise, her eyes staring in puzzlement directly into the camera. Then Pavin drummed the hard point of his tongue incessantly against the stem of her tense, unprepared and swollen nub.

After the moment's stillness it was all the more arousing, and this time Sara actually screamed as the pleasure flooded over her for a third and final time and her muscles bunched in ecstatic release.

Flora, who had just been preparing to touch the unbearably sensitive gland deep within the American, had to withdraw her finger. She glared at the rosy-faced and now sated Sara with barely concealed anger.

'You were meant to last longer than that!'

Sara shook her head. 'I'm sorry, miss. I couldn't.'

Pavin lifted his head from the pillow. 'Let the girl go, Flora and untie me. I think you'll have to admit defeat again this year!'

As Sara hurried from the room, Flora released Pavin from the bed. He was still hugely erect, and as soon as he was free he was pushing Flora up against the wall, his head bent to her breasts as he sucked on her already swollen nipples through the black lace bra.

It seemed as though he couldn't wait to pay her back for what she'd put him through, and he tore the bra from her with his teeth, letting the frayed edges of lace dangle against the sides of her breasts as he bit and sucked on them ferociously.

Flora was clearly enjoying his aggression, but when she bent herself forward from the waist in readiness for him to penetrate her he grabbed hold of her instead and bundled her onto the bed, her head hanging down from the foot of it.

Then he positioned himself across her upper torso and his huge hands grasped the breasts that were now damp, swollen and heavy from his mouth and pushed his rock-hard erection between the two globes.

'I want you inside me!' gasped Flora.

Pavin ignored her. He knew what he wanted, and he'd waited a long time for it. His hands pressed hard on the outsides of Flora's breasts, and he thrust his penis in and out between them until at last he felt the hot liquid rising up through his shaft. Then he withdrew from between the breasts and as his seed finally spilled out of him he directed it so that it covered Flora's nipples and areolae, massaging it into them as it fell. Only when the last drops had disappeared did he release her.

Flora gazed up at him. 'What about me?' she asked with a smile.

Pavin smiled back at her. 'This was my treat, remember? You'll have plenty of fun during the next two weeks.'

The expression of incredulous dismay on Flora's face almost made the whole thing worthwhile for Deborah, but just as the other woman rolled onto her face to hide her dismay, Pavin took a small vibrator from the bedside table and slowly but expertly used it all over her body and genitals until she too had reached a full and satisfying climax.

As Flora's face, still taut from her orgasm, filled the screen, the film came to an end and then they were all left in total darkness for a few seconds before the lights came on and on Deborah's left she distinctly heard the small muffled sighs of total pleasure coming from Elizabeth.

Once the lights were on drinks were poured for everyone, but Brian and Elizabeth took theirs away to

227

their room. 'Obviously their kind of film!' laughed Martin.

Deborah looked across the room to where Pavin was talking animatedly to Flora. 'I'm not sure it was mine.'

He looked thoughtfully at her. 'Why don't we take a stroll round the grounds? I could do with some fresh air and it's still light out there.'

Deborah decided that was a good idea. Somehow the cloying sexual tension in the room, the obvious excitement engendered by the film, were too overpowering for her and since Pavin clearly wasn't ready to go to bed a walk was a welcome diversion.

As they strolled across the courtyard Martin took hold of her hand. 'You didn't like that, did you?'

'It was very sexy,' she replied cautiously. 'I could quite see why everyone enjoyed it.'

'But you didn't?' he persisted.

'No, not much.'

He sat down on a wooden bench, its slats weathered by age. 'You know, it doesn't do to get emotionally involved with people like us.'

'But most of you are involved emotionally; you bring your partners here!'

'We were in steady relationships before we took these holidays. You've fallen for Pavin since the holiday began.'

'I fell for him the first night we met,' she confessed. 'It was purely physical at first, but now it's more.'

'And that's what's making it difficult for you?'

Deborah nodded. 'I suppose so. What I don't understand is why I can easily take pleasure from other people myself, but I don't like watching Pavin do the same thing.'

Martin stared off into the distance. 'It's partly the very fact that you're not in a secure relationship with him. If you were then all the rest would just be fun. As it is, you and Flora are really in competition with each other. Pavin knows this. It probably amused him to sit with you watching himself and Flora having a thoroughly good time.'

'He isn't like that!' protested Deborah. 'He genuinely believes this holiday is simply for fun. He never meant me to get as involved as I have, and nor did I.'

'Well, you are and you can't alter that, so what do you intend to do once you get back to London? This kind of lifestyle is rather a hard act to follow.'

'I think I'll travel,' said Deborah decisively. 'I've never had the courage before, but after this I don't think it will seem much of a risk. I'll try working my way round the world.'

Martin laughed. 'You'd be snapped up before you'd gone through Europe. Besides, will Pavin prove that easy to forget?'

'I've no idea, but I'll have to try won't I? Unless you think he's intending to employ me himself?'

Martin looked genuinely shocked. 'Heavens, no! I wasn't suggesting anything like that. He really isn't that keen on having the British working for him. He likes the women but can't work out what makes the men tick. I think he prefers people to shout and make a loud noise when things go wrong. Because I don't, he imagines I don't realise what's happening. That's why I'm in public relations, you know. He said since I was always so damned agreeable he'd put it to good use and I could be agreeable to potential opponents or troublemakers!'

'But you like him?' asked Deborah.

'Everyone likes Pavin. I like these holidays too. They always cheer Celia up. She's very Celtic you know; dark and brooding. Without the breaks I'm not sure I'd keep her happy.'

Deborah was surprised. 'Surely you don't intend to go on taking these sort of holidays as you get older?'

'Why not? Pavin's still going strong and he's forty-

229

two. I've some way to go before that and as long as I'm still in his employment I hope I continue to be invited. I'd find Brighton a bit boring, don't you think!'

'So, what would you advise?' asked Deborah.

'That you try not to take anything too seriously; get as much personal satisfaction from your last couple of days as you can and then busy yourself in the publishing world again. There must be work for someone like you, and after a while all this will seem like a kind of dream.'

Deborah stood up and turned back towards the castle. 'I'm sure you're right, but it won't be possible. You see, I'm not the same person any more. I shall have to travel, or move abroad permanently. I need a different kind of life now. Pavin's ruined me for the one I used to lead! But I definitely shall make sure I get as much satisfaction as I can before I go.'

'Well, as long as you do what you really want it's sure to work out,' said Martin with a smile.

'One thing,' added Deborah. 'Do you think Pavin will marry Flora?'

'I used to think so, now I'm not so sure. We'd better be getting back, the breeze is cooler than I expected.'

In the library there was only Flora, Pavin and Celia left. All the others had gone to bed.

'Where were you?' demanded Celia.

'He took me out for some air; I felt a bit faint,' said Deborah.

Flora smiled knowingly. 'Film too much for you?'

'No, I'm overtired from earlier exertions,' responded Deborah sweetly, and had the satisfaction of seeing the other woman's smile fade.

Pavin laughed. 'I thought you two Brits had run off with each other for a quick midnight swim. You'd have needed wet suits though, the water's freezing.'

'I quite like the idea of Deborah in a wet suit,' laughed Martin as he and Celia left.

Pavin pulled Deborah to him and hugged her. 'Why didn't you tell me you were going outside?'

'Aren't we free to do as we like here?' asked Flora sharply.

Pavin looked at her over Deborah's head. 'Sure we are, but you know as well as I do that we usually say if we're going off with just one other person.'

'We were only taking a stroll!' laughed Deborah, revelling in the feeling of being held so tightly against him and knowing too that Flora must be highly irritated.

'She's in no danger from Martin,' retorted Flora, deciding that it was time she joined Richard who at least was always pleased to see her. 'He likes his women small and dark.'

'He's no different from the rest of us,' retorted Pavin. 'He likes women, just as you ladies all like men! Come on, Debs. Time for bed.'

When they were lying side by side in the darkness, Deborah decided to ask Pavin something that had been puzzling her from the moment the film began. 'Didn't you mind being tied up?' she asked softly. 'You're normally in such a powerful position, didn't you hate it?'

'I loved it, honey. Believe me, there's nothing like giving up all responsibility and letting two lovely ladies take care of you, even if you are turning it into a kind of challenge.'

'Would you have enjoyed it even if you'd lost?'

He was silent for a moment. 'Maybe not; I'll have to wait until I do and then I'll know. If I don't then I shan't play it again. That's one advantage of running your own party, you can always drop the games you tire of!'

She snuggled against him and closed her eyes in preparation for sleep. 'Sometimes I don't think you're anything more than an overgrown schoolboy, Pavin.'

He guided her hand to where his penis was beginning to stir. 'Very overgrown, I'm afraid. We'd better get to

231

sleep before I have to do something about this. Sleep well, honey.'

Rather to her surprise, she did.

The next morning, Pavin decided to have a lie-in and remembering that it was a quiet day with nothing special planned, Deborah dressed casually in a pleated button-through linen skirt and cotton camisole top. She thought that she might try walking right round the island before lunch.

During breakfast everyone discussed their plans. Some of the women wanted to simply swim and laze around in the steam room but Tansy was persuaded to join Paul, Martin and Richard in the dungeon. 'We don't want to waste the plastic surgeon's efforts,' said Richard. 'What about you, Debbie?'

'I thought I'd like to walk right round the island,' replied Deborah.

'On your own?'

'I'll go with her,' volunteered Brian.

Everyone waited for Deborah's response. She wasn't sure what to say. Brian held an attraction for her that she tried to deny, knowing it was the kind of attraction that led to destruction. She was about to refuse his offer, and then suddenly remembering her talk with Martin, decided to accept. She would soon be gone, and was highly unlikely to meet up with Brian again. She would let herself spend some time alone with him and find out exactly what it was that drew her to him.

'I'd like that,' she said slowly.

'As long as you're sure,' said Richard, and then they all went their separate ways.

'You know, I didn't expect you to accept my offer, especially after what happened at Puffin's Cove,' confessed Brian.

'I wasn't going to, but I changed my mind.'

They walked for some time in comparative silence,

Brian occasionally pointing out a rare arctic skua in the sky, one pursuing a tern until it dropped the fish it was holding in its beak. She saw oystercatchers, ringed plovers and redshanks as well as a beautiful hen harrier.

'You know all about feathered birds too!' she laughed when he'd finished describing the nesting habits of the short-eared owl with great enthusiasm.

Brian laughed. 'Since coming here I've kind of gotten into this stuff more. It relaxes me, something that nothing else has been able to do.'

'Not even marriage to Elizabeth?'

He grinned. 'Marriage to Elizabeth is bliss and all I could ever want but it is not and never will be relaxing!'

After he'd shown her a long and rather frightening chambered cairn, or 'burial ship' as Brian called it, the couple sat down on the surrounding grassy area and raised their faces to the sun.

'It hasn't rained once since I got here!' exclaimed Deborah. 'I always imagined the Orkneys to be drab little islands.'

'They're bleak as hell in winter, but a genuine haven in the summer,' he responded, rolling onto his back and pulling her down beside him. 'Why did you agree to me coming with you then?' he added.

'Because I wanted to find out what it is about you that I find attractive,' retorted Deborah.

Brian laughed. 'That's honest! Maybe it's my lean and hungry look?'

'I lived with a man who had a lean and hungry look, and this isn't the same kind of attraction. I know very well you'd be bad for me, Brian, but I often find myself looking at you and wondering what it would be like to be Elizabeth. To have you in my bed and close to me every day.'

'You're right about one thing, I'd be bad for you,' he said slowly. 'I've been at this game too long. I need more than ordinary women can give in order for my interest to be sustained. Besides, when I look at you I know we're bad for each other too. You see, I could get to like hurting you and I think I could get you to like it. Then where would we be?'

'Where you and Elizabeth are.'

He shook his head. 'Not so, Debbie. Elizabeth is a genuine masochist. You're not, so I'd be changing you, twisting your nature and that isn't good for anyone.'

'Make love to me,' she said suddenly. 'Don't think about who I am or what I want, just do it.'

'I only make love to Elizabeth, Debbie. I have sex with everyone else. It's good sex, and I'm involved, but it isn't making love. I want you to know that before we begin.'

'That's all right,' said Deborah, feeling a wild abandonment rising up inside her and astonished at her own behaviour. 'It won't be lovemaking for me either.'

'I know,' said Brian. 'You keep that for Pavin, only he probably doesn't realise it yet. You are sure about this, Deborah? Once we start, there's no going back. Don't try calling a halt on me at the last minute.'

'I won't. I need to know what you're like, and why I want you the way I do. I'll be leaving soon, this might be my only chance to find out, and that's what this holiday's for, isn't it? To do the things we want but wouldn't usually have the chance to try?'

Brian propped himself on one elbow and looked down at her, his eyes so dark they looked black and his face very pale. 'All right, Deborah. You've convinced me. I'll show you exactly the kind of person I am. Who knows, you might learn something about yourself as well.'

Chapter Fourteen

*D*eborah closed her eyes, waiting for some kind of touch from Brian's lips or hands to indicate that they were going to begin their sexual enjoyment of each other, but instead he roughly tore at the buttons on her skirt and then rolled her off it, her long legs splaying out on the coarse grassland. After that he put his thumbs down each side of her briefs and jerked them down her legs, twisting her knees as he struggled to get them off and over her feet.

Within a matter of seconds she was bare from the waist down, and then he was tugging at her camisole top, pulling it up over her head and dragging her arms down through the openings without any care or thought for her comfort.

Only when she was entirely nude did he pause, and she opened her eyes to see him balanced over her, his weight taken on his arms as he drank in the long, lean lines of her pale body.

He was still fully clothed, and when he lowered himself onto her the zip of his jeans rubbed against her abdomen. She tried to protest but he placed a hand across her mouth and continued to rub himself up and down her, until raising himself up again on his arms in order to see how his efforts had brought the blood to the surface of her whole body area. She was now flushed red and her nipples were far darker and harder than before.

She looked and felt slightly dazed by the speed with which he'd moved, and he took advantage of this to tear off his own clothes while she remained unmoving on her back. Then he lay on his side, propped up on an elbow and with his free hand he reached out and took one of the protruding nipples between his fingers. He held it lightly at first, but then his grip increased until the first tremors of pleasure turned into a sharp, shooting pain that radiated right through the breast.

Deborah gasped, and at once Brian covered her mouth with his, his tongue invading her lips and teeth, thrusting into her, plundering every soft part of her gentle mouth. At first she resisted, but then as the pain from her imprisoned nipple grew unbearable, she responded with equal savagery and her tongue thrust into his mouth, down between his teeth and deep into his throat until she felt him bite on her tongue and this made her jerk her head away as his mouth finally left her.

Her nipple was released too, but as his legs imprisoned hers between his lean but strong legs, he used the same mouth that had just plundered hers to fasten on to her other, as yet untouched breast, and now he was biting and sucking on that while his free hand scratched lightly across her belly and the sensitive inward curves of her waist.

Deborah had never before had her flesh so savagely attacked in this way. Lovebites had always been gentle, playful nips, not the kind of demanding pain-inducing marks of domination Brian was inflicting and yet she knew, as deep down a part of her had always known she would, that she was responding to him.

236

Her hands went round his back and her nails scratched at the skin across his shoulders, digging in so hard that even Brian was aware of the pain and his mouth attacked her breast with renewed ferocity. The hand that had been scratching at her belly moved lower, he spread her legs wide with his own and without even testing to see if she was aroused thrust three fingers into her opening.

Deborah was aroused, she was more than ready for him and her body bucked against the fingers as they moved rapidly in and out of her until very quickly she was shuddering with her first orgasm. Brian felt her internal muscles contracting around his fingers and knew that she'd been right; deep inside the cool blonde was a creature as capable of wild savage sex as he was and for this short time they could undulge themselves.

Even as her last tremors were dying away he was turning her onto her front, and now the breasts and tender abdominal skin that he had already marked were rubbed hard against the prickly, scrubby brushland that characterised the island and she felt as though a thousand tiny pins were sticking into her.

Brian pressed against her back, forcing the breasts down harder until he heard her cry out with the pain and then he lifted a tube of jelly-like lotion from the pocket of his jeans and spread it all round her buttocks and into the surrounding creases until she was squirming with delight.

Her buttocks were marked by the pressure of the scrubland earlier and the jelly cooled and soothed them, but at the same time Deborah knew that soon Brian would be using it to lubricate another area; a hot, tight area that was already tensing with fearful desire for his attentions.

Grateful that he'd brought the tiny vibrator that Elizabeth so loved with him, Brian swirled the tip of that in some of the jelly that was covering Deborah's buttocks and then tried to slip it into her tightly puckered opening but Deborah was ready for him and she drew in her muscles so that it was almost impossible for him to do as he wanted.

She was revelling in it all. She wanted the vibrator inside her as much as he did, and she wanted to go on feeling the weight of him pressing her sore but stimulated flesh into the island's earth, but she sensed that resistance was something he both liked and expected from her at this point.

Brian sat astride the tops of her thighs and pushed a hand between her belly and the ground, then pressed upwards so that her buttocks were automatically raised. As they raised, Deborah forgot to keep her internal muscles contracted and immediately the vibrator was slipped into the opening and switched on.

He moved it with cunning calculation, letting it touch each of the highly sensitive walls in turn, then bringing it right back to the entrance and allowing it to vibrate there until her bowels began to clench with a desire to move and she felt herself heaving with the effort of constraining them.

Then, knowing how she felt, he allowed the vibrator to move deeper inside her until finally it came to rest against the T-bar at the base.

This meant that he could leave it in place, still vibrating, and turn her over once more. The face that looked up at him was wild with desire and a kind of uncivilised sexual hunger he had rarely seen on a woman's face before.

He caught hold of her long, wonderfully-shaped legs and thrust them sharply upwards. Deborah felt as though they were going to tear at the groin so high did he stretch them, but then all at once they were resting on his shoulders and despite the discomfort she was grateful because she could imagine that this would enable him to penetrate her deeper than anyone had ever penetrated her before.

'Yes!' she moaned as he came closer, watching her red, trembling breasts which still bore the marks of his teeth and noticing her swollen mouth, bruised from his savage kisses earlier. 'Please, do it to me now!'

Taking his weight on one arm he drove into her with as much power as he could, and at the same time as his penis filled her vagina and the vibrator titillated her rectum, his fingers, in complete contrast, tenderly peeled back her outer sex lips and then skimmed across her inner moist surfaces. They swirled and pressed in such a skilled way that her orgasm grew nearer and nearer as her clitoris strained from its sheath longing for the merest suggestion of a touch from him.

Brian wished that he had a camera; that he could record for ever Deborah's total abandonment to his savage plundering of her body, but he knew that even a photo wouldn't fully show the transformation that had taken place in her.

As one hand continued to delicately arouse her vulva, his mouth closed harshly about the most inflamed nipple and once more flashes of pain filled her sensitive breast area, but she didn't care. She was a mass of pulsating, frantic desire and when at last he allowed his thumb to caress the very tip of the swollen bud while at the same time pulling her nipple out to its full extent and holding it there so that the areola was puckered into a small gathering of flesh, Deborah exploded.

She screamed an almost primitive cry of release into the air and it was drowned in the cries of the birds as they lazily circled in the sky above them. As she screamed so her muslces pulsed, the walls of her rectum closed tightly around the vibrator and Brian felt her gripping his penis with a fierceness that matched the way he was gripping her breast, so that he too bucked

239

and convulsed in the throes of a wonderfully intense climax. He too cried out to the elements.

When it was over they drew apart quickly, both of them startled by the easy way in which they'd fallen into a pattern together. After a time Brian pulled on his clothes. 'We'd better carry on walking or we won't be back for lunch and they'll send out a search party.'

'I knew it would be like that,' Deborah murmured.

He glanced at her flesh, still marked by his loveplay. 'It was better than I expected,' he confessed.

Deborah began to fasten her skirt. 'It isn't what I normally want,' she explained, hoping no one would notice the tear in her camisole top. 'It's just something I had to do once.'

'I know. Like going on a Big Dipper or trying white-water rafting.'

'I suppose so.'

He pulled her to her feet. 'Pavin's right for you; we'd destroy each other. If this is how it begins, imagine how it would end.'

He was right, and Deborah knew it, but she would always be pleased that at least she'd had the experience. Such total, pagan abandonment of the senses wasn't someting everyone could try. She'd enjoyed it, but it wasn't something she would ever attempt again.

After a quick lunch, Deborah decided that she needed a rest before the evening's barbecue and took one of Pavin's books of erotica from the library in the east wing. She then spent the afternoon lying on a lounger beside the pool, enjoying the tropical-style heat and the collection of short, highly arousing stories, while in the pool Pavin, Richard, Flora and Celia enjoyed themselves in their own version of water sports.

At six o'clock they all went off to their rooms to get ready for the evening and, for the first time since her morning walk, Deborah was alone with Pavin. He

240

seemed slightly subdued for him. She wondered if it was his work or the fact that she'd chosen to go off with Brian which was the cause.

He soon let her know. 'Why did you choose Brian?' he asked abruptly as he threw himself down on the bed.

'Because I felt like it,' she replied. 'Isn't that the only reason necessary here?'

He didn't turn his head to look at her. 'Sure, but I can't help wondering why him.'

'I was drawn to him and I didn't know why; I wanted to find out.'

Pavin gave a soft laugh, deep in his throat. 'And did you find out?'

'Yes, I did.'

He rolled onto his side and now they were lying face to face. 'Did you enjoy the experience?'

Deborah hesitated, wondering whether honesty was necessarily the best policy. It was all very well to talk about total sexual freedom and lack of jealousy, but the very fact that Pavin was questioning her suggested he was unusually curious about the answer. The last thing she wanted to do was put him off her, but on the other hand he claimed that this holiday was his idea of perfection, in which case he might simply want to know the answer in order to gain some kind of private pleasure from her reply. In her mind her response took on the importance of the answer to an exam question and she tried to think how best to phrase what had occurred between her and Pavin's right-hand man.

'Yes, I did enjoy it,' she said at last. 'He has this intensity, a harshness to his sexuality that's so urgent it's positively dangerous, and I needed to experience it just once.'

'Once was enough?' asked Pavin, sounding as though he found that difficult to believe.

'Yes, because I responded too well. I nearly matched

him some of the time and that isn't the way I want to be. I accept it's a part of me, that sometimes I might be attracted to that kind of man because of this, but it isn't who I really am.'

'You mean, you'd enjoy meeting up with him another year, on this island say for another holiday session, but you don't want his kind of lovemaking the whole time?'

Deborah nodded, her eyes held by the piercing gaze from the American's blue eyes. 'I'm not an Elizabeth; Brian would destroy me.'

'You don't think he'll destroy her?'

'No!' exclaimed Deborah. 'Don't you see, if anything Elizabeth could destroy Brian because he needs her so much. He also loves her.'

'Loves her?' This time Pavin sounded incredulous.

'Before we began he said that he only made love to his wife. That everything else was purely sex.'

'Is that so? Then I guess you're right, honey, Elizabeth holds all the cards. It's strange, I spent the morning with her, and I could see the attraction in her submission, her total abandonment to the pleasure of pain, but I also knew that I couldn't live with someone like that. There has to be more for me.'

Deborah wished he hadn't told her. All at once the green-eyed monster, jealousy, was back and she had trouble maintaining eye contact with Pavin. 'What did you do together?' she asked softly.

'Hey, that's an out-of-bounds question! I didn't ask you for a blow-by-blow account and I don't expect to give you one. Let's be thankful we found they don't suit us but they do suit each other and leave it there.'

Deborah ran a hand over his chest, letting her nails scratch delicately over the skin and knowing full well that this always aroused him. 'Who does suit you?' she whispered.

He grabbed her hand and folded it tightly in his, scrunching her fingers up so that she had to pull away because he was hurting her. 'I think I'll have to say I'm not too good at judging that; after two divorces I'd look pretty damned stupid if I gave a firm answer!'

Deborah knew then that he wasn't going to tell her what she wanted to hear, at least not yet, and possibly never. She decided to lighten the mood. 'Is it shorts and bikini tops this evenimg, or wet suits?' she asked laughingly.

'Shorts and bikini tops; wet suits might come later! Are you having a bath first, or shall I?'

'Why don't we take one together?' she suggested.

Pavin shook his head. 'Not tonight; I'm saving myself for the barbecue. We'll keep the bath for our last night tomorrow.'

Deborah turned her head sharply away. 'Don't remind me about tomorrow.'

Pavin rested a hand on her shoulder. 'Come on, Debs! Let's enjoy the time that's left to us.'

She nodded, too full up to speak because she was beginning to think that in spite of everything, despite fitting in so well with all his friends and their own wonderful lovemaking, Pavin had no intention of taking their relationship further once the holiday was over, and she didn't know how she was going to get him out of her mind.

Pavin watched her go off to the bathroom and lay back on the bed, his hands folded behind his head. It was all going very well, even better than he had hoped at the start. So far, Deborah hadn't put a foot wrong and he was keeping his fingers crossed that their last twenty-four hours would be as successful. If they were, then his future looked a great deal happier than it had on the night he'd gone, as reluctantly as Deborah, to the publishing party in London.

The small cove where the barbecue was being held had been decorated with innumerable multicoloured fairy lights, the wires draped over the rocks. And in the sand, tall wooden posts held Chinese lanterns which glowed brightly attracting every moth in the vicinity.

'It's beautiful!' said Deborah as she and Pavin descended the cliff path. 'You must feel so proud of your island.'

He squeezed her hand. 'I am, and I'm pleased that you like it, Debbie. Am I forgiven for buying up your country's history now?'

She laughed. 'Of course; that was a really rotten thing to say. My only excuse is that I was in a vile mood at the time.'

'You're forgiven! Hey, Elizabeth, that's one hell of an outfit!'

Elizabeth, smiling gently, waved at them from where Brian and Richard were trying to get the barbecue alight. Her flesh-coloured bathing costume clung so tightly to her that it looked as though she was naked, and the effect was heightened by the fact that tiny holes had been cut to allow her nipples to protrude. Deborah was relieved to see that the other women were all dressed in shorts and tops while the men were in casual trainer bottoms and T-shirts.

'As usual Richard's having trouble getting the barbecue going,' said Flora, coming up to Pavin and resting a hand possessively on his upper arm. 'Will you see what you can do or we'll be here for hours!'

'Sure, then we'll leave the chef to see to the food while we all play blind man's buff,' called Pavin, striding off to join the group round the barbecue.

'Blind man's *buff*!' laughed Deborah.

Flora shook her head. 'The way we play it you end up in the buff, Debbie. That's why we use this cove, it's nice and sheltered. Is Pavin making sure you get safely back to London when you leave, only he hasn't asked me to make ticket arrangements?'

'We haven't discussed our plans after we leave here,'

244

said Deborah sweetly. 'Elizabeth, you've left your nipple rings off!'

Elizabeth nodded. 'That's because of the sand, it gets in the joins and messes up the spring fastenings. We learnt that last year. I've kept the other one on though,' she added softly. 'It's better protected, and I love the feel of it against this tight costume.'

Deborah could well imagine how it must feel and a frisson of excitement ran through her at the other woman's words. She realised that she was looking forward to this game Pavin had mentioned. It seemed that she was more than ready for some of the island's pleasures again.

Very quickly Pavin had the barbecue going, and the chef from the kitchen was left to see to the food while the rest of them formed a large circle. Pavin took a black silk scarf out of his tracksuit trouser pocket and held it aloft.

'Now, for the benefit of Debbie, who hasn't played before, I'll run through the rules of the game. One of the circle is blindfolded and then brought into the middle of the ring. I turn them round three times and then the rest of the players weave in and out in an ever-moving wheel, while the one who's been blindfolded tries to "tag" one of them. Once a player's been tagged he or she can then start sexually stimulating the blind-folded player in any way they choose and they keep going until the person being stimulated makes a guess at their seducer's identity.

'If the guess is correct then the two change places. If not, the blindfold stays on and the game continues until a correct guess is made. I don't play, mainly because we've learnt by trial and error that I'm too easy to identify, simply because I'm bigger than everyone else!'

Deborah felt the excitement rising in her. Here, on this isolated island in the slowly fading light of a late midsummer night, she would be sharing sexual pleasure with a group of like-minded people out in the elements, where nothing except sensual enjoyment mattered. A quick look around at the other faces in the group showed that they too found this a stimulating game.

Pavin smiled at Elizabeth. 'Lizzie, I'm sure you'd like to be the first victim, wouldn't you, honey?'

Elizabeth's pert nipples hardened visibly and she nodded, walking into the middle of a quickly-formed circle and then standing in front of Pavin as he fastened the scarf round her head, checking that her eyes were totally covered. He spun her round fast three times and as she stumbled and tried to regain her balance, the rest of the group started a slow, almost tribal dance, weaving in and out, the men moving one way and the women the other.

Deborah could imagine what it must be like for Elizabeth, stumbling around in total darkness, with no idea where anyone was and only the sound of the waves breaking gently on the sand in her ears.

Lizzie stretched out an arm and half-fell against the group, her slim fingers immediately extending so that they grazed against Tansy's shoulder. Immediately Pavin helped Elizabeth to lie down on her back, so that she had no way of judging the exact height of the person she'd touched while they worked on her.

Tansy looked down on the tightly encased form of Elizabeth and flicked her tongue over her lips. She enjoyed Brian's wife's body; enjoyed its incredible responsiveness and the way she positively encouraged aggression in others.

Silently Tansy knelt on the sand next to Elizabeth and then bending down she let her tongue circle the hard nipples where they protruded through the costume. She took special care to let her tongue flick hard against the holes where the nipple rings usually hung and Elizabeth moaned softly.

246

'Any idea yet, Lizzie?' said Pavin, but Elizabeth shook her head, trying to concentrate on what was being done to her so that she could identify the person quickly. She knew that as the game progressed it became far less tender than this quiet beginning.

Tansy put her hands on the tops of Elizabeth's bare legs and hooking two fingers of each hand inside the high-cut leg of the costume tugged upright as hard as she could. The tiny clitoral ring was pressed against Elizabeth's swelling nub and she gave a startled cry at the unexpected movement while her legs began to move restlessly on the sand.

'You must make a guess now,' Pavin instructed her.

Elizabeth thought hard. It was obviously a woman, but she could think of only one who would go straight for such direct erotic stimulation. 'Flora!' she gasped.

'Wrong!' laughed Pavin.

Tansy stood up, well satisfied with her performance, and Elizabeth was again spun round and this time she had more trouble keeping her balance because her legs were slightly weak with her growing sexual desire.

At last she tagged Martin. As she lay down, Martin's hands peeled her costume straps off her shoulders and then he nibbled softly at the red marks left behind, pulling slightly on the skin so that the olive-skinned girl writhed with delight.

Next he sucked on the protruding nipples, drawing them in past his teeth, making sure that they were grazed slowly but steadily the whole time and the rest of the circle watched as Elizabeth's body began to twist and turn in front of them. She pushed upright, trying to press more of the areola into Martin's mouth but he ignored her and instead lay face down on top of her, one leg between her open thighs, and rubbed, so that the clinging lower part of the costume dragged the ring back and forth making her clitoris move with it and the

247

resulting friction triggered a climax in Elizabeth, whose body arched helplessly before falling back on the sand.

'Well?' asked Pavin as her body quietened.

'That was Martin!' she gasped.

Pavin took off the blindfold as Martin stood up to take his turn as victim.

'Obviously something he's done before!' he remarked, and they all laughed.

Deborah watched as Elizabeth pulled the straps of her costume back up and came to stand close to her. 'What was it like?' she asked curiously.

'It's fabulous!' enthused Lizzie, glancing across the circle to where Brian was watching her closely. 'I hope I get another turn. I love the feeling of helplessness when the blindfold goes on and Pavin spins me round.'

'Do we all get a turn?' asked Deborah anxiously, her body so tight with excitement she dreaded hearing that this might not be the case.

'Not usually; we almost always run out of time. Don't worry, you'll get a go. Pavin will want to see how well you play.'

Before Deborah could ask her what she meant Martin was being turned around and the circle started moving once more.

He kept his balance more easily than Elizabeth and quickly tagged Brian. It was obvious that Brian didn't intend Martin to guess who he was because he merely slipped the trainer bottoms from the other man's legs, letting his hands glide over the outside of his thighs and calf muscles as he did so, and then after removing them he licked lightly on the pad of each of Martin's big toes.

'That's Celia!' Martin said confidently, and Celia smiled at Brian across the circle.

'Wrong,' Pavin announced, amused at how easily Martin had been taken in. 'Another spin, I think.'

This time the huge, grey-haired American deliberately pointed Martin in Deborah's direction and within a few seconds he had managed to tag her. Since he was now totally nude, Deborah crouched over his prone body and tongued across each of his hip bones in turn. This had the effect of bringing him instantly erect, and with growing excitement Deborah took each of his swelling testicles into her mouth in turn and sucked on them.

Martin gasped, his body jerked violently and his breathing grew rapid. 'Guess,' instructed Pavin.

Martin knew who it was meant to be, Pavin had told him before the evening began, and he only hoped that somehow or other Deborah had been where his boss had intended. 'Debbie?' he said, trying to sound uncertain.

There was a round of applause, and Deborah realised that it wasn't because of Martin's correct guess but for her; now she would get to be the victim for the first time, and they were all anxious to see how she played the game.

Her sexual arousal, which had been growing steadily during the first two rounds of the game, meant that when she stood in front of Pavin to have the blindfold fastened she was trembling slightly with anticipation. He let his fingers massage the nape of her neck in a brief, caressing movement before turning her around.

'I wish I was taking part,' he murmured softly. 'I'd love to be the first one to touch you tonight.'

Deborah wished that he was playing as well, but before she could respond with even the slightest of touches he was turning her three times and then she was lurching around on the soft sand, blindly groping for some human contact.

The others circled her, their eyes bright. It was always fun to have someone new join them, to learn the secrets of another person's body, and Deborah had certainly allowed them to learn a lot about her. There wasn't a man or woman there who didn't want to be the first to touch her this evening and when she finally managed to tag Celia on the arm the rest of them felt a pang of disappointment.

Pavin's hands grasped Deborah's shoulders. 'Lie back,' he whispered. 'Just feel what's happening to you and try to picture who can be touching you.'

Her mouth was dry. Everything was so quiet, even the sea was too far out for her to hear the small waves on the beach and no one in the group was making a sound. Everything was concentrated on Deborah and what Celia would do to her body.

Celia had come prepared for the game. In the pocket of her shorts she had a small spray of the Evian water that she normally used to set her makeup. She withdrew it without a sound and then carefully, using only her teeth, she drew the edge of Deborah's cut-off tank top upwards until the young blonde woman's midriff and breasts were totally exposed. She then pointed the head of the spray downwards and pressed lightly on the button.

As the unexpected water fell in a fine spray over her warm, tense flesh Deborah gasped aloud, and now she felt her seducer blowing softly on the damp areas so that they began to turn very cold. Immediately Deborah's nipples were hard while her stomach shook with the titillation.

'Guess,' said Pavin, watching her shaking body. Deborah tried to imagine who could have had the forethought to bring such a thing with them. The teeth that had accidentally grazed her flesh at one point felt like a woman's and so she made a guess. 'Flora?'

'Wrong. Off we go again.'

He grasped Deborah under her arms, lifted her to her feet and spun her round even more quickly. This time she fell to her knees and had to struggle up again in order to try and locate a fellow human being. Suddenly she was beginning to feel lonely and disorientated and she hoped that this time she would guess who her seducer was.

When Paul was tagged, Pavin smiled to himself. He doubted if Deborah would guess Paul. He was far too skilled a player to give himself away. They all wanted Deborah's turn as victim to last as long as possible.

Paul, who recalled Deborah's fascination with Brian and the fact that she'd been out with him on her own earlier that day, decided to behave more in Brian's fashion. She would still remember his touch, his ways, and it should be easy to fool her.

Harshly he dragged her shorts down her long, shapely legs and when he saw that beneath them she was wearing only a G-string, he knew that he could fool her. He dug the fingers of his hands into the top and jerked upwards, splitting her sex lips apart and bringing intense pressure to bear on her yearning, damp flesh. Deborah groaned, it felt so good that her juices felt hot with desire as they flowed from her and there was the instant bunching sensation in the pit of her stomach that told her she was close to coming.

Pavin, standing above her, watched her body responding to Paul's treatment and felt himself becoming painfully erect. He longed to take her there on the sand himself, but there was plenty of time for him to enjoy her later. Right now she belonged to them all and her abandonment to this was exactly what he'd hoped for.

Keeping the G-string cruelly tight against her inner flesh, Paul then pushed a hand up beneath her top and gripped one breast, digging his fingertips in around the outsides exactly as he knew Brian did.

The tightness of his grip, the glorious streaks of red-hot pain that changed swiftly to glorious pleasure and the incessant pulling against her inner sex lips brought Deborah to an immediate climax and she went rigid on the sand as her back arched and her shoulders pressed down into the beach.

'Who is it?' Pavin asked, even before her last tremors had died away.

At least now she would be free, thought Deborah. It had been exciting and stimulating, but she wanted to see again, and so she quickly gasped, 'Brian!'

'Wrong.'

She couldn't believe her ears. 'No! I can't be. It was Brian, I know it was.'

'I hope you're not suggesting I'm cheating?' queried Pavin, pulling her limp body upright once more. She didn't reply. Knowing that he wouldn't lie she suddenly realised that everything had been done deliberately in the way Brian would have done it, simply to confuse her.

This time when she stumbled over the sand, her legs heavy and aching, she realised that if she wasn't careful they could keep her as the victim all the evening. They all knew the way they behaved and could duplicate these patterns. She would have to look past the obvious and try for someone the complete opposite if she wanted to be freed.

The third time, she tagged Elizabeth. Brian's wife knew what was expected of her. Normally her role was submissive, she was never the sexual aggressor, but Deborah was not expected to guess and so she must play the game differently.

While Pavin was lying Deborah down, spreading her legs wide so that her sex was only protected by her G-string, Elizabeth quickly dipped her hands into a tiny pool of water that had collected in a rock close by and then rolled them in the soft sand. When she was kneeling beside Deborah's body she tugged the tank top upwards until Deborah's arms were above her body but still caught in the garment, which meant that virtually the whole of the Englishwoman's body was exposed.

Next she leant down and massaged the mixture of salt water and grainy sand all over the blonde's breasts, paying special attention to the nipples, their peaks now so hard and pointed; rolling the sand over them until the grains were embedded in every tiny crevice.

Deborah began to moan. It felt so strange, her skin prickled and burned and filled her with a despairing need for a kinder touch, a soothing lotion or the cooling water that had been sprayed on her earlier. Yet at the same time this same sensation increased her desire, and her clitoris began to throb. Elizabeth knew very well what Deborah would be experiencing. Now she dipped her still-damp hands into the sand again and very slowly started to spread the coarse grains over the inner thighs which trembled beneath her hands.

Deborah hardly dared to breathe in case the arousing but wickedly pricking mixture was put between her thighs, onto her most vulnerable places, but Elizabeth had her attack well planned. Once the thighs were covered, forcing Deborah to keep her legs apart or risk having the sand touch her sex lips, she massaged what was left even more firmly into the base of her victim's stomach, pressing and moving the tissue so that between her widely spread legs Deborah could feel her clitoris being indirectly stimulated, rubbing up and down inside its protective hood and then felt the covering flesh rotating around the entire clitoral area. The burning heat grew and grew deep within her and she knew that she was going to come again in front of them all.

This time her head tossed from side to side in the sand as her upstraining breasts continued to feel the incessant pinpricks of the sand and her lower belly was massaged so cunningly until at last she felt the tightness rising to a crescendo of release. 'Yes! Yes!' she gasped, and her hips twisted away from Elizabeth in her final climactic paroxysm.

'Who was that then, Deborah?' asked Pavin, his voice surprisingly steady considering his rising desire for Deborah as she lay at his feet racked by her second orgasm.

Deborah thought quickly. The ideas, the way it had all been done, seemed like Brian's, but the touch had been that of a woman. She went to say Flora, and then stopped herself. Flora was too obvious, she must choose the opposite. A picture of gentle, docile Elizabeth, awaiting her own torment with such eagerness, sprang into her mind and she decided to take a chance on total role reversal.

'Elizabeth!' she said clearly.

Pavin was very surprised; he had expected her to name Flora, but he realised that she'd worked out how they'd been playing the game with her and admired the way she'd kept sufficient control of her senses to guess her seducer.

'Correct. Very well done, Debbie. Right, I think the food's ready now. After we've eaten entertainment is voluntary!'

Deborah shivered as Pavin gently untied the blindfold and removed it from her head. She blinked in the slowly fading light. At first she felt terribly self-conscious but then, realising that everyone else had gone, she let out a quiet sigh of relief.

'You played well,' said Pavin, kissing her gently on the forehead when what she longed for was a passionate kiss on her mouth. 'I hope you enjoyed it as much as we all did.'

Deborah nodded. 'The blindfold and the open air made it utterly incredible, and because I couldn't see I was frightened and all the sensations were more intense.'

'Of course, that's why it's done.'

'The trouble is . . .'

'What?' he asked, but his laughing eyes told her he already knew.

'The more I play these games, the more you all teach me the different ways I can be stimulated, the more sex I seem to need.'

'That's even better! I'll try and take care of that for you later. Right now, let's eat.'

They had charcoal-grilled sausages stuffed with dried apricots and wrapped round with rashers of bacon, pieces of chicken in a spicy breadcrumb covering and small steaks marinated in red wine and spices, plus numerous salads and sticks of French bread. It was all washed down with glasses of chilled Chardonnay or ice-cold beer and then when they had eaten enough, Pavin and Deborah slipped away from the cove and walked quietly up the cliff path to the castle.

Deborah had never wanted Pavin as badly as she did at this moment, and she could tell by the pressure of his arm round her and the way he kept stroking the side of her face and her bare arms that he felt the same.

The stairs to their room seemed endless.

Chapter Fifteen

*A*s soon as they entered the bedroom, Pavin peeled
Deborah's tank top over her head and then
crouched down to ease the tight G-string from between
her damp, clinging inner lips. He let his tongue glide
briefly up along the parting, and she nearly fell to the
floor at the delicious weakness that assailed her as a
result.

'You need a bath to get that sand off,' he said softly.
He then carried her through into the bathroom and
filled the huge tub with steaming water before pouring
in some scented oil. Within seconds the entire room
was flooded with the fragrance of jasmine and through
the steam she saw him removing his own clothes and
then he was lifting her up and lowering her into the
scented depths.

Deborah slid down until everything but her face was
concealed, then watched as Pavin joined her, his huge,
tightly muscled body making the water rise dangerously
near the top of the bath so that Deborah had to sit up in
order not to swallow any.

As she'd originally suspected, the bath had been
designed in order to accommodate Pavin and a com-

panion, and so at last they were able to sit together in the warm intimacy of a tub and Deborah watched him rest his leonine head back against the opposite end, his eyes half-closed.

'Didn't you want to play the game with us in the cove?' she asked, indolently dipping a sponge into the water and running it down the valley between her breasts.

'No, I enjoyed watching. You've no idea how exciting I found it seeing you pleasured at my feet.' He stretched out one leg and this time his toe was able to slide freely up between her sex lips without the constraint of leggings between them.

Deborah felt her breathing quicken and she spread her legs slightly. He let his foot move lower and his big toe eased into the entrance of her vagina, rotating softly against the most sensitive part.

She could feel her whole sex mound swelling with need and pressed against his foot, trying to ensure contact between the centre of all her feelings and his toe but he evaded her and instead pushed her legs together so that they were inside his own.

'Later!' he laughed. 'Kneel up and I'll wash you.'

She knelt with her back towards him, her long hair dark with the dampness of the water. She was expecting the softness of the sponge, so the harsh stimulation of the loofah came as a shock and she jerked away, but he wrapped one arm round her and continued to scrub at her back, between her shoulder blades and then down to the sensitive spot at the base of her spine.

When she was tingling all over he got her to turn towards him, and now he applied the same treatment to her shoulders, arms and abdomen until every visible portion of flesh, apart from her breasts, was glowing brightly.

Next he handed the loofah to her, and she proceeded to clean him in the same way, watching how his

257

muscles bunched with pleasure as the blood pounded through his veins. And then when she'd finished and they both stood up face to face in the water she felt his erection nudging at her lower belly.

'Soap it for me,' he said huskily.

Very gently now she took some bath gel and mixed it with a little water until her palm was full of suds, then she slowly covered his erection with the bubbles, sliding her hand up and down the shaft with a lingering movement that had him clenching his teeth in ecstasy.

By the time she'd finished, the head of his shaft was gleaming a dusky purple colour and his testicles were tight and full but he ignored his own need and instead cleaned Deborah just as carefully as she'd cleaned him, his fingers gliding in and out of every nook until she was squirming like an eel as desire raged through her.

Finally he decided that they were both clean enough, and climbing out of the bath he carried her soaking wet through to the bedroom and then laid her on the coverlet but instead of wrapping her in a thick towel he used a hair-dryer on her body, letting the warm air play over her by now almost unbearably aroused flesh.

The droplets of water evaporated, but Deborah's skin responded by bunching tightly causing her nipples to pucker and her breasts to swell while within the skin her flesh seemed to expand so that it felt as though she was growing too large for it to contain her.

When the warm air played over her pubic hair she cried out for Pavin to take her, to fill her and put an end to the ever-growing ache that was pulsating somewhere behind her pelvis, but he simply laughed and carried on down her legs. When he parted each of her toes in turn and let the warm air caress the thin membrane of skin between them she thought she'd faint with the eroticism of the act, so acute were the resulting sensations within her.

At last, when Deborah was reduced to making small

mewing sounds of despair as she waited for a chance to reach her climax, Pavin, whose own self control was being sorely tested, put the hair-dryer down and took her burgeoning clitoris between two fingers. At such direct contact it tried to retract but couldn't, and now the hot sparks of electricity shot through Deborah's stomach and down her aching thighs.

For a moment, Pavin toyed with this mass of screaming nerve ends. Deborah gasped, he eased his grip a fraction, let his nail caress the stem of the bud and as she cried out tightened his hold once more so that the clitoris stayed trapped.

By now Deborah could hardly bear it. Every fraction of her body felt close to exploding, there were glorious jolts of pleasure shooting through her, her heart was racing and her juices flowing copiously from her vagina but still he continued to toy with the soaking little nub.

'Yes! Yes, please!' she screamed, forcing her hips off the bed and this time he decided to end it. He gripped the taut bud tightly and then skimmed the imprisoned tip with the pad of his thumb.

As Deborah finally climaxed her legs drew sharply together and her whole body went stiff. Her eyes rolled back in her head and a mist seemed to fill her head as sensation after sensation rocked her body like a tidal wave. All the time she continued to climax, Pavin, having released her clitoris, kept his hand between her tightly-clenched thighs, cupping her sex with the palm of his hand and maintaining a soft but steady pressure that would ensure she kept going for as long as possible.

Deborah wondered if she was ever going to stop coming. Her muscles were aching with the spasms they were being forced to endure and yet still the ecstasy continued and she could feel Pavin holding the centre of this bliss within the palm of his hand.

Finally she was still, and immediately Pavin pushed

a pillow beneath her hips and entered her, sliding easily into her moist passage. She was so damp he decided it would be better for them both if he changed his angle of penetration. He withdrew, got her to draw her legs up tight to her chest, then lay across the bed on his side and entered her at an angle of ninety degrees, which meant that he was stimulating the side walls of her vagina. No man had ever done this to her, and she very quickly discovered that it meant she experienced entirely different sensations, so that her body was rapidly excited again by this new technique and the arousal of newly discovered erogenous zones.

Pavin sensed that she was enjoying it, that he was going to take her with him to another climax but he couldn't wait very long and within seconds of Deborah tightening around him in a rigid internal convulsion of vaginal muscles his aching testicles at last released their load and Pavin too shuddered and shouted in triumph as he finally climaxed.

'I wanted you so much,' confessed Deborah just before they fell asleep. 'All I could think of after that game in the cove was what we'd do once we were alone together.'

Pavin wrapped himself closely around her back, moulding his body to hers so that they were like two spoons. 'Tomorrow, I want you to spend the day on your own,' he murmured.

Deborah stared into the darkness of the room. 'On my own? But it's my last day.'

'You're allowed to speak to the others! The thing is, in the evening as it's your last night we have a rather special dinner and I want you fresh for that.'

'Why? Is there another new game for the last night of my holiday as well as the first?' she asked teasingly.

Pavin hesitated, still unsure quite how she would take this last piece of information about her holiday on Pavinsay. 'No,' he said slowly, 'not a game. After dinner, I want you to give yourself to every man here, as a farewell gift you might say.'

He felt her body tighten in his embrace. 'Just me? What about the other women?'

'They've all done it on their first visit. They'll be expecting this, and no doubt they'll thoroughly enjoy watching.'

Despite herself, Deborah felt a frisson of dark excitement run through her. 'And you?' she asked softly. 'Will you enjoy watching?'

He laughed against the tender skin of her neck. 'It will be the highlight of the week for me. I want to see the way you respond to each of them, how your body reacts to their different caresses and methods of arousal. It will teach me more about you than I could ever learn on my own.'

'What if I won't?'

'I'll explain you've decided to eat alone and that will be the end of the matter. We leave the next morning anyway. They'll be disappointed, but it's how you feel that counts. Does the idea excite you, Debbie? Tell me the truth, don't you want to be free to abandon yourself to them all, just once?'

As he asked, his hand stroked the curve of her spine and she never knew if her shiver was as a result of that or at the prospect of what lay ahead.

'Yes,' she responded, her voice so low he could hardly hear her. 'I think it's the most exciting thing you've suggested yet.'

Pavin's eyes closed and he drifted off to sleep. The last hurdle was nearly cleared.

The following day, Deborah followed Pavin's instructions of the previous night to the letter. She went for a walk round the beautiful island on her own, watched some of the others in the pool, swam herself when they'd gone and read books from the library.

The group were friendly, and chatted whenever she wished, but she could sense that they knew what lay ahead of her and were withdrawing slightly, allowing her time to gather her strength and courage for the evening.

She decided to wear the pink and blue dress she'd worn on the first night, because she knew that the feel of it against her naked flesh would help to put her in the mood even before the meal was over. Just as she was putting it on, Pavin, wearing his dinner suit and a white bow tie, drew her over to the bed.

'Lie down, honey. I want to make tonight as good as possible for you. This will help.'

'What is it?' she asked, struggling to sit up but he pushed her down flat on her back again and then slowly drew her dress down, painted her areolae and nipples, and then went lower to anoint her secret inner lips with a cool ointment. 'What does it do?' she demanded when he'd finished.

'It's the ointment I used on you once before, the one I get out East. By the time the meal's over you'll want all the men as badly as they want you.'

Deborah stared at him, her eyes huge in her face. 'No, Pavin, that's not fair! I remember how it made me feel. I could barely control myself once that was on. I . . .'

She stopped. Already the insidious chemicals were doing their work and her breasts and vulva were beginning to glow with a deep-reaching heat that she knew would increase with every minute that passed. Her nipples swelled against the fabric of her dress and she caught her breath at the myriad sensations that swept through her.

'Pavin, please, take it off! It makes me need . . .'

'That's the idea,' he said briskly. 'I'm sure I heard the gong, we'd better go down.'

When Deborah walked into the room every person

there turned to gaze at her. The men's eyes were excited and full of desire, the women's curious. Pavin pulled out Deborah's chair and as she sat down he saw her neck muscles tense as the blood coursed through her sensitive vulva and she wriggled slightly. He smiled. She'd soon learn that it was better to keep still.

All through the courses, Deborah felt herself becoming more and more aroused. Her breasts were thrusting against the bodice of her dress so firmly that both Richard and Brian could hardly take their eyes off her, while between her legs her clitoris throbbed and pulsed with desire. She could hardly stand it, and every time she saw Pavin smiling down the table at her she wanted to scream at him for the torment he'd put her through.

But as the meal ended and it was time for her to do what was expected she was suddenly grateful for the terrible hunger he'd kindled in her. When they moved to the blue drawing room and the women sat around to watch, Deborah knew that if she hadn't been so consumed with desire she could easily have lost her nerve and run from the room. As it was her hungry, demanding body kept her there, waiting for the first of the men to take possession of her.

It was Richard who was to take her first. He walked her into the centre of the room and slowly released her swollen body from the confines of the dress. Beneath it she was totally naked, not even wearing hold-up stockings this time, and he gave a sigh of pleasure.

A high ladder-backed chair was brought forward for him and he sat on this, then turned Deborah so that her back was to him and gripped her between his thighs. He was fully clothed and the feel of the harsh material of his dinner suit against her flesh made her long for a similar touch against either her burning breasts or between her legs, but she could only wait.

Richard bent her forward so that her fingers were brushing against her toes and he could tease the skin

263

beneath the tight rounds of her parted buttocks. With her breasts dangling down, the blood filled them even more, and Deborah was so aroused that she wondered if it was possible to come simply due to the ointment and the heaviness of her breasts.

She could feel Richard touching her behind, where her flesh was cool and she wanted to scream at him to reach round and touch her nipples, bring her some relief from the dreadful burning ache that was consuming them, but he seemed totally focused on the part revealed to him. He lubricated his fingers from between her moist thighs and then spread her own juices round the entrance to her rear opening.

Slowly he slid two fingers inside her tightly puckered hole, and Deborah's need was so great that she contracted tightly around them. 'No, press down,' he said firmly and she was forced to release him and lose the slight stimulation he'd been providing.

Now he was ready to insert the warm, pulsating oval-shaped vibrator that he had ready and he pushed her head still lower so that he felt that she was finally able to take the whole of it into her rectum.

As Richard eased it inside her, Deborah gasped with shock. Because of its shape it was far more difficult for her to take in and all her muscles instinctively tried to expel it while a painful ache started to knot her bowels. 'Breathe slowly, let it settle,' Richard told her, and at last she found that it was possible to keep it inside her.

Now she was allowed to straighten, and as soon as she did the oval object began to vibrate more fiercely inside her, and her belly shook with the indirect stimulation of her nerve endings. Because she was so swollen and hot between her thighs these vibrations were sufficient to trigger a climax and to the astonishment of everyone watching, before Richard could even slide a hand beneath her to massage her vulva, she had come in shuddering gasps while beads of sweat covered her top lip.

'A magic touch, Richard!' laughed Pavin. 'Leave the vibrator in her for now, and let Martin have his turn.'

Deborah remained standing in front of them all, her buttocks shaking from the movements deep within them, her breasts upright and swollen and her sex lips puffy with desire as she waited to see what Martin would do with her.

She wasn't afraid, nor ashamed. All that drove her on was the need for sexual satisfaction, and she even took pride in the look of surprise that she could see in the eyes of the watching women, especially Flora.

Although there were no visible signs of the ointment Pavin had used on Deborah, Flora suspected that in some way he had encouraged her sexual hunger in order to ease her through the initial embarrassment of the evening, and she was furious. He had never done that for anyone else, and if she was right it had to mean that he felt more for this blonde young woman than anyone else he'd brought to Pavinsay.

Martin laid Deborah down on her back across the seat of the chair so that her hair brushed against the carpet while her eyes gazed steadfastly at the opposite wall. She was aware of nothing but her body.

Like Richard, Martin was fully clothed and from his trouser pocket he drew a shining piece of mahogany wood, from which extended three thin thongs of leather, each one knotted near the end. He suspended this above Deborah's face so that she could see it for herself.

'I'm going to whip you with this, Deborah,' he said gently. 'I shall draw it across that gorgeously tight, swollen body of yours and then flick it across your breasts and between your thighs and every time I do I want you to thank me. Is that clear?'

Deborah stared up at him, hardly able to believe that

265

it was Martin and not Brian who was doing this. Not that it mattered. If he'd only known it, she was grateful to him. Her breasts were screaming for that kind of touch, she'd have begged him to do it if he'd asked, never mind thanking him afterwards. Once again she realised how much she owed to Pavin for helping her get through this.

Martin drew the soft leather thongs along the side of the tightly-stretched tendons of her neck, trailed them between her visibly needy breasts, started to move towards her stomach and then lifted his hand and struck her a stinging blow across the top of her right nipple.

The burning glow of desire caused by the ointment was doubled by the contact. Tongues of flame seemed to lick through her swollen tender tissue and her outer lips opened still wider as she strained on the edge of a climax.

'Thank me,' Martin reminded her softly.

'Thank you! Thank you!' Deborah gasped, and Elizabeth trembled at the words. How she longed to be in the other woman's place. She could imagine so well the bliss of being on the receiving end of such exquisite torment.

Martin was impressed. Deborah had sounded genuinely grateful and so he let the whip caress the tightly-stretched skin of her waist where she was bent backwards on the chair and then flicked it sharply against the inner thigh of her left leg. The leg jerked outwards, her sex mound trembled and he saw the clitoris emerge from its protective covering, swollen, red and moist.

The flames from Deborah's thigh spread into her vulva and for a moment she thought that she would come, but they died too soon and she nearly cried with frustration.

'Thank you! Thank you!' she shouted, hoping this

would encourage him to move the glorious sharpness of the leather thongs closer to her clamouring nub.

It did. His hand shaking with his own excitement, Martin dangled the whip against her other thigh for a few seconds and then at last let it rise and fall against her open sex, so ravenous for enough stimulation to finish the work the ointment had begun. Deborah screamed aloud with gratitude. Her feet drummed on the ground, her hair brushed to and fro against the soft blue carpet and they all watched the ripples travel across her body as she climaxed again and between her thighs a slick of moisture appeared.

'Thank you!' she gasped, scarcely able to get the word out, and at this Martin raised the whip and struck her again. She was once more racked by intense contractions while at the same time he moved round to where her head was hanging back and releasing his thrusting, swollen penis he slid in between her lips and used the softness of her mouth as though it was her vagina.

Still swamped by the dying embers of her climax, Deborah sucked at him greedily, trying to show him how much he'd pleased her, and when her tongue whirled beneath the sensitive skin beneath his glans Martin's hips moved faster and faster and then he came with startling force and Deborah swallowed and sucked until she had finally milked him dry.

When he returned to his seat, Martin didn't look at Pavin. He had a nasty feeling that he might see something other than appreciation in his employer's eyes. Deborah had seemed to enjoy herself too much, but it was hardly his fault, he reasoned. Often he got quite the opposite reaction.

Pavin didn't mind in the least. He was watching Deborah with an almost detached interest, taking in the way she was abandoning herself so entirely to the evening and feeling his desire for her grow all the time,

267

not just for momentary possession but for keeping her beside him constantly.

Deborah stayed lying on her back across the chair until Brian and Paul lifted her up. They had worked together before on evenings like this and knew exactly what they were going to do.

The chair was taken away, the pulsating vibrator removed from her rectum and then she was made to undress each of the men in turn, until at last she was able to stand naked between them, her back pressed against Paul and her still swollen and throbbing breasts up against Brian's chest.

The men pressed close to her. Paul's erection could be felt pressing against her buttocks whilst Brian's was nudging against her hip, but they had no intention of penetrating her yet.

After a few minutes standing between them she was left while they collected a piece of hessian, which they then proceeded to rub all over her tender body so that the raw, despairing nerve endings were stimulated yet further and the heat that had been located mainly in her nipples and genitals was now all over her.

Once that had been accomplished they laid her flat on her back on the carpet and covered her eyes with a black mask. Then, moving silently, they fetched a piece of tarpaulin with tiny holes cut in it at random intervals and this they held tightly outstretched about three feet above her unsuspecting body, before Pavin nodded for Tansy to fetch the watering can.

The first thing that Deborah heard was what sounded like rain falling very near, and her burning flesh made her long for some of it to fall on her and dampen down the fire the men had ignited within her.

But she knew it was only a fantasy, and when the very first drop of water found its way through one of the holes and fell without warning onto her stomach she gave a startled cry. Before she had time to realise exactly what was happening, drops were falling all over her but never in the same place twice because the men moved the tarpaulin very slightly all the time.

Water hit her on one burning nipple, but not the other. It slid into her belly button but not lower. It struck her two or three times in her pubic hair and then lower, on her knees and feet, but not between her thighs where she was so unbearably hot that she would have sold her soul to feel the cool bliss of the liquid touch her.

She groaned, she begged them to let it touch her where she wanted and her body flinched and strained alternately as it waited and then felt a droplet before the waiting began again and all the time the tension in her was rising and rising and she began to sob with desperation.

Just when she thought she would go mad with need, a heavy drop of water fell directly onto her exposed clitoris. The shock of it, combined with the relief from the terrible burning heat, triggered her orgasm and the men let the water continue to fall there so that her climax went on and on until she heard herself begging for them to stop because she was aching from the wrenching frenzied spasms.

Finally the tarpaulin was removed and leaving her covered by the black mask they pulled her onto all fours, crouching like a dog and, as Brian slid into her soaking front passage from the rear, doggie-fashion, Paul got onto his knees so that he could push his bursting organ between her breasts and then he was massaging her swollen orbs frantically with his hands. rubbing them up and down his shaft.

Brian's movements finally gave her the lasting relief she'd craved ever since the ointment was put between her thighs and Paul's hands gave her breasts the same necessary stimulation so that between them they at last satisfied her body's needs and with a strange keening sound she felt her body explode in its final orgasmic spasm only to be followed a few seconds later by the men climaxing, one deep within her and the other between her wonderful, sensitive and deliciously feminine breasts.

The three of them collapsed in a heap on the carpet and the watching women looked at each other. As Pavin rose to collect Deborah's limp body from the tangled heap the women all knew what Flora had suspected for a long time. Now only Deborah, at present too exhausted to care, was in ignorance.

Sara was waiting in their bedroom and quickly ran a bath for Deborah, then gently washed the exhausted young woman before helping her dress in a light summer skirt, blouse and linen jacket because it was now one o'clock and the night air was cool.

'Where are we going?' a stunned Deborah asked Pavin when he reappeared in their room, dressed in slacks and a sports jacket. 'I thought we were leaving in the morning.'

'No, we're going now.' His face was shuttered, giving nothing away.

'What's the matter? Did I do something wrong?' she cried, trying to remember exactly what had happened in the blue drawing room but only able to conjure up the incredible sensations she'd discovered rather than the acts that had caused them.

'Wrong? I told you, nothing's wrong as long as no one's hurt. You were wonderful, exactly as I expected. Is her case packed?' he added in an aside to Sara. The maid nodded. 'Excellent. Get one of the footmen to bring it out to the helicopter. Richard will see to the usual end-of-holiday arrangements next weekend.'

'Very good, sir.' If the maid was surprised by her employer's hasty departure she was too well trained to show it.

270

Deborah and Pavin travelled in almost total silence by helicopter to the Orkney mainland, and then they transferred to his private plane. It was only once that was airborne that the American seemed to relax. At last he turned and smiled at the bemused fair-haired young woman at his side.

'All right, honey?' he asked.

She shook her head. 'No, how can I be? I don't know why we rushed off, or even where I'm going. Are you travelling back to London with me or are you off to the States?'

He seemed surprised. 'I'm coming with you of course.'

'But what about your business crisis?'

Pavin exhaled slowly and then took one of her cool hands in his. 'Debbie, what did you discover during your week's holiday?'

'That I was a far more sexual person than I'd realised and that there's nothing to be ashamed of in being sensual.'

'Great! Do you want to know what I learnt?'

She gave a small smile. 'That English women aren't so very different from American ones?'

His smile faded. 'No, something more important than that. I learnt that my instincts were right that first night we met. You and I are meant for each other. The holiday confirmed it for me. You will be the perfect third Mrs John Pavin.'

Deborah stared blankly at him. 'I'll be what?'

He lost his usual air of self-assurance. 'I realise you might not want to be my wife, honey. I mean, my track record's not good and perhaps you enjoyed the holiday in general but not my company in particular. I don't know any of that. I can only tell you what I know, and that's that I want to marry you, Debbie. I want us to be together all the time, I don't want to let you go.'

'But why the rush? Why the dash from the island?'

His face tightened. 'I couldn't stand sharing you any longer. Once you're mine, if you agree to be mine that is,' he added hurriedly, 'then I'll happily take you back next year, but it all got too much for me and I had to get you away. There's no business crisis, just a special licence for the day after tomorrow if you agree to marry me.'

At first Deborah couldn't believe she was hearing him right; that he'd actually had to leave his island, give up his own ideas on sexual freedom because of jealousy, but the proof was there on his face and she knew he was telling her the truth, however painful it was for him.

She flung her arms round his neck and clung on to him as tightly as she could. 'I thought you wanted to get rid of me, that I'd never see you again. I never guessed that you felt the same for me as I did for you. You always seemed so detached, so in control.'

'I'm a good poker player, I can disguise my feelings!'

'Of course I'll marry you,' she sighed, wriggling closer. His arms tightened and one hand began to edge its way beneath the hem of her skirt. 'How else would I get back to Pavinsay next summer?' she added teasingly.

His answer was to let his clever fingers ease their way past the edge of her French knickers and then he was gently manipulating her flesh, stroking her softly along those moist inner channels that he so adored and as Deborah felt her muscles start to bunch with the beginning of a climax she made a small vow to herself.

She might be the third Mrs John Pavin, but she was going to make quite sure that there was never a fourth one, not while she was alive to keep him content.

After the ripples of her climax had died away he pulled her head down against his shoulder and began to talk to her about a penthouse suite he planned to buy in London.

'What about Flora?' she asked suddenly. 'Won't she be terribly upset?'

'She'll marry Richard: they're tailor-made for each other and that way we'll all meet up again next summer on Pavinsay. It should be interesting, don't you think?' he added thoughtfully.

Deborah imagined the scene and knew beyond any doubt that it would be more than interesting. It would be another unbelievably erotic summer holiday.

BLACK
lace

NO LADY
Saskia Hope

30-year-old Kate dumps her boyfriend, walks out of her job and sets off in search of sexual adventure. Set against the rugged terrain of the Pyrenees, the love-making is as rough as the landscape. Only a sense of danger can satisfy her longing for erotic encounters beyond the boundaries of ordinary experience.

ISBN 0 352 32857 6

WEB OF DESIRE
Sophie Danson

High-flying executive Marcie is gradually drawn away from the normality of her married life. Strange messages begin to appear on her computer, summoning her to sinister and fetishistic sexual liaisons with strangers whose identity remains secret. She's given glimpses of the world of The Omega Network, where her every desire is known and fulfilled.

ISBN 0 352 32856 8

BLUE HOTEL
Cherri Pickford

Hotelier Ramon can't understand why best-selling author Floy Pennington has come to stay at his quiet hotel in the rural idyll of the English countryside. Her exhibitionist tendencies are driving him crazy, as are her increasingly wanton encounters with the hotel's other guests.

ISBN 0 352 32858 4

CASSANDRA'S CONFLICT
Fredrica Alleyn

Behind the respectable facade of a house in present-day Hampstead lies a world of decadent indulgence and darkly bizarre eroticism. The sternly attractive Baron and his beautiful but cruel wife are playing games with the young Cassandra, employed as a nanny in their sumptuous household. Games where only the Baron knows the rules, and where there can only be one winner.

ISBN 0 352 32859 2

THE CAPTIVE FLESH
Cleo Cordell

Marietta and Claudine, French aristocrats saved from pirates, learn their invitation to stay at the opulent Algerian mansion of their rescuer, Kasim, requires something in return; their complete surrender to the ecstasy of pleasure in pain. Kasim's decadent orgies also require the services of the handsome blond slave, Gabriel – perfect in his male beauty. Together in their slavery, they savour delights at the depths of shame.

ISBN 0 352 32872 X

PLEASURE HUNT
Sophie Danson

Sexual adventurer Olympia Deschamps is determined to become a member of the Légion D'Amour – the most exclusive society of French libertines who pride themselves on their capacity for limitless erotic pleasure. Set in Paris – Europe's most romantic city – Olympia's sense of unbridled hedonism finds release in an extraordinary variety of libidinous challenges.

ISBN 0 352 32880 0

BLACK ORCHID
Roxanne Carr

The Black Orchid is a women's health club which provides a specialised service for its high-powered clients; women who don't have the time to spend building complex relationships, but who enjoy the pleasures of the flesh. One woman, having savoured the erotic delights on offer at this spa of sensuality, embarks on a quest for the ultimate voyage of self-discovery through her sexuality. A quest which will test the unique talents of the exquisitely proportioned male staff.

ISBN 0 352 32888 6

ODALISQUE
Fleur Reynolds

A tale of family intrigue and depravity set against the glittering backdrop of the designer set. Auralie and Jeanine are cousins, both young, glamorous and wealthy. Catering to the business classes with their design consultancy and exclusive hotel, this facade of respectability conceals a reality of bitter rivalry and unnatural love.

ISBN 0 352 32887 8

OUTLAW LOVER
Saskia Hope

Fee Cambridge lives in an upper level deluxe pleasuredome of technologically advanced comfort. The pirates live in the harsh outer reaches of the decaying 21st century city where lawlessness abounds in a sexual underworld. Bored with her predictable husband and pampered lifestyle, Fee ventures into the wild side of town, finding an an outlaw who becomes her lover. Leading a double life of piracy and privilege, will her taste for adventure get her too deep into danger?

ISBN 0 352 32909 2

THE SENSES BEJEWELLED
Cleo Cordell

Willing captives Marietta and Claudine are settling into an opulent life at Kasim's harem. But 18th century Algeria can be a hostile place. When the women are kidnapped by Kasim's sworn enemy, they face indignities that will test the boundaries of erotic experience. Marietta is reunited with her slave lover Gabriel, whose heart she previously broke. Will Kasim win back his cherished concubines? This is the sequel to *The Captive Flesh*.

ISBN 0 352 32904 1

GEMINI HEAT
Portia Da Costa

As the metropolis sizzles in freak early summer temperatures, twin sisters Deana and Delia find themselves cooking up a heatwave of their own. Jackson de Guile, master of power dynamics and wealthy connoisseur of fine things, draws them both into a web of luxuriously decadent debauchery. Sooner or later, one of them has to make a life-changing decision.

ISBN 0 352 32912 2

VIRTUOSO
Katrina Vincenzi

Mika and Serena, darlings of classical music's jet-set, inhabit a world of secluded passion. The reason? Since Mika's tragic accident which put a stop to his meteoric rise to fame as a solo violinist, he cannot face the world, and together they lead a decadent, reclusive existence. But Serena is determined to change things. The potent force of her ravenous sensuality cannot be ignored, as she rekindles Mika's zest for love and life through unexpected means. But together they share a dark secret.

ISBN 0 352 32907 6

MOON OF DESIRE
Sophie Danson

When Soraya Chilton is posted to the ancient and mysterious city of Ragzburg on a mission for the Foreign Office, strange things begin to happen to her. Wild, sexual urges overwhelm her at the coming of each full moon. Will her boyfriend, Anton, be her saviour – or her victim? What price will she have to pay to lift the curse of unquenchable lust that courses through her veins?

ISBN 0 352 32911 4

FIONA'S FATE
Fredrica Alleyn

When Fiona Sheldon is kidnapped by the infamous Trimarchi brothers, along with her friend Bethany, she finds herself acting in ways her husband Duncan would be shocked by. For it is he who owes the brothers money and is more concerned to free his voluptuous mistress than his shy and quiet wife. Alessandro Trimarchi makes full use of this opportunity to discover the true extent of Fiona's suppressed, but powerful, sexuality.

ISBN 0 352 32913 0

HANDMAIDEN OF PALMYRA
Fleur Reynolds

3rd century Palmyra: a lush oasis in the Syrian desert. The beautiful and fiercely independent Samoya takes her place in the temple of Antioch as an apprentice priestess. Decadent bachelor Prince Alif has other plans for her and sends his scheming sister to bring her to his Bacchanalian wedding feast. Embarking on a journey across the desert, Samoya encounters Marcus, the battle-hardened centurion who will unearth the core of her desires and change the course of her destiny.

ISBN 0 352 32919 X

OUTLAW FANTASY
Saskia Hope

For Fee Cambridge, playing with fire had become a full time job. Helping her pirate lover to escape his lawless lifestyle had its rewards as well as its drawbacks. On the outer reaches of the 21st century metropolis the Amazenes are on the prowl; fierce warrior women who have some unfinished business with Fee's lover. Will she be able to stop him straying back to the wrong side of the tracks? This is the sequel to *Outlaw Lover*.

ISBN 0 352 32920 3

THE SILKEN CAGE
Sophie Danson

When University lecturer Maria Treharne inherits her aunt's mansion in Cornwall, she finds herself the subject of strange and unexpected attention. Her new dwelling resides on much-prized land; sacred, some would say. Anthony Pendorran has waited a long time for the mistress to arrive at Brackwater Tor. Now she's here, his lust can be quenched as their longing for each other has a hunger beyond the realm of the physical. Using the craft of goddess worship and sexual magnetism, Maria finds allies and foes in this savage and beautiful landscape.

ISBN 0 352 32928 9

RIVER OF SECRETS
Saskia Hope & Georgia Angelis

When intrepid female reporter Sydney Johnson takes over someone else's assignment up the Amazon river, the planned exploration seems straightforward enough. But the crew's photographer seems to be keeping some very shady company and the handsome botanist is proving to be a distraction with a difference. Sydney soon realises this mission to find a lost Inca city has a hidden agenda. Everyone is behaving so strangely, so sexually, and the tropical humidity is reaching fever pitch as if a mysterious force is working its magic over the expedition. Echoing with primeval sounds, the jungle holds both dangers and delights for Sydney in this Indiana Jones-esque story of lust and adventure.

ISBN 0 352 32925 4

VELVET CLAWS
Cleo Cordell

It's the 19th century; a time of exploration and discovery and young, spirited Gwendoline Farnshawe is determined not to be left behind in the parlour when the handsome and celebrated anthropologist, Jonathan Kimberton, is planning his latest expedition to Africa. Rebelling against Victorian society's expectation of a young woman and lured by the mystery and exotic climate of this exciting continent, Gwendoline sets sail with her entourage bound for a land of unknown pleasures.

ISBN 0 352 32926 2

THE GIFT OF SHAME
Sarah Hope-Walker

Helen is a woman with extreme fantasies. When she meets Jeffrey – a cultured wealthy stranger – at a party, they soon become partners in obsession. In the debauched opulence of a Parisian retreat, and a deserted island for millionaires, they act out games of master and servant. Now nothing is impossible for her, no fantasy beyond his imagination or their mutual exploration.

ISBN 0 352 32935 1

SUMMER OF ENLIGHTENMENT
Cheryl Mildenhall

Karin's new-found freedom is getting her into all sorts of trouble. The enigmatic Nicolai has been showing interest in her since their chance meeting in a cafe. But he's the husband of a valued friend and is trying to embroil her in the sexual tension he thrives on. She knows she shouldn't succumb to his advances, but he is so charming. With Dominic and Carl – two young racing drivers – also in pursuit of her feminine charms. Karin is caught in an erotic puzzle only she can resolve.

ISBN 0 352 32937 8

A BOUQUET OF BLACK ORCHIDS
Roxanne Carr

The exclusive Black Orchid health spa has provided Maggie with a new social life and a new career, where giving and receiving pleasure of the most sophisticated nature takes top priority. But her loyalty to the club is being tested by the presence of Tourell; a powerful man who makes her an offer she finds difficult to refuse. Captivated by his charm, but eager to maintain her very special relationship with Antony and Alexander, will she be making the right decisions?

ISBN 0 352 32939 4

JULIET RISING
Cleo Cordell

At Madame Nicol's exclusive but strict 18th-century academy for young ladies, the bright and wilful Juliet is learning the art of courting the affections of your noblemen. But her captivating beauty tinged with a hint of cruelty soon has its effects on the menfolk nearer the college. Andreas, the rugged and handsome gardener, and Reynard, a chap who will do anything to win her approval, even be a slave to her tireless demands.

ISBN 0 352 32938 6

DEBORAH'S DISCOVERY
Fredrica Alleyn

Deborah Woods is trying to change her life. Having just ended her long-term relationship and handed in her notice at work, she is ready for a little adventure. Meeting American oil magnate John Pavin III throws her world into even more confusion as he invites her to stay at his luxurious renovated castle in Scotland. Once there, she learns his desires, and those of his friends, are more bizarre and complex than she had realised. What looked like being a romantic holiday soon turns into a test of sexual bravery.

ISBN 0 352 32945 9

THE TUTOR
Portia Da Costa

Like minded libertines reap the rewards of their desire in this story of the sexual initiation of a beautiful young man. Rosalind Howard takes a post as personal librarian to a husband and wife, both unashamed sensualists keen to engage her into their decadent scenarios. Cataloguing their archive of erotica is interesting enough, but Rosalind is also expected to educate the young cousin of her employer. Having led a sheltered life, the young man is simmering with passions he cannot control.

ISBN 0 352 32946 7

WE NEED YOUR HELP . . .
to plan the future of women's erotic fiction –

– and no stamp required!

Yours are the only opinions that matter.

Black Lace is the first series of books devoted to erotic fiction by women for women.

We intend to keep providing the best-written, sexiest books you can buy. And we'd appreciate your help and valued opinion of the books so far. Tell us what you want to read.

THE BLACK LACE QUESTIONNAIRE

SECTION ONE: ABOUT YOU

1.1 Sex (*we presume you are female, but so as not to discriminate*)
     Are you?
       Male   ☐
       Female   ☐

1.2 Age
       under 21   ☐   21–30   ☐
       31–40   ☐   41–50   ☐
       51–60   ☐   over 60   ☐

1.3 At what age did you leave full-time education?
       still in education ☐   16 or younger   ☐
       17–19   ☐   20 or older   ☐

1.4 Occupation _____

1.5 Annual household income
  under £10,000 ☐ £10–£20,000 ☐
  £20–£30,000 ☐ £30–£40,000 ☐
  over £40,000 ☐

1.6 We are perfectly happy for you to remain anonymous; but if you would like to receive information on other publications available, please insert your name and address

_____

_____

_____

_____

SECTION TWO: ABOUT BUYING BLACK LACE BOOKS

2.1 How did you acquire this copy of *Deborah's Discovery*?
  I bought it myself ☐ My partner bought it ☐
  I borrowed/found it ☐

2.2 How did you find out about Black Lace books?
  I saw them in a shop ☐
  I saw them advertised in a magazine ☐
  I saw the London Underground posters ☐
  I read about them in _____
  Other _____

2.3 Please tick the following statements you agree with:
  I would be less embarrassed about buying Black Lace books if the cover pictures were less explicit ☐
  I think that in general the pictures on Black Lace books are about right ☐
  I think Black Lace cover pictures should be as explicit as possible ☐

2.4 Would you read a Black Lace book in a public place – on a train for instance?
  Yes ☐ No ☐

SECTION THREE: ABOUT THIS BLACK LACE BOOK

3.1 Do you think the sex content in this book is:
     Too much   ☐   About right   ☐
     Not enough   ☐

3.2 Do you think the writing style in this book is:
     Too unreal/escapist ☐   About right   ☐
     Too down to earth   ☐

3.3 Do you think the story in this book is:
     Too complicated   ☐   About right   ☐
     Too boring/simple   ☐

3.4 Do you think the cover of this book is:
     Too explicit   ☐   About right   ☐
     Not explicit enough ☐

Here's a space for any other comments:

SECTION FOUR: ABOUT OTHER BLACK LACE BOOKS

4.1 How many Black Lace books have you read?   ☐

4.2 If more than one, which one did you prefer?

4.3 Why?

SECTION FIVE: ABOUT YOUR IDEAL EROTIC NOVEL

We want to publish the books you want to read – so this is
your chance to tell us exactly what your ideal erotic novel
would be like.

5.1 Using a scale of 1 to 5 (1 = no interest at all, 5 = your
ideal), please rate the following possible settings for an
erotic novel:

Medieval/barbarian/sword 'n' sorcery ☐
Renaissance/Elizabethan/Restoration ☐
Victorian/Edwardian ☐
1920s & 1930s – the Jazz Age ☐
Present day ☐
Future/Science Fiction ☐

5.2 Using the same scale of 1 to 5, please rate the following
themes you may find in an erotic novel:

Submissive male/dominant female ☐
Submissive female/dominant male ☐
Lesbianism ☐
Bondage/fetishism ☐
Romantic love ☐
Experimental sex e.g. anal/watersports/sex toys ☐
Gay male sex ☐
Group sex ☐

Using the same scale of 1 to 5, please rate the following
styles in which an erotic novel could be written:

Realistic, down to earth, set in real life ☐
Escapist fantasy, but just about believable ☐
Completely unreal, impressionistic, dreamlike ☐

5.3 Would you prefer your ideal erotic novel to be written
from the viewpoint of the main male characters or the
main female characters?

Male ☐ Female ☐
Both ☐

5.4 What would your ideal Black Lace heroine be like? Tick as many as you like:

Dominant	☐	Glamorous	☐
Extroverted	☐	Contemporary	☐
Independent	☐	Bisexual	☐
Adventurous	☐	Naive	☐
Intellectual	☐	Introverted	☐
Professional	☐	Kinky	☐
Submissive	☐	Anything else?	☐
Ordinary	☐	_____	

5.5 What would your ideal male lead character be like? Again, tick as many as you like:

Rugged	☐		
Athletic	☐	Caring	☐
Sophisticated	☐	Cruel	☐
Retiring	☐	Debonair	☐
Outdoor-type	☐	Naive	☐
Executive-type	☐	Intellectual	☐
Ordinary	☐	Professional	☐
Kinky	☐	Romantic	☐
Hunky	☐		
Sexually dominant	☐	Anything else?	☐
Sexually submissive	☐	_____	

5.6 Is there one particular setting or subject matter that your ideal erotic novel would contain?

_____

SECTION SIX: LAST WORDS

6.1 What do you like best about Black Lace books?

_____

6.2 What do you most dislike about Black Lace books?

_____

6.3 In what way, if any, would you like to change Black Lace covers?

_____

6.4   Here's a space for any other comments:

_____
_____
_____
_____

Thank you for completing this questionnaire. Now tear it out of the book – carefully! – put it in an envelope and send it to:

Black Lace
FREEPOST
London
W10 5BR

No stamp is required if you are resident in the U.K.